Holmes & Watson

THE CASE OF THE

One Bridge Too Far

ROBERT LAY

Holmes & Watson
The Case Of The One Bridge Too Far

gibletbelle.com
gibletbelle@gmail.com

Copyright © 2025

Text: Robert Lay

Senior Editor: V.M. Lay

Cover design/illustrations:
Gabriella Southworth, gabriellalyn.myportfolio.com

Giblet & Belle–Lily And The Great Vampire Hunt illustrations:
Natalia Junqueira, Dawn Book Design, dawnbookdesign.com

Interior Design and Layout:
Danielle Smith-Boldt, Miss D's Designs, missdsdesigns.wordpress.com

ISBN 979-8-9924473-5-4

This Book Is Dedicated To

ACCEPTANCE.

We accept who you are
without judgement
and are glad you are here.

Table of Contents

Epigraph

"To Trust thyself:
every heart vibrates to that iron string.
Accept the place the divine providence has found for you,
the society of your contemporaries,
the connection of events."

SELF RELIANCE.

—Ralph Waldo Emerson
1841

Cast of Characters

Holmes: Orange tabby cat & recovering addict with a brilliant mind, and who is unmatched as a detective.

Tyler Watson Baumann: Ex-con who partners with Holmes to start their consulting detective agency.

Cassidy Macgregor: Evaluated as a genius at ten years old with special abilities who joined the Holmes & Watson agency out of college.

Christopher Macgregor: Brother to Cassidy and pursuing a veterinary degree.

Russell & Shirley Macgregor: College Professors, and parents of Cassidy and Christopher.

Anne Gaumont: Retired chief homicide detective and co-founder of the Holmes & Watson agency, along with Tyler Watson.

Miss Cynthia Delacourt: Heir to one of Philadelphia's founding families. Art collector and cousin of James Xavier Gund.

Isabella De Leòn: Granddaughter of the leader of the De Leòn cartel out of Colombia.

James Xavier Gund: Patriarch of the Gund Family and leader of their business empire. He lives on a guarded estate in central Texas.

Carlos (Carl) De Leòn: Father of Isabella. Left the family in his teens to start his own life.

Abigail De Leòn: Wife of Carlos and mother to Isabella.

Antonella De León: Abuela (Grandmother) to Isabella and mother to Carlos De Leòn. She runs the De Leòn cartel since her husband and two other sons were killed by rival gangs.

Irene Adler: White cat who has an intimate history with Holmes and bested him. He refers to her as "That Female."

Mycroft: Holmes' brother with an equally brilliant mind, but without the drive displayed by his brother.

Ethan Kelly: Special Agent in Charge (SAC), FBI New York Field Office.

Mike Hann: FBI Special Agent and in charge of the Counterintelligence Desk in the New York Field Office.

The Fixer: Political fixer and cleaner. Steeped in mystery, he works directly for James Xavier Gund and his father before him.

Dieg: The former Patron of the St. Louis territorio for the DeLeòn cartel.

Mittens: Senior Protector for Torrington, CT., mentor to Belle, the new Protector, and counsel to Holmes.

Belle: Current Protector in Torrington, CT. She was trained by Mittens.

Giblet: A fussy tabby tomcat, and Belle's best friend.

Protectors: An ancient order of cats who have been watching over and protecting human beings since our ancestors started the first settlements. Only a few people are aware of these cats, who operate from the shadows. Every community has a Protector.

Prologue

The computer screen was divided into four individual boxes, each labeled with the name of one of the other families of the Circle. Within each box was one person, the designated family representative for today's meeting. To say this meeting was private didn't begin to cover the lengths these people went to keep their business clandestine. End-to-end encryption to start with, followed by a virtual private network (VPN) that was located on a private satellite in geosynchronous orbit over the United States. Getting a satellite into orbit without anyone knowing about it was, in itself, beyond the abilities of many nations. However, for the four families of the Circle, it represented only a minor inconvenience and a respectable outlay of cash.

"Okay, that's it for old business. I will now open the floor for new business," the individual named Phillack said to the group.

"Hold on. I want to know what Gund is going to do about the assassin he tried to employ? He's still in Federal custody, right?" a man named Landewedock asked aggressively.

"Prescott," Gund began, using the man's first name. "The person you are referring to had a fatal heart attack two days ago. He is permanently out of the picture."

"I heard he had files on jobs he did for you and the Circle. Can you confirm this?" another person named Camborne questioned.

"Most of the jobs Pelotas did were outside the United States and were not Circle business. However, the two jobs he did for the Circle were handled entirely through intermediaries. The Circle has nothing to worry about." Gund didn't have to say that those intermediaries were also taken care of; no loose ends were the standard practice for businesses of these families.

"What about the files?" Landewedock pressed.

"They have been retrieved, and I destroyed them," Gund replied, letting his irritation show at being questioned.

"Any more questions on this topic?" the representative for the Phillack family asked. Landewedock looked like he wanted to ask additional questions on the topic, but, after a moment, shook his head. "Very good. I believe we have an update on our plan to control the new President."

Camborne began with background, "As you know, the Circle has had a plan in development for a number of years, whereby we would have a man elected to the Presidency that we control completely. Unlike prior administrations, where we could only influence events, albeit not always successfully, this popinjay would be completely controlled by the Circle, doing what we want from the Oval Office." Camborne paused and saw the other members of the Circle nod.

"Therefore, with Phillack's help, we found and recruited James Tyrone Pennyfold, a second-rate businessman and media personality. The man is perfect, coming from a dysfunctional home where his parents didn't love him. He suffers from low self-esteem, feelings of insecurity, and has difficulty forming healthy relationships. He hides the worst of his diffidence under a veneer of malignant narcissism."

"I know him," Landewedock admitted. "He's an idiot. A number of years ago, he tried to get me to invest in a business, but the venture was doomed to failure. How will you get this man elected?"

Camborne smiled into the camera, "Yes, he is all of those things and more, but he is excellent in front of a crowd. He puts on a show that the unquestioning electorate loves. With our cable news network, we will bolster his candidacy 24/7 and fund his campaign through intermediaries. When he is elected, we will own him. And the best part is, the man doesn't even realize it. His narcissism is so ingrained that we can get him to do anything through the use of blandishment."

Gund half listened to the report, but his mind was elsewhere. The Pelotas matter was more troublesome than he had admitted to his contemporaries of the Circle. One of the Assassin's files had Gund's name in it. That particular file was now in his desk drawer, having been liberated from the Justice Department as soon as Pelotas had his heart attack. Even though his name only appeared once in the file, that was one time too many. Furthermore, Gund couldn't be sure that Pelotas hadn't mentioned him in other files or spoken his name to other people.

To ensure his anonymity, he would need someone he trusted to conduct the investigation. That meant he would have to expedite the return of The Fixer. There was work to be done.

CHAPTER I

The Case of the Doomsday Cult

"Are the samples ready?" Holmes asked for the third time, pacing back and forth outside the airlock at the Holmes & Watson offices.

"I've got the film samples ready, but the solution processing sample is taking a longer time to complete," Cassidy Macgregor replied, her voice muffled by the respirator. She hated being in the hazmat suit because, among other things, she couldn't scratch her nose. "I'm working as fast as I can."

"You alerted your professor about us coming over today?"

"You know I did," Cassidy answered, raising her voice. "Dr. Watkins promised access to the mass spectrometer. And, before you ask, yes, the lab will be cleared." She knew why Holmes was double-checking everything; the detective was worried. When Holmes was worried about something, he was fastidious about details. There was also another reason Holmes had been in a foul mood lately; it involved a stalled case that had flummoxed the detective for the last eight months. "Dr. Watkins was curious about why we need the lab empty."

"What did you tell him?"

"That we had a substance sent to us. We were worried about what it might be, and for safety's sake, we didn't want anyone around when we tested it."

"Good," Holmes meowed, poking his head into the airlock.

"STOP," Cassidy ordered when she saw what Holmes was doing. "Nobody comes into the airlock unless they are suited up, and we don't have a hazmat suit for a cat." She watched as Holmes withdrew and sat back down outside. "Almost there," she said in an attempt to calm the cat's nerves.

The orange tabby nodded. He knew she was right. When the envelope arrived at the Holmes & Watson firm the day before, it was Cassidy who noticed the letter didn't look right. Granted, the whole firm was on edge as they began investigating this doomsday cult that their client's son had become involved with. But it was Cassidy's excellent instincts that prevented Watson from opening the envelope and exposing them all to what was inside.

It took almost twenty hours and multiple stops at various specialty businesses to obtain the supplies needed to create a containment room in the lab and protective gear for Cassidy to wear. Many of the shops looked at the young woman and her orange cat suspiciously when they came in and bought the various equipment. When it was done, the lab in the Holmes & Watson office became a sealed plastic bubble, equipped with a negative-pressure airlock, which fed through a filter specially made for trapping viruses and bacteria.

For Cassidy's protection, she was covered in a full-body impermeable hazmat suit, with chemical-resistant gloves and a full-face mask with an ABEK2-P3 respirator, capable of stopping nerve agents. "…And the kitchen sink," Cassidy grumbled when she put on the suit. But she also knew it would be foolish not to take these precautions.

Using forceps and a scalpel, Cass opened the envelope but didn't remove anything; instead, she used a long swab to wipe the interior of the envelope. Sure enough, when she withdrew the swab, a fine powder coated the end. Cass deposited the swab into a test tube and sealed the end with a rubber stopper.

Looking carefully, Cass saw that the only thing in the envelope was a single white card. Once again, using the forceps, she pulled the card out enough to read what was on it; the cult's call to arms: **Ad coelum per sacrificium**—*To heaven through sacrifice.* "I hope Watson is careful. I'm worried about him staking out these lunatics by himself," Cassidy admitted.

"Watson will be safe as houses. I've trained him and he knows my procedures," Holmes meowed. "You need to worry about you."

"Finished," Cassidy announced as she carefully loaded the samples into the white, air-tight container and locked the lid. The universal biohazard symbol adorned the lid and sides of the container.

The envelope and instruments Cass used were placed in a separate biohazard container. The junior member of the Holmes & Watson firm stepped into the airlock, which was now occupied by a plastic kiddie pool. Gently, she hosed off the hazmat suit and the samples box as the water was collected in the pool. Then stripped off the hazmat suit, revealing the underwear she had on underneath. The hazmat suit was placed in a yellow biohazard bag, sealed, and eventually taken away by the appropriate agency.

"The bloomers, too," Holmes added.

"Fine." Cassidy removed her bra and panties, which she also placed in the bag. "Happy now?" she asked, standing naked in front of the cat; the scars she received last year from a particularly vicious stabbing were still clearly visible on her abdomen. "Only Izzy gets to see me like this."

"You silly humans and your modesty. Shower off, and we'll get going."

The shower was another hose with a spray nozzle. Cassidy stood over the floor drain in the back room, rinsing off herself and the samples box once again. Finally, clean, wet, and cold, she dried herself and put on an old sweatshirt and sweatpants for the drive over to the university.

Watson was sitting in his car, over a block away from the cult's compound, but with a direct line of sight. The compound, a former fast-food restaurant purchased with money obtained from the cult's followers, was located at the end of a road in an industrial section of Providence, RI. As soon as they bought the property, the cult blackened all the windows and erected an eight-foot fence and topped it with a double coil of razor wire. A single guarded gate allowed people to enter; one way in and one way out.

It was a mild late fall afternoon with hardly a cloud in the sky. *I should be home with Mom or practicing my Krav Maga* Watson thought irritably, *instead of watching these nut-jobs.* Still, it was a critical case. No telling how many people they would kill if they got the opportunity.

The Benevolent Followers of The Ascension believed that mankind had become wicked and that God was going to cleanse the earth. Those unworthy would be cast into Tartarus, while their followers would find themselves in Elysium.

"This is what happens when you let a Classic's major start a cult," Homes had commented with his usual dry wit.

Unfortunately, God had not started the purification of the world on schedule. Therefore, Malachai, the cult leader, said they would help God by kick-starting the process. Among their members was a husband-and-wife team of chemists, who had fallen hard for the message the Benevolent Followers of The Ascension had prophesied. It was their twisted genius that resulted in the deaths of a number of stray dogs and three homeless men found around Providence, each showing a different kind of physical distress.

Holmes, Watson, and Cassidy visited the crime scene of one of the dead homeless men. While Watson distracted the police detective with questions, Cassidy and Holmes looked at the dead man, blood crusted around the man's nose and mouth. "What do you make of this, Macgregor?" the cat meowed softly.

Cassidy squatted down to examine the body, but made very sure not to touch it. "Toxin of some kind. The blood crusting around the nose and mouth is worrisome," she said, thinking back to her classes in organic chemistry and forensics. "What do you think?" she asked Holmes.

"I think this is a dress rehearsal, and we had better figure it out before opening night," the orange tabby meowed, lost in thought.

That had been the second homeless man found. However, it was the third dead homeless man who was so worrisome to the local authorities and confirmed Holmes's fear that they were dealing with a group intent on a mass casualty event. After the third body was recovered and taken to the morgue, the two people who collected the body, as well as the Medical Examiner, all came down with severe symptoms that required hospitalization. Fever, cough, and vomiting were initially dismissed as a virus. However, when the Medical Examiner, who spent the most time with the body, began having blood in his urine, Holmes correctly deduced, "The cult is working on a bio-weapon where even a dead body can transmit the toxin."

"I knew there was going to be trouble when we took this case," Watson said to no one in particular, sitting at his desk in their offices on Baker Street.

"What have you told the client?" Cassidy asked from one of the wing-back chairs.

"That we finally got an interview with their son, Matt," Watson said. "He said he was not being held against his will and that we should tell his parents that they were going to pay for their sins. We left our card with him."

"Charming lad," Holmes added from the other chair in the sitting area of the office.

Watson went through the mail until he found a letter from the Connecticut Electric Company. "Why are they writing us? I moved all correspondence to email, like they asked," Watson announced to no one in particular, picking up the letter opener.

"STOP!" Cassidy screamed, rising to her feet.

"What? Why?" Watson asked, looking confused, holding the envelope in one hand and the letter opener in the other.

"We know the cult is working on some sort of bio-weapon. And the cult knows that we are looking into their organization for our client," the junior member of the Firm reminded them. "Holmes, look at that envelope before Watson opens it."

The orange tabby left his chair and went over to the desk. Watson placed the envelope gingerly on the corner of the desk and backed away. Holmes looked at the letter for fifteen seconds before meowing, "Bloody Hell. This is a fake. The font does not match previous correspondence from the power company." That Holmes could remember such an obscure piece of data, like the font used by a local utility, was a testament to his unparalleled powers of observation and retention.

"We need to take precautions before we open that letter," Cassidy declared.

"You're right," Holmes added. "Watson, carefully take that envelope back to the lab and put it in the evidence container. It's air-tight."

"No. Grab the tongs and put the letter in the biohazard container. It's properly labeled. Then wash your upper body thoroughly several times and change clothes," Cassidy added. "I'm going to make a list of items we need before we can examine whatever is in the envelope."

That was twenty-four hours ago. Since then, Watson had driven to Rhode Island to keep an eye on the building the cult called home. If it looked like they were going to execute their plan, he would call for help and leave the area immediately. For what seemed like the hundredth time, Watson reached over and patted the full-face gas mask that was on the passenger seat. According to Cassidy, the full-face mask with an ABEK2-P3 respirator should protect him from even nerve gas. However, Watson had no interest in testing that theory. Just in case, and as a backup, an auto-injector of atropine, with the largest needle Watson had ever seen, sat next to the mask.

"If you think you have been exposed, inject yourself with this," Cassidy instructed, handing him the auto-syringe. "And get to the hospital."

"Where do I inject myself?" Watson asked in horror, staring at the needle beneath the plastic cover.

"Straight into your heart," Holmes meowed, seeing Watson's expression.

"ARE YOU FRICKEN SERIOUS?" Watson exploded.

"No. You inject yourself in the thigh," Cassidy said soothingly. "Holmes is being funny."

"Just tooling with you, old man," the orange tabby replied.

"Yeah. You're as funny as a crutch," Watson replied. Now, twenty-four hours later, he was considering what to do about a bathroom when his phone rang. It was Cassidy's number, but it was Holmes who was on the other end of the line. "We're on our way to the lab at the college. Anything to report?"

"No. A few more people have arrived, but nobody has left."

"Understood. We will call you as soon as we have news," Holmes promised.

"Wait. I need someone to check on Mom," Watson said. "The day nurse will be leaving in another couple of hours, and I won't be home." Tyler's mom was eighty-five, and in the last month, her health had deteriorated significantly.

"Watson, I'll ask Izzy to stop over," Cassidy said over the speakerphone.

"That would be great if she'd do that. Thank you," Watson said. "I can call a night nurse to come over early."

"We're at the university. We'll call you as soon as we know something."

Inside the lab, Cassidy put on new protective gear and prepared to introduce the samples into the mass spectrometer. Her former professor, Dr. Watkins, stood aside, ready to help but knowing that Cassidy knew what she was doing; after all, in his twenty-three years of teaching at the university, Cassidy Macgregor had been his best student. Although it was beyond him to understand why she brought her cat into the lab.

Inside the hermetically sealed glove box, the sample container was opened, and the first sample was placed in the vacuum chamber of the mass spectrometer. The pump was then started to reach a pressure of 10^{-5} to 10^{-8} Torr (on an absolute scale, a unit of atmospheric pressure). When the pressure was reached, the sample was vaporized while an electron beam created charged ions. Those ions were accelerated towards the detector while a powerful magnet caused the heavier ions to separate from the lighter ones. The results of this complicated process appeared as a vertical bar graph on the computer screen, which Cassidy, Holmes, and Dr. Watkins watched.

"Look," Cassidy said, pointing at the graph on the screen. "There are two polypeptide chains, here and here," pointing at the A-chain and B-chain. "Each has a molecular weight of around 32 kDa." Cassidy quickly did the math in her head and said, "The total molecular weight is around 64 kDa. That's ricin, isn't it?"

"Yes. That's the molecular weight of a ricin protein." Dr. Watkins agreed.

Holmes meowed. "Those fools are using ricin." Cassidy nodded, but Dr. Watkins looked at the cat suspiciously.

"Wait, there's something else," Cassidy said, looking at the readout. "What is that?"

Dr. Watkins looked over her shoulder and replied, "That is a viral glycoprotein. If they figured out how to couple it with the ricin, it would allow the toxin to penetrate the cell membrane even faster." When Cassidy gave him a questioning look, Dr. Watkins went on, "Normally, the ricin takes about four hours to penetrate the cell membrane. However, a viral glycoprotein can significantly shorten that time. The body couldn't defend against that. This is a super-toxin."

"They want an apocalypse," Holmes announced. "Time to call our friends."

"Why is your cat meowing?" Watkins asked.

"It's nothing," Cassidy assured him. "I'm calling the authorities." Cassidy cleaned up her workspace and went outside the lab to make a call. One hundred forty-three miles away in New York City, Ethan Kelly's government-issued cell phone rang. When he saw who was calling, he grunted and answered, "You know, there are other good people in law enforcement you can call when you have a problem." Kelly was being flippant, but he knew Cassidy or Watson would never waste his time, so this was probably serious.

Cassidy grinned and countered, "But we trust you. The cult has developed an even more deadly variant of ricin. We have proof from the test we ran with the mass spectrometer."

"Okay," Kelly said, making notes. "What else?" Ethan Kelly was the SAC of the FBI Manhattan Field Office and was the one who directed the distraught family to Holmes & Watson when the FBI couldn't help them with their son and the cult.

"Watson is keeping an eye on the compound. Make sure whoever responds knows that, and make sure your people know they are walking into a potential mass casualty biohazard." Cassidy was interrupted by meowing. "Oh, you're right."

"Excuse me?" Kelly asked.

"Not you," Cass said into the phone. "But we will also need our lab decontaminated. The original letter is on the lab table in a white, air-tight sample case. I left a key to the office in a lockbox on the doorknob. 348 is the combination." Cassidy paused, then added, "Please tell your people to be careful."

"I will. I will let you know what we find when we raid the place." Kelly said and then hung up.

Holmes and Cassidy nodded to each other after the phone connection was broken. The next call was to Watson, informing him of the situation. "Do not approach the cult's compound," Cassidy told him. "You don't have the protective clothing," Holmes added.

"And just what do you expect me to do?" Watson asked, irritated.

"Keep an eye on the cult, but don't approach. The authorities should be there soon," Holmes meowed. "Be careful, call us if you need anything. Izzy is at your mom's house." Watson thanked his partners and broke the connection.

"Well done, Cassidy," Holmes said to their junior partner. "Now, let's make sure the lab is clean so Dr. Watkins will be inclined to let us back in if we need it in the future."

The sun had set, but Watson hadn't left his post. He was about to call Cassidy for an update when a van without headlights rolled silently up behind his car. *They must have turned off their engine and coasted the last block,* Watson thought to himself. Soon, his car was surrounded by men in Mission-Oriented-Protective-Posture uniforms or MOPP gear. Each was carrying a M4A1 CQBR (Close Quarters Battle Receiver). Unlike the traditional M4A1, the CQBR had only a 10.3-inch barrel, making it ideal for special circumstances, such as clearing out a building. In addition, each had a full-face mask dangling from around their neck. Those specific masks were designed to stop everything, including nerve gas. They set a perimeter as one who appeared to be in charge approached and tapped on his window. "Are you Tyler Watson?" the man asked.

"Yes," he replied. "Who are you?"

"Lieutenant Barnes, U.S. Army Biological Warfare Laboratories response team." He flashed his ID and went on, "We were briefed on the way here. Has anyone left the compound?"

"No. A few more people arrived, but no one left. They're all in there," Watson reported as another van rolled up with its lights off. "I hope that those outfits of yours are good," He said sincerely.

"They're designed for a Level IV biological event. That's about as serious as it gets," the lieutenant assured the detective. "Thank you, Mr. Watson. We'll take it from here," he replied as he brought his radio up and began to give orders. Soon, a second van rolled silently up, and more men piled out. Some set up a perimeter, while others started approaching the compound.

"It's all yours," Watson agreed as he started his car and turned his wheel hard over to do a U-turn and get out of there. On his way home, he called Cassidy to inform her that the authorities had taken over and that he was on his way home. Two and a half hours later, a very fatigued Watson arrived at his home. The first order of business was to send the night nurse home, and then he went upstairs to check on his mom.

At about the same time, Cassidy was letting herself into her apartment in West Hartford, which she shared with her girlfriend, Isabella DeLéon. It looked like Izzy had fallen asleep in the recliner when she got home from Watson's house. Cassidy smiled; she loved watching Isabella when she slept. She looked so pretty and peaceful. After a minute, she bent over and kissed Izzy's forehead and whispered, "Hey, girl."

Izzy's eyes fluttered open and focused on Cassidy. "Hey, yourself," she answered. "How'd it go?" she asked in a sleepy voice.

Cassidy smiled and said softly, "Oh, you know. Just another day at the office." Reaching down, she drew Izzy up into a tight hug, then she led the woman she loved down the hall to bed.

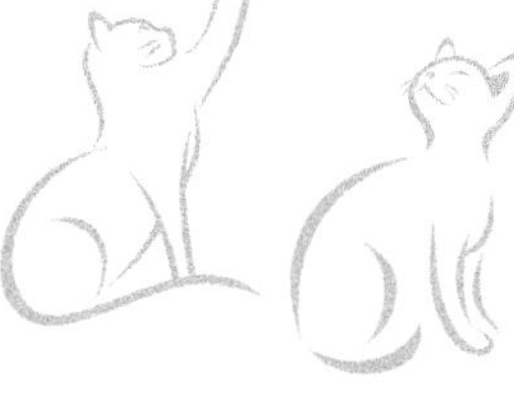

CHAPTER II

Early Warnings

Isabella awoke first, as she usually did, and slowly got out of bed without waking Cassidy. Naked, she crossed the bedroom to where her robe hung on the bathroom door. Usually, she didn't sleep in the buff, but neither one of them had bothered with pajamas after their lovemaking last night; both contented and exhausted.

At times, it was hard for Izzy to remember that they had only been together for a year. Their improbable relationship: Cassidy Macgregor, an investigator, mind reader, and genius who could speak to cats, and Isabella DeLéon, granddaughter to the leader of one of Colombia's largest cartels. A Hollywood screenwriter couldn't come up with such a dubious cast.

Izzy's father, Carlos DeLéon, had left his Colombian family thirty years before because he didn't want any part of the gangster life. Settling in Connecticut and Americanizing his first name to Carl, he worked very hard to keep his American family safe and away from the Colombian family's business. What Carl had not planned on and didn't know was that Izzy had joined the FBI's Financial Crimes Unit right out of college and was then selected to infiltrate his Colombian family's operation in St. Louis; all because of her last name. So, when Carl couldn't contact his daughter for several weeks, he hired Holmes & Watson to locate Isabella.

It was fortunate that he had. When Izzy's undercover went sideways, Holmes & Watson were there to rescue her, and in addition, free a number of women who were being trafficked. Still, there were repercussions. The Acting Director of the FBI, Gable Finch, wanted to use a successful undercover as a stepping stone to elected office. When the undercover blew up, the secret big money funding Finch worried that Isabella would expose their hand-picked candidate, and by extension, themselves. Their solution to protect Finch was to hire an assassin with the alias Pelotas to find and kill Isabella DeLéon.

Catching wind of the plot, Holmes and Watson found and stopped the assassin. Unfortunately, he wasn't the only one looking for Izzy. Diego, the former boss of the DeLeon Cartel in St. Louis, vowed his own revenge against Izzy. When he tracked Izzy and Cassidy to Torrington, Connecticut, he managed to seriously wound Cass before he was stopped. It was in the midst of these whirlwind events that Izzy and Cass had fallen in love.

Living together for the last ten months had been the happiest time in Isabella's life. No longer with the FBI, Izzy was using her degree in forensic accounting to conduct due diligence for companies that could afford her services. So far, business has been good.

From the kitchen, Izzy heard Cassidy waking up, so she took her cup of coffee and walked back to the bedroom. "So, you solved the case of the cult yesterday?" she said to Cass.

"Yes," Cass replied, puzzled. "I thought I was the one who could read minds. How did you know?"

"The sex is always better when you solve a case," Izzy admitted with a grin, causing Cass to turn scarlet. "What's on your agenda today?" Izzy wondered.

"For one thing, you and I are going to Watson's house. Your former FBI colleagues would like to discuss your case from last year with us," Cass replied, staring at a text on her phone to Ethan Kelly.

"Is there a problem?" Izzy asked, a frown settling on her face.

"Not sure," Cass answered. "We'll know after we meet," she guessed as she typed out an acknowledgement to Agent Kelly.

"We'll go in separate cars," Izzy remarked. "I have to come back to finish the books on the Franklin Murphy merger."

Cassidy nodded and rose from bed to begin her day.

Tyler Watson was making lunch for his mother and watching the local midday news. It was all over the airwaves; apparently, the members of the Benevolent Followers Of The Ascension had committed mass suicide last night. Federal Government authorities were called in to deal with the situation because Providence, or even the whole state of Rhode Island, didn't have the resources. Authorities went to great lengths to assure the public that nobody was in danger, and the people going in and out of the cult's headquarters in hazmat suits were doing so just as a precaution.

While Watson watched, Holmes came into the kitchen and jumped on the counter. He sat and watched the TV coverage for a while, then turned and meowed at Watson, "Except that is not how it happened at all, is it?"

"What do you mean?" Watson asked while putting some mayo on the sandwich he was constructing.

"Up for a flutter? A fiver says that it wasn't suicide," Holmes meowed.

"First, you don't have any money. Fiver or otherwise," Watson replied. "Second, we'll find out later what happened with the cult. Cassidy called, and Ethan Kelly wants to talk to all of us, including Izzy. He's driving up from New York and will be here about 1:00 p.m."

Holmes accepted the news with a nod of his head and jumped off the counter. But before he left the kitchen, he purred, "You just don't want to be in financial debt to a cat."

At exactly 1:00 p.m., Ethan Kelly's blue bureau car pulled up outside Watson's home. The young black man met Kelly at the door and showed him inside. Kelly saw Izzy and Cassidy sitting on the couch, and Watson's orange cat was lying on the coffee table. He accepted the armchair that was offered while Watson got a chair from the kitchen table. Without engaging in pleasantries, the FBI agent got right to the point of his visit. "Pelotas is dead." Pelotas, the assassin, had been in federal custody since he failed to kill Izzy last year. Everyone fell silent at the news and exchanged worried looks. However, it was Holmes's reaction that startled Kelly. The cat stood up and walked to the end of the coffee table to stare hard at the agent.

Finding her voice first, Izzy asked, "What happened?"

"The prison doctor said it was a heart attack. Pelotas was fine at lunch, and by dinner, he was dead." Kelly was prevented from continuing because the orange cat staring at him let out a long and loud meow.

"What did the autopsy reveal?" Cassidy asked.

"There wasn't an autopsy. The body was transferred to a local mortuary and was cremated before anyone at the FBI or Justice Department was notified." Kelly let that news sink in, then said, "The mortician claimed it was a mix-up with the paperwork, and the wrong body was cremated." Kelly tried to maintain eye contact with the people sitting around him and ignored the cat that stared at him with flattened ears and a bit of a scowl.

"And you believe that?" was Watson's dubious reply. "Where was Pelotas being kept? He was supposed to be in segregation and not the general population. Right?"

Kelly was quiet for a long time, much longer than necessary to simply answer Watson. The cat again meowed angrily at Kelly, which seemed to break the agent out of his silence. "That's the disturbing thing. Pelotas was being kept at Joint Base Andrews in the Military Police lockup because the Justice Department hadn't finished questioning him."

Holmes actually hissed at that news, causing Kelly to ask, "What in the hell is wrong with this cat?"

When Cassidy stared at Kelly, she saw flashes of images; there was more to this. "What else are you not telling us?" she asked.

Kelly looked very uncomfortable but finally admitted, "Some of Pelotas's files you found for us have gone missing from the Justice Department."

Watson let off a loud expletive, and Holmes hissed again. Both of them knew that anyone with access to these files would have to be high-ranking within the Department of Justice. Holmes looked at Watson and meowed, "Our enemies have increased tenfold," to which Watson nodded.

It was Izzy who tried to calm down the tension in the room. "Ethan, why did you come all the way to Torrington? You could have told us this over the phone."

"Izzy, you three were the last ones to associate with Pelotas before he was arrested. And Watson here figured out where he kept his records stash. Did Pelotas do or say anything that would lead you to believe there is more than a conspiracy to elect Gable Finch to the Senate?" What Kelly didn't say, but everyone present guessed, was that he was worried for their safety as well because of their association with the Assassin. The three of them were loose ends.

Watson, Cassidy, and Isabella all shared an uncomfortable look and remained quiet until Holmes meowed once again. Watson then answered, "Sorry, we don't have anything we can add that you don't already know."

Izzy asked, "Have you talked to Gable Finch about this?"

"That man's an idiot. I don't think he even understands that what he did was wrong. All he says is that it was all The Fixer's fault." Ethan then added, "He's scheduled to go on trial next year."

"If I were you," Watson began, "I would guard Finch only with people that you trust and never let him out of your sight."

Kelly nodded and stood up, "I have a fair drive back to New York, so I think I will be going. Keep an eye on each other, and let me know if you think of anything that will help our investigation."

Kelly watched as Watson's cat meowed again, and then Watson asked, "Before you go, do you know how the cult members in Rhode Island died? Did they commit suicide?"

The FBI agent shook his head. "According to the Army team that went inside, it looked like one of them accidentally broke the pathogen container, and it got out before they were ready. Bodies were stacked up at the door like cordwood, apparently trying to escape. The CDC said the cult developed a very nasty toxin. We appreciate your help with that."

"Is that gratitude official?" Watson asked, knowing the answer.

"Of course not. Holmes & Watson, who? It's all politics," Kelly answered, being honest.

The cat meowed again, and Watson looked down at his cat and mumbled, "Smart ass. I'm not paying you five quid."

Kelly watched the exchange between Watson and the orange cat and added one more thing before he left. "Pelotas did tell me one thing when we were alone. He said that your cat is not normal. Care to explain what he meant by that?"

Watson didn't make eye contact with Kelly when he answered, "Sorry. I've no idea."

After the door closed, everyone looked at Holmes, waiting for him to begin. The orange cat was quiet for a moment, then meowed, "I think it is time we showed Cassidy and Izzy the room."

Watson's house had three bedrooms. The largest was for his mother, and the other two were for him and his sister, Mary. Since his sister had left right before her eighteenth birthday, after a falling out with her mother, her bedroom had remained closed off and unused. Lately, however, the abandoned room has taken on a new purpose.

Watson unlocked the bedroom door and pushed it open for Izzy and Cassidy to enter. Holmes ran between their feet, stopped in the dead center of the room, and proudly meowed, "Welcome to The Conspiracy."

The bedroom was empty of furniture, but across the walls, wrapping around the room, was an investigative timeline. Cassidy saw that it all began before the Civil War and went right up to the present day. Branching off the timeline, at various points, were written notations, and in some cases, there were what appeared to be printouts of articles. However, in some places along the chronological timeline, some decades were blank. "The file I examined in the Assassin's lair spoke of a family called the Gunds. They employed Pelotas on two occasions, and from what I was able to gather from the file, he was not supposed to know the name of his actual employer, and only work through The Fixer, but Pelotas found out by accident."

Cassidy asked the cat, "Who are the Gunds?"

The earliest mention of them was a name: Andrés Ulysses Gundisalvus, before the name change to Gund. He came to Texas with his wife when it was still under Mexican rule. That family continues to this day. I deduce that they are an immensely wealthy family that controls a significant portion of the United States' economy and politics.

"Oligarchs?" Izzy questioned.

Mary?
Hell Before Lunchtime
1861
Chronicle
Page 2
Sil·loa
Head
Line
Shiloh,
KY

"More than that," Holmes meowed, and Cass translated. "The Gunds control cotton, pork, and other major foodstuffs that the US uses on a daily basis. They have their fingers in a lot of pies."

Holmes walked over to one section of the wall, lifted his paw, and indicated several news stories from various reputable news sources. "A congressman losing his seat in a sex scandal," he said at the first report.

"Nothing unusual about that," Watson replied.

"Right, you are, Watson. But then, a private jet going down in clear weather on its way to an American football game with the leadership of a defense contractor…the same men who were being investigated by the dead congressman's committee." Holmes watched as his compatriots understood the connection.

Moving to the last news story, Holmes meowed, "And the sale of this company when its CEO developed a fast-acting form of brain cancer. The man was dead in four weeks, and his company was sold to the very same defense contractor from the prior article." Holmes paused, then continued, "All separate incidents, but if you examine them, it is as if a disembodied ventriloquial voice gave orders, and they came to pass."

Holmes began pacing back and forth in the bedroom, organizing his thoughts before saying, "Too much, too much for one powerful family. Everything I have found tells me that the Gunds are only the tip of the spear. I have found similar circumstances of events being manipulated in the media, defense contracting, and the health industry."

Cassidy had paused along the timeline and was reading about a county council election in St. Louis, where the challenger had won despite the polling indicating otherwise. "Holmes," she summoned him to a different place on the wall. "This was a local race for the County Council in St. Louis. Why is it on your wall?

"Because, Macgregor, that member of the County Council was holding up the expansion of a biogenetics firm's lab in their district. The Councilwoman was concerned about a genetics lab being in a populated area, especially if they had an accident. That lab, Genome Infinitum, is owned by a company that exists only on paper in the Cayman Islands, which in turn is owned by Gund Worldwide, Inc."

"You're saying that the Gunds took the time to fix a local election?" Cassidy asked.

"I checked the polling; it was mathematically improbable that the councilwoman would lose her election."

Then Holmes said to everyone, "These people will do anything to further their aims. What you see represents ten months of work."

Cassidy continued translating what Holmes was saying for Izzy as she looked closely at the timeline. Towards the end, she saw Pelotas's name and her name. "You mean the Gunds were behind everything that happened last year?"

"Yes. I believe they were," Holmes meowed.

"That's where we were last year when you got out of the Hospital," Watson said. "Holmes and I went to Texas to see what we could find out about Mr. James Xavier Gund. Turns out we found very little. Nobody around there would talk to us, and there was surveillance everywhere. I feigned car trouble on the highway so Holmes could reconnoiter the property."

"I went over two miles through the Texas scrub before I could see their house. The estate is enormous. I actually saw Gund on his patio. I have no doubt he is ultimately the man behind the attempt on your life." Holmes finished, staring at Izzy.

"Hasn't anyone been able to investigate this man?" Izzy asked.

"Being incredibly careful not to leave a paw print behind, I was able to establish that at least a dozen people have tried to interfere in Gund's affairs through the years, and none were successful. I can't stress this enough: Don't discuss our investigation with anyone. The danger is very real."

"The others tried to investigate the family and failed, huh?" Cassidy replied.

"No," Holmes answered. "They all tried and died."

CHAPTER III

Stagnation

Eight weeks had passed since Holmes, Watson, Cassidy, and Izzy had received the visit from the FBI, and the lack of progress on the Gund case was showing on the orange cat. Watson was sitting at his desk at the Holmes & Watson offices on 221 B Baker Street, checking his email, when Cassidy came in. "Hey," she said by way of greeting.

"Hey, yourself. Here are the pictures of our subject, who's on total disability," Cassidy said as she passed Watson the thumb drive. "He skis very well."

"Is he still staying at the lodge in Vermont?" Things had been slow at Holmes & Watson lately, so to keep money coming in and give Cassidy something to do, Watson decided to take a couple of insurance cases. The latest one involved a man who was on total disability from his company after falling down the stairs in front of a business.

"Yeah. I got some good shots of him coming down the mountain."

"Well done. Be sure to finish your expense report so we can bill the client when we send them the pictures," Watson reminded her.

"Where's our fuzzy orange leader?" Cassidy asked, looking about.

"Where else. Sitting in the bedroom, staring at the walls and thinking about the Gunds. Every once in a while, he gets on the computer, but then he goes back to looking at the timeline." Watson thought, then added, "He even sleeps in the room. I'm worried about him."

"Is he careful with his searches online?" Cassidy asked with concern.

"He is running his searches through two separate VPNs in series, plus we're paying the VPNs with an offshore account taken out with a fictitious name," Watson assured Cassidy. "I think we're fairly safe."

"His mind is running on a closed loop right now. he needs the stimulation of a new case to clear his mind," Cassidy suggested. "When I was stuck on a problem in college, I did something nonsensical to clear my head."

"What did you do?" Watson asked, curious.

"I would go to the art museum in Hartford and watch people look at art."

"You wild child," Watson said with a grin. "How did your parents ever control you?"

"You forget, I could see what they were thinking when they looked at art. It was fascinating to see what a painting made them feel." Cassidy said earnestly.

"Well, don't keep me waiting," Watson said. "What did people think about when looking at art?"

"It really depended on the piece. People's thoughts were all over the place."

"Where's Izzy today?"

"She's back at our place doing due diligence for a company out of Boston. They're attempting a merger."

Watson nodded his head. He was glad she was home and not traveling. "Is she being careful?"

"We both are, thank you."

Watson nodded and went back to scrolling through emails, looking for a good case. Every once in a while, he would pause at an engaging subject line and hit enter. So far, none of the potential cases would interest Holmes, so he kept scrolling. When he came to a subject line: ***Mrs. Cynthia Delacourt of Philadelphia–Missing Art,*** he hit enter and began reading. "Yes. Yes, this looks like a winner." Then, turning, he called to Cassidy, who was in the lab. "Read this," he asked.

Leaning over Watson, Cassidy put her hand on his shoulder and scanned the email, her hair brushing against his cheek. Watson noted the soft fragrance of flowers, which was undoubtedly a floral shampoo. *She has certainly changed a lot in the last year since falling in love with Izzy. The Cassidy Macgregor from two years ago wouldn't have given a darn how she looked or smelled, considering both a distraction to her work and studies.*

Not for the first time lately, Watson felt a profound wave of loneliness that he hadn't anybody special in his life. He consoled himself with the knowledge that caring for his mother, looking after Holmes, and his work as a detective were three full-time jobs. Besides, he had good friends, and compared to how many years he had been locked away, this was heaven. Still, having that special person in your life sure looked like a lot of fun.

"I like it," Cassidy said, breaking him out of melancholy. "Old Philadelphia money, priceless art missing. I think we have a winner."

"Great. Let's go and coax the little furry pain in the ass to take the case." Together, they left the office and headed to Watson's house.

The line for international arrivals at JFK airport was running about twenty-five minutes, an average wait for this time of day and this day of the week. The experienced global passenger had their arrival documents ready as they approached the Customs and Border Protection (CBP) officers. The novice traveler could always be spotted by the way they fumbled for their paperwork after reaching the CBP desk. This group, passengers from Lufthansa Flight 400, Frankfurt (FRA) to New York (JFK), was excited to clear Customs and be on their way after an eight-hour and twenty-minute flight. One passenger, dressed in a suit that needed a good ironing, was so engrossed in reading his phone that he needed a tap on the shoulder to realize he was next in line. Putting his phone in his pocket, he approached the desk and handed his blue United States passport to the CBP agent.

The Customs agent took the paperwork and thumbed through the pages of the passport, noting stamps that dated back several years, mainly to Germany but also to the U.K. and France.

"What do you do, uh, Mr. Dirkson?" the agent asked, using one of her go-to questions for passengers. She checked the passport photo, and it matched the man standing in front of her: sandy brown hair, thin eyebrows, a flat nose, and glasses.

"I sell oil and gas valves. Mostly to power companies," the man named Dirkson replied. If the customs agent had asked, Mr. Dirkson could have provided a list of companies he called on, literature from his company on their products, and a business card that had his picture and company name.

"Do you have your declaration form?"

"Oh, yeah. Here you go," Dirkson said as he handed over Form 6059B. Dirkson kept his phone in his hand in case they wanted to see it. The customs agent scanned the document, and apparently, Mr. Dirkson hadn't done any shopping while he was away. Typical for the business traveler.

"Where do you live?" the agent asked, usually her final question.

"Willowbrook. North of Houston," Dirkson answered, giving the bored impression he'd gone through these questions on many occasions.

The customs agent glanced at her colleague, who shook his head, indicating he wasn't interested in searching this traveler's phone. Handing back the passport to the gentleman, the agent said, "Welcome home, Mr. Dirkson."

The traveler took his passport and put it in his suit coat pocket, along with his phone. "Thanks," he said before heading off, probably to catch another flight.

When Dirkson reached the JFK main concourse, he pulled out his phone again and dialed a number from memory. The phone rang twice and connected. Nobody answered, and none was expected. Instead, a beep told him that the call was being recorded. "I'm back. I should be there in about six hours." Hanging up the phone, Dirkson put it back in his pocket and went to the next ticket counter for the domestic flight to Houston. The Fixer, Joseph Goebel, had returned.

Holmes sat on the coffee table while Watson and Cassidy both tried to convince him to take the new case. "Holmes, it has everything. Priceless artwork that was stolen. A family whose lineage goes back to pre-Revolutionary War, in a mansion where George Washington once slept." Cassidy paused, then added, "What more could you ask for?"

"Washington was a damnable rebel leader," Holmes grumbled. But then he asked, "What was the painting that was stolen?"

"According to the email, it was a commissioned portrait work for the family from an artist named Sir James Thornhill," Watson said, reading from his phone. "The last time it was seen in public was when the family loaned it to the Philadelphia Museum of Art in the 1990s for an exhibition."

"I've never heard of Thornhill?" Cassidy admitted.

"He painted the dome of St. Paul's Cathedral in London, as well as vast murals for castles and manor homes," the cat recited from memory. "He didn't do much portrait work."

Cassidy reached out and ran her hand down the orange tabby's back. She was one of only two people in the world who would ever attempt such a feat. "Come on, Holmes. The case will clear your mind and let you see the Gund case with fresh eyes. Remember, Einstein said he did his best work while he was a patent clerk."

"That's a truism," Holmes said in a snippy meow. "But what about you, Watson. Can you be that far away from your mother in her condition?" Since the beginning of the year, Tyler's mother had continued to decline. She hardly left her room anymore and required round-the-clock care.

"I will stay here and mind the store. Cassidy can go with you."

Holmes knew that Watson and Cassidy wouldn't leave him alone until he agreed to take a case and get him out of his doldrums. "Fine. Make arrangements," he meowed. "Let's go see what the flap is all about."

That night, Cassidy was in the bedroom she shared with Izzy, packing an overnight bag for her trip to Philadelphia the next day. "How long are you going to be gone?" Izzy called out for the second bedroom, which they used as an office.

Cassidy was folding a pair of khaki slacks and a woman's white Oxford shirt; those went into the bag. "Just overnight is the plan. This is the get-to-know-you trip where we see if it is our kind of case, if we can help them, and if they like us."

"Why don't you take the train? There's a nonstop, and it would save driving," Izzy questioned while working on the audit job.

"Because if they decide they don't want to hire us, we can come straight back. I could be home for dinner," Cassidy said while going through her drawer looking for a pair of black socks. "It's only a four-hour trip by car."

She found the socks in her drawer, but each pair had a hole in the toes. Walking across the hall to the office and sticking her head in the doorway, she asked, "Do you have a pair of black socks I can borrow until

I can replace these?" as she held up the socks that were soon to be thrown out. When her girlfriend didn't respond, Cass called her name, "Izzy?"

Without turning away from the screen, Izzy said, "Uh, yeah. Top drawer of my dresser, right side."

Cass walked back to the bedroom and went to Izzy's dresser. "You really concentrate when you're looking at spreadsheets. Those things put me to…"

Izzy was typing away on the spreadsheet when Cassidy stopped talking in mid-sentence. However, that wasn't what caused Isabella to say, "Shit!" and jump from her seat and run to the bedroom. Too late. Cassidy was standing there by her dresser with an open black velvet ring box, staring at the white gold and diamond ring within. "What's this?" Cassidy asked in a calm voice, wanting to understand. Isabella DeLeón stood in the doorway, wringing her hands, a palpable look of fear on her face. When she didn't respond, Cass asked again, "Izz?. Tell me."

Izzy walked in and sat on the corner of the bed, her hands continuing the wringing motion that told people who knew her that she was nervous. When Cass came over and sat next to her, she broke her silence. "Next month is our one-year anniversary of the night we met and kissed for the first time."

"So we're not counting the first time we saw each other, and you held a gun on me?" Cassidy said playfully, trying to lighten the mood, but it didn't work. Izzy began to cry.

"It's okay, just tell me."

Izzy began talking in a rush, "Next month, we have a reservation at that nice restaurant for our anniversary, and I was going to ask you to marry me because I love you more than anything, and I never want to be away from you, but I'm afraid you won't want to get married, and I will have ruined everything," When she finished, Cass didn't say anything. Instead, she got up from the bed and crossed the room to her dresser. Izzy began crying harder because she knew this was not a good sign. *I blew it,* she thought.

Cass went to her dresser and returned with a blue velvet box. Opening it, Izzy saw a diamond ring encircled by green emeralds, the same color as her eyes. "Isabella DeLeón, will you marry me?" Cassidy asked, smiling. "I was waiting for next month also."

Izzy stared at the ring in disbelief, then cautiously extended her index finger to touch it. *Yup. It was real,* she thought. Throwing her arms around Cassidy, she wrapped her girlfriend in a fierce hug, holding her tight and not letting go. "Is that a yes?" Cass asked, smiling. Then added, "Izzy, dear. I can't breathe."

Loosening her grip, Izzy replied, "Yes. I will marry you. Of course, I will. Will you, Cassidy Macgregor, marry me?"

"Yes. Absolutely, "Cass replied. And then they lost themselves in a kiss of love and happiness. After a few minutes, or perhaps longer, who could tell, Izzy said, "Let's call our parents with the news." She stood up and held her hand down to the woman she wanted to spend the rest of her life with. Cass took the offered hand, and together, they went to the front room to make their calls.

In Cass and Izzy's condominium parking lot, a white van was parked. The van was white, the most common color, with darkened windows that prevented anyone on the outside from seeing in. The graphics on the sides of the vehicle proclaimed that it belonged to an organization that provided transportation for the elderly. Since the complex had a large number of retired persons, it was reasonable that one of their vans might be parked there.

However, if someone were to take a closer look at the graphics, they would see that they are magnetic stickers, easy to remove or change. Then, if they could see inside the van, they would not find seats for passengers, but rather an air mattress for rest, a cooler with water and

MREs, and a small, portable toilet for relief. The two people manning the van tonight were on alternating four-hour shifts and had enough provisions to last two days without needing to leave, although for the two in the van tonight, their shift would end at six a.m.

The two men in the van were physically fit and professional. They had been trained to ignore the discomfort of their surroundings, including smells and other annoyances, while on this assignment. One of them was sleeping while the other stood watch. The lights were on in the target unit, which told the man that their quarry was still awake. Glancing at his watch, he figured that would change in the next hour or so. Until he was relieved by his partner, he would not take his eyes off the objective. Even though he didn't know the specifics of why he was watching this particular condo unit, he would ensure that his part of the mission was completed; all other considerations, including his own life, were secondary.

CHAPTER IV

Marching Orders

Cassidy knocked on the door as she let herself into Watson's house with her key. It was six a.m. and overcast, and the plan was for her and Holmes to get an early start so they would arrive in Philadelphia well before their 11:00 a.m. appointment. She heard Watson's voice from the kitchen and proceeded sure-footed through the dark living room. "Good morning," was her cheerful greeting as she entered the kitchen, smiling.

"Are we ready to go?" Holmes asked, looking up from his breakfast, noting, among other things, that Cassidy was dressed very smart for today's meeting.

"All gassed up and ready," Cassidy said far too cheerfully for it being so early, her left hand fiddling with the collar of her blue pinstripe blazer. "Our appointment is plugged into the GPS, and the weather is good." Watson looked up at her and nodded, then returned to his laptop and continued to read the paper.

"I'm gonna refill my coffee," Cassidy said, now holding her travel cup in her left hand, shaking it out in front of her.

"Yeah, sure. Go ahead," Watson replied without looking up from his reading. As soon as the cup was topped off, Cassidy sat down on a kitchen chair, crossed her legs, and began drumming her left hand on the kitchen table.

"Oh, for Cat's sake. Watson, please notice the ring on Cassidy's left hand, or we will never get out of here," Holmes meowed.

"Uh. What?" Watson asked, finally looking up from the computer. For her part, Cassidy held out her left hand for him to see it, wiggling her fingers and displaying an uncharacteristically large grin on her face for so early in the morning. "What's this?" he asked.

"I'm engaged!" Cassidy exclaimed as if keeping it inside one more second would have been impossible. "Izzy and I are getting married!"

Watson looked up with a blank look on his face as if he didn't understand what he was being told. Reaching out, he took Cass's hand in his and looked closely at the ring. "It's beautiful," he told her with a smile. Then, rising to his feet and drawing Cass up with him, he gave her a warm congratulatory hug. "I'm so happy for you."

"It happened last night. We were each going to propose to the other on our anniversary next month, but I found Izzy's ring by accident, and I showed her the ring I bought, and it just sort of happened!"

"That's great, isn't it, Holmes?" Watson said to their partner.

The orange cat curled his lip and raised an eyebrow, then finally meowed, "Yes. Congratulations." Then, changing the subject, he added, "I think we had better get going for our appointment."

"You're right. Let's go," Cassidy said, heading for the door. From the living room, Watson heard, "You both are going to be in the wedding, Izzy insisted. Holmes, you will look so cute in a little bow tie," she continued talking as she walked through the front door.

Watson and Holmes shared a look, and Holmes meowed, "Four hours in a car with a newly-engaged female. Kill me now."

Watson laughed and then got serious. "Call me when you meet the client. Let me know if we should take the case." The orange tabby nodded before jumping off the kitchen table and following Cassidy out the door.

At 10:00 a.m. on the dot, The Fixer knocked on the outside door to Xavier Gund's private study. Since he had been working for the son, he had always used this private door and never the front doors of the house located on a vast ranch in central Texas. Once he was granted admission, Joseph Goebel walked over and stood before the desk, but didn't say anything. Gund appeared to be writing something, and The Fixer didn't want to disturb him. While he continued to get his thoughts down on paper, he pointed at the seat in front of the desk, indicating that The Fixer should sit. When he reached a stopping point, Gund picked up the cap and screwed it back on the top of his pen, then addressed his guest, "You do look different."

"Yes, sir," The Fixer replied, reaching up to test the residual tenderness of his new face. The clinic in Europe performed rhinoplasty by removing some cartilage from Goebel's nose and flattening it. Then they pulled the skin tighter around his eyes and did some work on his chin. All that, plus changing his hair color, made The Fixer look reasonably different from the way he did a year ago. A new set of documents bearing a new name completed the transformation.

Gund nodded, then asked, "Are you ready to get back to work?"

"Yes, sir."

"What do you think we should do about Gable Finch? Does he know anything that can hurt us?" Gund asked, getting immediately to the point.

"No, sir. I don't think so," Goebel replied. He had been brought up to speed with developments before he returned to the U.S. "Gable Finch has never met you and was always a pawn, to use or discard as you wish. If he were to have an accident, the authorities would be forced to investigate. We shouldn't give them a reason."

Out of curiosity, Gund asked, "Do you think I was wrong about silencing Pelotas?"

"No, sir. Pelotas was a trained intelligence agent and assassin. We have his files, but we don't know what else he might have known about you that he didn't write down. It was best that he had his heart attack. Besides, he had taken on many jobs for others; any of them could have ordered his death. The authorities are burdened with too many suspects to focus only on you."

"Okay. I called you back because I need you to begin a new project. Nobody, not the Circle, not my family, not God himself, if he asked, can know about this." The Fixer nodded, displaying a serious look on his face and wondering where this was going. "I want you to assemble a file on each of the three families of the Circle. I need you to investigate and find me a pressure point for each family that I could use if I need them to bend to my will."

The Fixer was quiet as he digested his boss's request. "You want," he began slowly, "to be able to compromise each of the three families of the Circle individually?" His tone betrayed his unease at the assignment.

Gund looked at The Fixer, noting the apprehension in his voice and knowing he would have to settle the issue before he could go on. "This is not necessarily something we will use. I think the best description would be a failsafe in case we need to bring a family back in line."

"Has something happened, sir, that I should know about?"

"No, nothing has happened," Gund told The Fixer, keeping the reason to himself. "I just need to know if you can do it?"

"Investigating the Circle without alerting them to what we're doing." The Fixer looked at his boss, who nodded. "Like your family, the other families have been in place since the Gilded Age, and they will have formidable defenses in place to prevent outside interference."

"My family predates the Civil War," Gund said with pride, the implication being that they were the strongest. "The other Families don't have the fire in their bellies that their ancestors did. They've grown soft, and with that comes danger for the entire Circle. I don't think you will have that much trouble developing a plan."

"It will take me some time to figure out an approach for each Family," The Fixer estimated.

Gund nodded and said, "This is your priority until you get it done."

"How much time do I have?" The Fixer asked.

"As much time as you need," Gund responded, to which The Fixer translated it to mean soon. "I won't keep you," he said by way of dismissal.

The Fixer nodded, rose to his feet, and left the way he came in.

CHAPTER V

Society Hill, PA.

Cassidy guided her car into the only open spot on Spruce Street in the Society Hill neighborhood of Philadelphia. Up and down the narrow, one-way cobblestone street were rows of adjoining eighteenth and nineteenth-century townhomes, elegant and meticulously cared for by their owners. In the spring, the street would be shady and picturesque, with trees planted about every twenty yards apart, down both sidewalks. However, on this cold February morning, there were no leaves to be seen, but Holmes did note that one hearty cyclist, clad in cold-weather gear, was getting his miles in on the bike path adjacent to the street. "Our destination is at the end of the block," Holmes meowed, and together, they set off.

201 Spruce Street was at the corner and appeared as the only stand-alone home on the block of attached homes. Three stories tall and in the early Federalist style, the house stood apart in both scope and grandeur, drawing the eye as a beautiful specimen of pre-revolution colonial architecture on a street already brimming with notable examples. Cassidy and Holmes took a minute to study the home before approaching.

By far, the focal point of the house's façade was the pair of imposing eight-foot-tall front doors, featuring a leaded glass fanlight across the top. A pair of real gas-lantern carriage lights flanked the tall doors on the left and the right. The copper used to build the lights had long since turned a blue/green color, showing its age. The mantle of the gas jet was pinched in such a way that the flame was spread out, like an illuminated leaf, instead of a narrow flame. "Reminds me of England," Holmes meowed, studying the lights.

A pair of double-hung sash windows was to the right of the doors, while on the left, a previous generation had removed the windows and replaced them with two sets of leaded French doors with wrought-iron French balconies. Although not original, the French doors added to the elegance of the house. All the windows across the front of the house had functional wood shutters. Originally, those shutters would be closed at night and opened in the morning by the serving staff. Finally, the third floor had three bonnet-dormer windows and was likely where the servants' quarters were initially located.

"Nice place," Cassidy finally commented as she and Holmes climbed the five granite steps and stood before the entry doors, now even more imposing when you stood right in front of them. A pair of twin cast iron door knockers with the face of a lion appeared to be the only way to summon the people inside, so Cassidy carefully lifted the heavy knocker arm and brought it down on the receiver twice. Each time, the metallic sound resonated through the large door, the wood amplifying the bang so anyone inside could not help but hear it. "Well, they either heard that, or they're dead," Holmes meowed wryly.

Not long after, they heard a latch being thrown, and the door swung open. A short, thin-faced man who was obviously a butler stood in the opening, glanced at Cassidy and then Holmes, and inquired, "Yes?" The butler didn't wear the livery of his profession like they did in Britain. Instead, he wore what could best be described as business casual: a dark blue jacket, charcoal grey slacks, and a white shirt with a black tie.

"Cassidy Macgregor of the Holmes & Watson firm," she said, holding out her card. "We have an appointment with Mrs. Delacourt."

"Yes, Miss," he responded with a British accent. Holding the door open for Cassidy.

Before she entered, Cass gestured to Holmes and said, "This is my emotional support cat," slipping into the standard explanation of why Holmes was there. "He comes with me. He is exceptionally well trained and…"

"That is not necessary, Miss," the Butler easily interrupted. "Madam Delacourt enjoys the company of cats. Please follow me." The Butler directed them to the sitting room on the left, off the entry hall. "Madam Delacourt will be with you momentarily," he informed them, and then closed the mahogany pocket doors.

When the door closed, Holmes meowed, "East Midlands, in or near Calverton."

"Don't you ever tire of placing a person's accent?"

"No," was the detective's reply.

The room where they found themselves was obviously the original parlor of the house, built primarily to receive visitors in its day. The layout was rectangular, with ten-foot cove-molded ceilings. At the front of the room were the French doors noted outside, which provided the people sitting in the parlor with an excellent view of the street. The far wall was dominated by a fireplace framed by a sculpted marble surround, obviously original to the house. At some point, the fireplace had been changed over to gas, and a comfortable fire was lit. At the other end of the room was a smaller, swinging door that led into the less public rooms of the house. Two couches were placed facing each other with a coffee table in the middle. Covering the walls were paintings of various sizes and subject matter.

As Cassidy and Holmes began walking around the room, it became apparent why the original windows had been replaced with French doors; they admitted much more light into the north-facing room than the original windows, and the light was needed to fully appreciate the impressive artwork that hung on the parlor walls.

"Here's a John Singer Sargent and a Thomas Cole," Cassidy said, reading the names on two paintings. Then, stopping before a six-foot-tall oil-on-canvas of a young woman, Cassidy read the name: "James Abbot McNeil Whistler. I know the artists, but I've never seen these works." Cassidy admitted to Holmes.

The cat walked up and sat next to Cassidy, "None of these paintings have been on public display," Holmes meowed. "I deduce they are all commissioned works for the family, which, as unknown works, makes the art in this room worth millions of pounds." Holmes then went to the Thomas Cole painting and examined it. "Note this oil on canvas. Not a true landscape because he incorporates architectural elements of a log cabin, as well as what appears to be a family and farm hands," he said to Cass. "The perspective is similar to his 1847 work, Home in the Woods; however, the geography is markedly different, with a farm, rolling hills, and no mountains." Cassidy looked closely at the painting, seeing what appeared to be a family on the log cabin's porch. Out in the field, black farmhands were depicted working the land.

Before Cassidy could respond, the pocket doors opened, and an elderly woman came in, supported by a modern aluminum cane. She was dressed in camel hair slacks and a cream-colored sweater over a simple white blouse. "Hello, Ms. Macgregor. I'm Cynthia Delacourt. Won't you please sit down?" She indicated one of the couches for Cassidy to take a seat as she sat on the opposite couch. Looking around, she asked, "I was told you had a cat with you?"

"Yes," Cassidy said. "Holmes, come here." The orange tabby, concealed by the back of the couch, jumped gracefully onto the couch and took a seat next to Cassidy.

"Oh, how lovely. He will have to meet my cat." Turning to the open pocket doors, Cynthia called out, "Ms. Adler, come here." A moment later, a slender, short-haired white cat walked gracefully into the parlor.

The cat seemed to glide along the floor like a ballet dancer and joined Mrs. Delacourt. The white cat settled in and studied Holmes with an enigmatic smile on her face. "Oh, look," the old woman said delightfully. "I think they're going to be friends."

Cassidy nodded and then admitted, "I love your house. You have exceptional artwork. I guess that your family acquired it over the years?"

"Yes. The whole family has always been very keen on supporting art and artists."

"May I record our conversation for my notes?" Cassidy asked, taking out her smartphone. Mrs. Delacourt nodded and smiled, waiting for the first question. "Where was the Thornhill hung?" Cassidy asked,

"My second-floor sitting room. Top of the stairs, on the right."

"When did you notice the painting missing?" was Cassidy's next question.

"A couple of weeks ago, I first noticed it was missing. I'm sorry to say I'm not as observant as I used to be."

"We will need a list of those people who have access to the second floor and contact information so we can interview them."

"No problem, dear," the old woman

"Do you have a picture of the painting?"

"Yes, let me get it for you." Mrs. Delacourt reached into her pocket and removed a small call button, which she then pressed. The butler arrived half a minute later. "Yes, ma'am?" he inquired.

"Sinkson, please bring the photo album with the Thornhill picture in it." The butler nodded and withdrew. "He'll have it in a minute," Cynthia promised. "While we're waiting, please tell me why a young lady decided to become a detective?"

"I was involved in the Torrington serial murder case when I was young, and I guess that just hooked me into detective work," Cassidy smiled. She was accustomed to being questioned about her career choice.

"How splendid," Mrs. Delacourt replied. "I think we are going to get along marvelously." Before she could continue, Sinkson returned with a dusty photo album that he laid on the coffee table and then withdrew.

"Here we go," Cynthia said, leaning over and opening the photo album. As she flipped the pages, Cassidy caught glimpses of famous people she recognized; Winston Churchill, Dwight D. Eisenhower, and even John Kennedy all seemed to have been photographed sitting in the same parlor where they were now. Cass turned to Holmes, surprised that the usual vocal cat was being so quiet. Holmes, however, was staring at Ms. Adler as if transfixed, while the white cat appeared to be enjoying the effect she was having on the detective.

"Ahh. Here we go," Cynthia said, finding the picture she was looking for. Turning the photo album around and towards Cassidy, she said, "Here is the Thornhill. I'm sorry the picture isn't better."

Cassidy could see the Thornhill; the photo seemed to have been taken while another visitor was looking closely at the painting. "Is that Lyndon Johnson?" Cass asked about the figure standing to the side of the artwork.

"Oh, yes. Lyndon used to visit quite often. We loved having him over. He was so funny and such a ham." Cassidy stared at Mrs. Delacourt and tried to frame her description in terms of the President she had studied growing up. Indeed, the terms "ham" and "funny" were not descriptions of what Cass had ever encountered in reading about President Johnson. Most of the portrayals described the man's ruthless approach to politics.

The painting depicted a young girl and a boy, both about ten years old, who were seated. The girl was wearing a white dress with long sleeves and had on a hat with a bow. The hat had two ribbons that knotted under the girl's chin with a flourish. The boy was wearing a black tunic and black britches. Rather than have the children staged in formal wear of the time, it seemed the artist wanted to depict them in casual, everyday clothes. Both children were smiling and looking at each other.

Cassidy looked at the photograph of the painting and then took a picture of it with her phone, but was distracted by her partner's conspicuous silence. Not trying to seem too eccentric, Cassidy said to Mrs. Delacourt, "This is a beautiful painting, but not very large. It looks to be about one and a half feet wide and about two feet tall in the frame. Still, it would not be something that would be easy to walk out with, unnoticed." Then, turning casually to Holmes to try to make him pay attention, she said, "Isn't this a nice picture?"

"I think Cassidy is worried about you, Holmes," the white cat purred. "You might want to rejoin the living." Ms. Adler then looked at Cassidy and winked.

"Problem, dear?" Cynthia asked, seeing a confused look on Cassidy's face.

"Uh, no," Cassidy said quickly, trying to hide her surprise at what the white cat said. Then, regaining her train of thought, she asked, "Who are the children in the painting?"

"That was Adelaide. She and her twin brother Andrés were children in the house in the early 1800s."

"Can you think of why someone would steal this particular painting?" Holmes meowed, finally participating in the interview.

When Cassidy translated the meows, Mrs. Delacourt replied, "I don't know." Cassidy looked the client in the eye and did not detect any subterfuge in her statement. But then, playing a hunch, she asked, "Why did President Johnson want to see this particular painting?"

"Oh, it was because we were talking about her brother, Andrés. He got married and moved to Texas to build a life there." Using her cane, Mrs. Delacourt got to her feet and walked over to the Thomas Cole painting of a log cabin on a farm. "This is Andrés and his family in Texas. According to the family lore, they had to pay the artist quite a lot to travel all the way from Philadelphia to Texas to do this work."

"So, President Johnson knew the descendants of Andrés Delacourt?" Cassidy observed.

"Oh, no, dear. The family name then was Gundisalvus. It didn't become Delacourt until Adelaide got married." Pointing with her finger at the image of a man on the log cabin porch, she said, "This is Andrés Ulysses Gundisalvus. But the family goes by Gund now."

Mention of the name broke Holmes out of his stupor. He got to his paws and stared at the tiny image Mrs. Delacourt was pointing at, Ms. Adler momentarily forgotten. "Gund, you say?" he whispered, then let off a long meow that Cassidy quickly translated. "Is there any of the family still in Texas?"

After the meow was translated, Cynthia said, "Yes. My cousin James Xavier Gund."

Holmes and Cassidy were staring at the painting when Ms. Adler meowed, "Finally worked it out, huh? Welcome to machinations and intrigue worthy of even you, Holmes," and then the white cat laughed in a very unsettling way.

CHAPTER VI

Joseph Goebel, Jr.

1988–HOUSTON, TEXAS: Twenty-five-year-old Joseph J. Goebel was sitting in the lobby of the Gund Organization, wondering when his interview would begin. He'd arrived twenty minutes early at the Gulf building, a distinguished Art Deco skyscraper in Houston, Texas, because he didn't like feeling rushed. Consulting the directory, he saw that his appointment was on the 35th floor, a prestigious level in the 37-story building. He also noticed that there were no other tenants on the 35th floor, which surprised him. He didn't think that Gund was a big enough company to occupy an entire floor.

Joseph's second surprise happened when he summoned the elevator, and the doors opened. *There's something you don't see much anymore,* he thought to himself. A gray-haired, uniformed elevator operator greeted Joseph Goebel and inquired, "What floor, sir?"

"35th floor, please," Joseph replied to the anachronism.

"Yes, sir," the operator replied. Then added, "The Gund Company… We don't get many people going there."

Joseph remained quiet, but filed that particular detail away for future reference. After a quick ride up to the 35th floor, Joseph stepped off the elevator and saw a pair of opaque glass doors that had—**GUND COMPANY**—stenciled on them. Nothing else. Shrugging his shoulders, he pushed open the right door and walked in. The company lobby was spacious and quiet. *This lobby is bigger than my apartment,* Joseph thought as he stood for a moment and got his bearings. There was an older woman who wore old-fashioned eyeglasses with a decorative chain sitting at the reception desk, typing away. She didn't look up when he approached, so Goebel announced himself, "Joe Goebel. Here to see Mr. Gund," he announced, shattering the silence and causing the receptionist to finally look up at him.

Goebel got the feeling that he was expected because the receptionist didn't show any surprise at the young man standing in front of her. She invited him to have a seat and told him that Mr. Gund would be with him in a moment. Then, she went back to her typing. Joseph nodded and looked around the conservatively appointed, wood-paneled lobby that reminded him of a couple of the stodgy law firms he had interviewed at. Picking a seat where he could keep an eye on the front doors, Joseph settled in and began to wait. After twenty minutes, Joseph Goebel wondered what was going on. So far, the phones hadn't rung, nobody else had come in, and except for the sound of typing, there was dead silence. Joseph wondered if he and the receptionist were the only people on the 35th floor.

Joseph Gobel questioned again why he had agreed to an interview for a job he really didn't want, in a town where he didn't want to live, to practice corporate law, which bored him to tears. True, there was curiosity about his father and his role in all of this. Why would the man about whom Joseph knew almost nothing set up an interview for a son who was a stranger to him?

Joseph Gobel Sr. left his young wife the week after the boy was born, departing as enigmatically as he had arrived in his mother's life the year before. Never to return, the only proof that Gobel Senior was still alive was the weekly check that came to cover the mother and son's living expenses. First, the funds arrived via a cashier's check in a plain white envelope without a return address, and then as a direct deposit into his mother's bank account. However, the missing father must have been keeping track of his son, because when Joseph began college, the money to cover tuition also began to arrive.

It was one month ago that Joseph Goebel interacted with his father for the first time, in the form of an unexpected phone call. "This is Joseph Gobel, Sr., your father," the man on the other end of the call said by way of a greeting to his son. "I've arranged a job interview for you with Kerwin Gund in Texas. You need to go and hear what he has to say," his father insisted without any emotion or small talk.

For some unknown reason that he couldn't identify, Joseph didn't doubt that the man on the other end of the call was his father, even though he had never heard the man's voice before. It was something about the way he talked, the cadence, that seemed very familial. Throughout his life, Joseph had seen only one picture of the man who named him. It was from twenty-five years ago; thin, sallow face, black eyes, and unsmiling.

Standing there, holding the telephone receiver in his hand, Joe wondered what the man looked like now. He had a whole slew of questions he wanted to ask this man, so much so that they formed a logjam in his mind. But when the son finally did speak, it was with a statement, not a question. "I don't want to do corporate law. It is undoubtedly the most mind-numbing field there is."

"Meet Kerwin Gund anyway. He might surprise you. A plane ticket and instructions have been sent to you," his father said before Joe heard a click over the phone.

"Wait. Where have you been? Why did you wait until now to contact me?" Joe asked, but it was evident that the caller was no longer there. The entire conversation lasted less than fifty words and took under two minutes to complete. Gone out of his life again as mysteriously as he had arrived. However, true to his word, a certified parcel from that new company, Federal Express, arrived at his apartment. Within the sealed envelope were a plane ticket and instructions for this interview.

That was two weeks ago. Today, glancing at his watch, Joseph Goebel Jr. noted that Kerwin Gund was thirty-five minutes late for their interview. "I might be surprised if this interview ever gets off the ground," Joseph mumbled, but not loud enough for the receptionist to hear. Even though this was a complete waste of time, Joseph did his due diligence on Gund and his organization in preparation for the meeting. And for the first time since he agreed to take the interview, he had been surprised.

Other than a superficial acknowledgment of the company's existence, none of the national reporting organizations had any significant information on the Gund company. Of course, the obvious answer is that if your company is a private concern and not traded on Wall Street, then you don't have to make quarterly reports. However, that logic broke down when Joseph found out through an old school contact that Lehman Brothers had a full partner dedicated to servicing the Gund's operation. Why Lehman would concern itself with a Texas family agricultural business, let alone assign a very senior partner to oversee it, was a mystery.

Joseph was checking his watch once again when a grey-haired man in a well-tailored suit came through the glass doors and made a turn towards the back offices. Without looking at the young man in the lobby, saying anything to the receptionist, or breaking his stride, the man barked, "You're Goebel. Follow me."

Joe Goebel was taken aback and wasn't exactly sure what to do. He wasn't even sure who the gray-haired man who had just marched through the office was; no picture of Kerwin Gund was in the materials his father sent. He looked over at the receptionist, a look of confusion on his face, when she bobbed her head, "Yes. That's Mr. Gund. You'd better follow him." Joseph nodded at the information, grabbed his briefcase, and quickly went after the man.

He saw Gund make a turn into an office at the end of the hall, and Joseph hustled to catch up. Like the lobby, Gund's office was wood-paneled, and the furniture looked expensive, well-maintained, but rather old. There was a large fireplace on one wall and built-in bookshelves on the other walls. The only acknowledgment that they were in the 1980s was the black phone on the desk. Other than that, no electronics or modern conveniences were found. "Sit down," Gund said to his visitor as he positioned himself behind the desk. "So, you're Goebel's boy?"

"Yes, Sir. Joseph Goebel Jr."

"Why do you want to work for me?" Gund asked.

"Sir. My father set up this interview, and I tried to tell him. I'm not interested in corporate law."

"What kind of law do you want to practice?"

"I want to work in politics," Goebel answered honestly.

"This isn't a corporate law job," Gund replied.

"Then, may I ask what the person you hire would be doing?"

"Whatever the hell I tell him to do," Gund snapped. Rather than elaborating on what he just said, Gund opened a desk drawer and pulled out a manila folder. Within was an expensive, lengthy report on the young man sitting across from him. Gund opened the report and began turning pages until he stopped at the one he wanted to see. "I know about you, Goebel. For instance, as an undergraduate, you worked on a campus election. You got your candidate elected as Student Body President by destroying the reputation of his opponent. Didn't you?"

Joseph didn't say a word. He simply looked at Gund and wondered why a man of his level would bother investigating his collegiate background. The election Gund referenced was in his sophomore year of college in Mississippi. A student he knew, Pete Barnes, was running against Melonie Hightower for Student Body President. Barnes was a strong candidate, but not quite as strong as Hightower. Melonie came from one of the original old families of Mississippi, back when it was still a territory, seventeen years before it was the twentieth state. To win the election, Goebel devised a dual push for his candidate. There would be the usual positive campaign highlighting Pete as the better candidate, featuring speeches around campus and popular events such as a BBQ cookout in the quad. That was the traditional and public face of the campaign.

However, behind the scenes, a covert, visceral campaign was orchestrated by Goebel and a couple of useful idiots who would do his bidding. The sole purpose of the second, clandestine campaign was to savage Ms. Hightower's reputation but not leave behind any evidence that could be traced back to Pete Barnes. Among the other things they did was to start a whisper campaign that Melonie had had an abortion on more than one occasion. What wouldn't have been given a second look at any school on the East or West Coast was considered positively scandalous at their fundamentalist college located in one of the most conservative regions of Mississippi. In the end, Pete Barnes won the election, and Melonie Hightower had to leave the school to escape the harassment. Joseph Goebel was elated at how easy it was to manipulate people's votes. "Do you know what happened to the girl you savaged?" Gund asked.

"Yes," Joseph replied, but didn't elaborate. He continued to stare at Gund with fascination.

Gund wasn't going to let Goebel off that easily. He needed to know what the young man was made of, so he said, "She killed herself. Slit her own wrists because the salacious rumors followed her home. How'd that make you feel?" Kerwin studied the young man across from him.

Goebel was silent. He was well aware that Hightower had killed herself, but as far as his feelings in the matter, he didn't have any. No remorse, no guilt, nothing. His candidate won, while the other candidate lost. If she couldn't handle politics, well, that was her problem. It was then that Joseph Goebel knew he was different; he couldn't feel any empathy for the people around him. After doing some research in the college library, he self-diagnosed his condition as Antisocial Personality Disorder (APD).

APD can be a crippling condition for people who have it, leading to disastrous decision-making and, for some, criminal behavior that results in jail time. However, Joseph learned early on that he could control his symptoms and turn them into an advantage. The campaign also taught Joseph that for him, there were three kinds of people: Those who were tools to further his goals, those who might be obstacles that needed to be overcome or eliminated, and those who were inconsequential and could be ignored. Even the candidate he supported meant nothing to him. It was a job. If Melonie Hightower had hired him, he would have gotten her elected somehow.

Turning a page in the file, Gund said, "Then, in your second year of law school, you worked for Senator Cummings' re-election. That was when you really upped your game to help your candidate." Joseph nodded but remained silent. He had interned for Senator Cummings, and it had been a brutal election cycle. Cummings was used to gliding into reelection, but not this year. Cummings' opponent was a young, accomplished candidate with a stellar platform and the ability to connect with voters. What made matters worse was that the opposing campaign's manager was brilliant and laser-focused on the issues that mattered to the electorate. Something had to be done to upset the campaign in the final weeks.

"How many weeks did the campaign manager for Cummings' opponent spend in the hospital after that traffic accident?" Gund asked, then studied the young man in front of him for a reaction or guilt, but there was none. Perfect. "You were supposed to work for Cummings after graduation, right? Chief of Staff, wasn't it?"

Joseph caught the use of the past tense in Gund's words about his upcoming employment. "Yes, sir," he answered, wondering where the interview was going.

"Well, you've been traded up. You will be working for me when you graduate. I need a new Fixer." Goebels studied Kerwin Gund but still held his tongue, waiting for him to elaborate. He didn't have to wait long. "You didn't know this, but Cummings works for me. I have funded his campaigns, and he does what I want him to do in the Senate. He offered you to me when my current Fixer passed away."

"Why do you need a Fixer? The Gunds own cotton farms and pork production?" Joseph asked. But when he saw the eyes of Kerwin Gund narrow at him, he quickly added "Sir" to the end of his statement.

"How much did you find out about my company when you did your research for this interview?" Gund asked.

"Not much, sir," Goebels said, being honest.

"Get comfortable. I'm going to fill you in about the Gund family, the Circle, and who really runs this country." Joseph Goebel sat quietly and listened to Kerwin Gund. After fifteen minutes, he began to realize that his life wasn't ever going to be the same.

PRESENT DAY: The Fixer was seated at a desk in his new condo, courtesy of one of Xavier Gund's numerous shell companies, trying to figure out how to accomplish the task that had been assigned to him. How do you compromise a family that has been controlling significant parts of the United States since the Gilded Age?

In the 1870s and 1880s, numerous robber barons vied for power across the country. These families were making fortunes in shipping, railroads, manufacturing, and mining, and each was becoming obscenely wealthy. They built massive homes on huge estates that covered hectares of land. They married their daughters off to European royalty and controlled the lives of their workers, yet after all that, they felt unfulfilled. What they craved more than wealth was the power to run the whole show.

Gradually, through attrition, deceit, or outright warfare, the other plutocrats were forced out. In the end, the four surviving Families established an uneasy truce. They decided to work together to further their goals and power: Landewedock, Camborne, Phillack, and, of course, the Gund family. Now, Xavier Gund wanted to be able to control it all.

The Fixer reached across his desk and grabbed a yellow legal pad. There was no way he was going to put this on any computer; they can be hacked too easily. First, he began making a list, including the family name, the primary industries they controlled, and their successor (if known). Then he added what they contributed to the Circle. Even though each family had diversified holdings, often in each other's businesses, these were industries where each family had the most influence, and in some cases, the industries that laid the foundation for their fortunes.

Landewedock–***Healthcare***. Prescott Landewedock and his family were behind the two biggest health insurers and drug makers in the country. Collectively, these two insurance companies controlled access or, more often than not, denied access to healthcare for over half the country while their drug companies inflated the price of every drug they made. The successor was going to be Annabelle, his wife, and the Landewedock family had considerable political influence.

Camborne–***Media***. This family controlled the broadcast, cable, and internet industries throughout the country, and it directed the editorial policies of multiple news outlets. The power of this family to control the narrative in the news was incredible. Their immediate successor was supposed to be the son, Eugene. The Circle liked Simon Camborne because it was said he could kill any story the Circle might not want published, even those in competitors' news organizations, with a single phone call.

Phillack–***Manufacturing & Real Estate***. Bertrum Phillack owned multiple manufacturing concerns across the United States. The Phillack family wasn't interested in building microwave ovens. Instead, they were the power behind the two most prominent defense contractors, everything from ships to aircraft and various weapons systems. It turns out that maintaining the U.S. and its allies' readiness for war was indeed highly profitable. There was talk that their successor was going to be the husband of Bertrum Phillack's daughter. However, that had not been okayed. The Circle still believed in a strict, unbroken bloodline succession only.

And just because he had listed the others, The Fixer wrote down his Boss, Xavier Gund–***Agriculture, Finance & Insurance, Absolute Power***. The Fixer knew something of his boss's family history, and sometimes he wondered what old Andrés Gundisalvus would have thought of the empire that sprang from his small farm, which had been started in the territory of Texas. Gund planned for his son to follow in his footsteps.

The Fixer stared at what he wrote down. *This was not going to be easy,* he thought.

CHAPTER VII

The Mandeville

It was a short drive over to the hotel that accepted cats in downtown Philadelphia. As it turned out, it was a much higher-quality hotel than the one usually used by the Holmes & Watson firm. Part of this was because Mrs. Cynthia Delacourt insisted that Cassidy stay somewhere nice while she was in town with her cat and had Sinkson call and make reservations at a place called The Mandeville. The other part was that Mrs. Delacourt didn't want a young woman to drive back to Connecticut in the dark. Cass wondered if she had been adopted.

Cassidy had spent most of the day at the Delacourt house, interviewing the butler, the cook, and the maid. Each had tried to be helpful, but none of them could tell exactly when the painting had disappeared. "It used to hang right here," Sinkson said, pointing at the wall. "But the paintings were reorganized, so there didn't appear to be a blank space."

The paintings in the sitting room and much of the house were hung the old-fashioned way using a picture rail. Each room and hallway had a wooden picture rail installed about six inches from the crown molding at the ceiling. A painting would be hung on two wires. One end of the wires would be fastened to the painting, and the other end would have hooks for the railing. It was a simple matter of unhooking a painting to remove it and sliding a different painting over to cover the blank space.

"Does Mrs. Delacourt entertain much?" Cassidy asked while Holmes listened.

"Not very much anymore," the maid confided. "She's eighty-seven, and many of her friends have passed. It's sad." The maid thought for a minute and then added, "I think you are the first guest she's had over in a couple of months."

"Who lives in the house besides Mrs. Delacourt?" Holmes meowed, and Cassidy asked Sinkson.

"Just me," Sinkson replied. "The maid and the cook come in each day." Cassidy nodded. With each interview, she used her gift to scan the person and attempt to detect falsehoods. However, each member of the staff seemed to genuinely like Mrs. Delacourt, enjoyed working for her, and didn't know anything about the missing painting, but all agreed that it had gone missing.

Throughout the day, Ms. Adler would appear at different times, sit and listen to what Cassidy was asking, or watch what she was doing. In a rare moment when it was just Cassidy and the white cat by themselves, she tried questioning her. "What do you know about the missing painting?" she asked.

Ms. Adler softly laughed in delight and shook her head. "Oh, this is marvelous. How long have you been able to talk to cats?" she purred.

"Since I was twelve. And I'm still waiting for you to answer my question," Cassidy reminded her.

"What a wonderful gift. I could use a person like you," the inscrutable cat meowed, avoiding the question, then turning and leaving with her tail swishing back and forth, a sign of deep amusement. A couple of times, Cassidy saw Holmes and Ms. Adler off by themselves in deep conversation. She promised herself that she would ask Holmes about this peculiar behavior when they got to the hotel.

At 4:30, Cassidy pulled into the circular drive of The Mandeville Hotel, and immediately, a doorman, who happened to be a young woman, came running to the driver's side and prepared to open her door. Cassidy signaled her to wait a second and turned to Holmes, who was sitting in the passenger seat. "You need a harness and leash if we are going into this place," She said, holding the two items. Holmes didn't answer, but the annoyed look he had more than made up for it. Cass gently slipped the harness over his head, then secured the strap going between his front legs to the belt around his middle. Once secure, she nodded at the doorwoman, and the door was opened.

"Welcome to the Mandeville," the doorwoman said with a wide smile. "Checking in?"

"Yes," Cassidy replied and walked around the back of the car to retrieve her overnight bag. As soon as the trunk was opened, the Doorwoman reached past her to get the bag. "Only the one, ma'am?" she asked.

Ma'am? Cassidy reflected with humor, then she said, "Yes, thank you."

"This way, please." The doorwoman let Cassidy and her cat move ahead through the revolving door and to the front desk. When they reached the desk, the doorwoman set her bag down and wished Cassidy an enjoyable stay before heading back to the front doors.

"Wait," Cass said, reaching for her wallet to give a tip, remembering that was what they did in those old movies that she and Izzy watched on Saturday nights together, curled up on the couch.

The doorwoman smiled and said, "No, thank you, ma'am. It's been taken care of."

Not understanding how it could be taken care of, Cass turned to the man behind the front desk, but before she could mention her name, she was greeted. "Good afternoon, Ms. Macgregor. Will it just be you and your cat with us this evening?"

"Uh, yeah. I believe a reservation had been called in for me?" Cass replied, then eyeing the name tag, she added, "Michael."

"Yes, ma'am. If I may see your ID," Then, engaging in small talk, Michael asked, "What is your cat's name?"

"His name is Holmes," Cass said as she handed over her driver's license and credit card. However, the man only compared the driver's license photo to her face; he left the credit card on the reception desk and then handed both back to her. Seeing the questioning look on her face, Michael said, "Your stay and all gratuities have been taken care of by Mrs. Delacourt." He handed Cass her room key. "A bowl of fresh salmon for Mr. Holmes and a litter pan are already in your room, and room service is available twenty-four hours a day. We hope you enjoy your stay." Michael motioned to a porter who approached, picked up her bag, and gestured toward the elevators. Five minutes later, Cass was in her opulent room, and Holmes was lying on the bed.

"Not exactly the River Des Peres motor lodge, is it, Holmes?" Cassidy asked with a generous smile, walking around the room. She turned on the light in the bathroom and saw the shower had a massaging shower head, a hand shower, and what was called a rain-can drench shower coming out of the ceiling. "I'm going to call Watson and tell him we may never come back." When Holmes didn't respond, she turned around and saw that the detective was awake and staring off into space. "You and I are going to talk about this attitude of yours right after I call our friends. That's a promise."

She sat on the corner of the bed and dialed Watson, and it rang several times before rolling over to voicemail. Instead of leaving a message, Cass hung up and dialed Izzy to let her know she wouldn't be home until tomorrow. After a couple of rings, Izzy answered. "Hey, Cass," she replied, but not with the usual smile in her voice. Furthermore, there were noises in the background where Izzy was, including the sounds of doctors being paged and codes being called. Sounds all too familiar to Cassidy.

"Why are you in a hospital?" Cass asked, her voice pitching up with worry.

"I'm fine," Izzy reassured her. "It's Watson's Mom. She had a pretty bad stroke. We're at the hospital."

"I will drive home right now," Cassidy replied, rising to her feet.

"I don't think…hold on, Watson wants to speak to you. Here he is." There was a brief pause as the phone was passed back and forth between them. "Hey, Cass," Watson's tired voice came over the line.

Cassidy switched the phone to speaker mode and set it on the bed so Holmes could also listen. "Tyler, I'm so sorry. What do the doctors say about your Mom?"

"They're running some tests, and they're going to do a CT scan. It doesn't look good," Watson replied, sounding like any son would when his mom was in a hospital.

"Holmes and I will come home tonight to be with you."

"Don't do that. There is nothing you can do. Izzy's here with me; you can come home tomorrow." Then, changing the subject, he asked, "Did the meeting go well?"

"Yes. We have the job. But that is not important right now. We'll leave Philadelphia in the morning," Cassidy assured him, then looked at Holmes to see if he wanted to add anything. The orange tabby seemed reluctant until Cass glared at him with such intensity that it was frightening.

"Watson. Your mother is a strong woman. If there is a way back from this, she will find it." Holmes looked at Cass, who nodded and encouraged him to continue. "Call us if there is any change. We will see you tomorrow."

Watson thanked them and handed the phone back to Izzy. She promised to stay with him and call if there was any change, and then she hung up the phone. Cassidy looked around the room and muttered, "Well, shit." The joy of the extravagant hotel room and new job had evaporated in the presence of the news from Torrington. Looking over at Holmes, she said, "I'm going to order myself some dinner from room service, and then you are going to tell me what the deal is between you and this Ms. Adler."

CHAPTER VIII

Ms. Irene Adler

NEW YORK CITY, SIX YEARS BEFORE: The orange cat ran effortlessly down the gangway at the Manhattan Cruise Terminal, weaving in and around people disembarking from their passage from Britain and making their way to customs. Ignoring startled comments from passengers who wondered if the animal had somehow escaped its owner, the orange cat ran out of the terminal and onto the shoulder of 12th Avenue, where he stopped and looked up. The skyline of New York dominated his view, beckoning him forward with an irresistible pull. Holmes was the happiest he had ever been; he was right where he needed to be as a detective. Catching a glimpse of the Empire State Building and triangulating his position from the map he memorized, Holmes set off for Lower Manhattan. His future as a detective awaited.

Two months later, Holmes was working for Mei Zhang, the matriarch of the Zhang family and owner of their restaurant in Chinatown: Zhang Garden, on Mott Street. The upper Yangtze Mandarin dialect spoken by the ninety-six-year-old, Madame Zhang, wasn't too hard for Holmes to understand since he had learned Mandarin as a kitten.

At night, after the restaurant closed, Madame Zhang, who called Holmes 橙貓 *(Orange Cat)*, would feed him leftovers from the kitchen and talk to him about her village outside of the city of Guiyang, capital of Guizhou province, in south-central China. Today, the province is best known for the city of Guiyang, also known as Forest City, a metropolis of over five million people situated in a lush landscape of dense forests, steep hills, and abundant greenery. But Madame Zhang remembered the area from when there were few roads in or out of the remote city, and as late as 1950, the primary mode of transportation was still the horse and cart. The Zhang family lived in a small village on the outskirts of Guiyang, off the Nanming River, where they grew rice.

Holmes would sit, sometimes for hours, listening to Madame Zhang talk about her life and what she had seen in China. She was too young to remember the Japanese and the brutality of their occupation. But she had many memories as a little girl during the Second Chinese Civil War from 1945 to 1949, when the Chinese Communist Party (CCP) and the Nationalist (KMT) fought for control of mainland China. It seemed the dust barely settled from the Civil War when they were plunged into the cultural revolution of the 1960s. It was then that Mei Zhang and her parents decided to come to the United States.

The Zhang family settled in Chinatown in New York City, in Lower Manhattan. 「紐約的一切都很新奇有趣，橘貓」 *(Everything in New York was new and interesting, Orange Cat)*, Madame Zhang said to Holmes. Lately, however, the stories told to Holmes have centered on the Zhang family's attempts to resist the local Wah Ching gang. The Wah Ching had started bearing down on the family and their business on W. 49th Street because they wanted to use their basement as a gambling den. Madame Zhang told Holmes she didn't know what the family was going to do. From the family's prior experience in China, there was a deep-seated distrust of the police. Therefore, people like the Zhangs were left to their own devices.

Holmes knew all of this from other shop owners, which is why he chose the Zhang Garden as the place to stop the Wah Chings before they could complete their plan to control all the businesses on the block. So while Madame Zhang told her stories to Holmes, he set his mind on solving the gang problem for them.

Holmes decided he could cover more ground and gather more intelligence if he had some help; that was where the Irregulars came in. A group of young, hungry alley cats led by a local, beat-up, one-eyed tough named Wiggins and his lieutenant, Sir Timothy Lawrence. Holmes did a double-take at the name, but ended up shrugging his shoulders, though he doubted Sir Timothy would be found in Burke's Peerage.

Holmes promised the Irregulars plenty to eat as long as they worked for him. Thus, while Holmes sat in the window of Zhang's Restaurant, the Irregulars spread out to find out everything they could about the Wah Ching gang. A week later, Holmes convened the first meeting to assess what they had learned. Wiggins started out the report in between mouthfuls of discarded fish from the restaurant, "Them Wah Ching gots a problem," he reported.

"Tell'em about the Triads," a tiny tabby cat named Pip meowed.

"He's gonna. Let'em finish," Maverick answered.

"Quit interrupting," Sir Timothy added.

"What's this?" a black kitten asked, pointing at a half-full takeout box.

"Chicken feet," Holmes meowed. "As you were saying?" Holmes meowed smoothly, nodding his head to Wiggins.

"Yeah, the Wah Ching and the other gang, the Triads, are in a war to control this block. All the other businesses are also being leaned on or promised a piece of the action if they go along."

"What's this?" the black kitten asked, pointing to a different box.

"More feet," Holmes replied as he sat and thought for a minute; multiple logic strings were calculated and then discarded when the ultimate outcome indicated failure. Finally, one string blazed in his mind, a plan, start to finish, and the result was *success*. A small smile crept onto his face, and Holmes meowed, "Right, lads. This is what we are going to do…" Over the next few minutes, the detective outlined the plan to rid the neighborhood of both gangs. When it was time to wrap it up, the British detective said, "All of you Johnny's, get a good night's sleep, and tomorrow, the game is paw."

As the Irregulars started to head back to the abandoned factory where they lived, Holmes pulled one aside, "Pip, who is that young white female cat that was here?"

"I dunno, boss. She'd shown up a couple of days ago. Says her name is Irene."

"Thank you, Pip. See you tomorrow." Holmes watched the little tabby dash off and then set about reviewing his plan one more time, looking for all possible countermeasures. However, his train of thought kept returning to the white cat named Irene. The coquettish look she was giving him kept breaking his line of thought, which was not something that Holmes was used to.

For the next several weeks, like a chess master setting a trap from which there was no escape, Holmes manipulated events and moved his pieces into place with subtlety and finesse. Throughout the time, the irregulars performed their duties flawlessly. It was during this time that the cat, named Irene Adler, would spend each evening with Holmes, engaging him in playful banter, moonlight walks through the quiet city, or playing a game of chess at one of the tables in the park, where her uncouth style of play managed several draws, much to the detective's surprise. Despite Holmes' rule against affection, their relationship did, in fact, become intimate.

It wasn't until the veil of total infatuation was lifted that Holmes realized how one-sided their sharing was. For instance, Holmes was sure Irene Adler was from somewhere in Britain, but her ability to mask her accent was as good as his. "Where are you from, Irene?" he would meow at her.

"Everywhere and nowhere," the white cat would laugh, annoying the detective. But instead of pursuing the line of questioning, he allowed her to change the subject.

When the night came to spring the trap, Holmes was nervous; it wasn't a feeling he was remotely used to experiencing. The trap consisted of bringing the two gangs together in confrontation and having the police arrive to arrest all of them simultaneously. While that was going on, Holmes would be visiting each gang's location for a bit of public service arson. He wasn't going to burn down the buildings, but rather give the police and fire departments exigent circumstances to enter those locations where, among other things, were the principal storehouses of each gang's drugs.

From his perch, Holmes watched as the two gangs walked into the crucible he had created, but almost immediately, the detective realized something was seriously wrong. Only a few of the foot soldiers from the Triads were there. The leadership, including the lieutenants, was nowhere to be seen. Holmes recognized that the trap he had created was appropriated by the Triads, and this was simply a feint, indicating that the core of the gang was elsewhere. When Holmes deduced where they were, it gave him a sinking feeling.

The next day, Holmes understood how bad he'd been played when the sign on the door of Madam Zhang's restaurant and several other businesses proclaimed that the establishments were under new ownership. The cats he had sent to start the fire at the Triad's headquarters reported that the building was empty when they arrived; no drugs and nobody remained. Adding to Holmes's humiliation was seeing *That Female,* Irene Adler, and the Triad leader together. Irene Adler gave Holmes a patronizing smile from the arms of the new owner of Zhang's restaurant.

PRESENT DAY: "That was the last time I saw *That Female.* She disappeared into the tapestry of New York. I underestimated her deviousness and her intelligence. Plain to fact, she bested me. Truly, it is the female of any species that is the most cunning. They will smile seductively at you while thrusting the dagger between your ribs." Holmes finished his muse and resumed his quiet contemplation.

The sun had set, and the single lamp Cassidy had lit made the hotel room feel cozy. She sat cross-legged on the bed, finishing her club sandwich from room service and listening to Holmes's tale. After a sip of her Diet Coke, Cass asked, "So how does this Irene Adler figure into a missing painting from an old Philadelphian's house, and how did she come to be here, in Philadelphia?"

"I don't know," Holmes said honestly. "But if *That Female* is involved, I naturally expect the worst."

CHAPTER IX

Watson

Cassidy bid a reluctant farewell to the Mandeville as she and Holmes climbed into her car for the drive back to Torrington. When she awoke to her phone's alarm, she called the front desk to ask that her Honda be brought around in thirty minutes. The person on the phone assured her it would, and then she went into the bathroom to wash her hair. When she came out of the bathroom, there was a discreet knock at her door. Cassidy glanced at the door and then at Holmes, who shrugged and said, "Answer it."

Looking through the peephole, she saw a uniformed waiter. Opening the door with a chain still on, she asked, "Yes?"

"Room Service, ma'am, with your Continental Breakfast," the young man intoned.

"I didn't order any breakfast," Cassidy replied.

"Yes, ma'am. This is compliments of the Mandeville."

"Okay. Please wait a moment," Cass asked, then went to her phone to call the front desk to confirm the waiter's story because she hadn't been able to read him through the partially open door. When the front desk confirmed the room service and even provided the waiter's name, Cass thanked them and went to let the young man in.

After the waiter left, Cassidy and Holmes took stock of what had been brought. As it turned out, a Continental Breakfast at the Mandeville consisted of coffee in a silver coffee pot. Hot water in a separate pot. A selection of teas, breads, croissants, pastries, and fruits, even a bowl of kibble for Holmes. "This is really a nice place," Cass admitted as she sniffed and then tasted the croissant. It was still warm, light, and buttery–perfect.

"Soon back to reality, I should think," Holmes said after trying the kibble.

"Yeah. But first, I am going to have a good cup of coffee," Cass replied, pouring the French roast into a china coffee cup. Then, she finished dressing while sampling a few items from the cart.

Once they were on Interstate 95, heading back home, Cass said, "We'll go straight to the hospital. Izzy texted me that there wasn't any new information."

"Agreed," Holmes replied. But his mind was elsewhere.

Three hours later, Cassidy pulled into Torrington General Hospital and parked. "I don't think I can sneak you in," she told Holmes.

"That's fine," Holmes assured her. You go ahead, and I will wait here for news."

Cassidy found Izzy and Anne Gaumont in the waiting room for the intensive care unit. "Hey, girl," she greeted her fiancé with a hug and kiss. "What do we know?" she asked the two women.

"Watson is in the room with the Doctor and his mother. The Doctor wants to go over advanced directives with him," Anne said.

"They want him to make a decision about a ventilator and other life-sustaining treatments," Izzy added. Then, looking around, she asked, "Where's Holmes?"

"He's either out by the car or trying to find a way to sneak in here," Cass said. Peering down the hallway, she saw Tyler walking towards them; his face looked like it had aged a hundred years.

When he walked up to his friends, he said, "She passed." All three women brought Watson into their embrace as he could no longer hold back the tears.

"I want an update," the angry voice declared over the phone.

"I understand, sir," The Fixer said quickly. "I have made progress." The Fixer paused, waiting for Gund to respond. As it turned out, he didn't have to wait long.

"I'm waiting, dammit. What did you find?" Gund barked.

The Fixer heard the tone and glanced at the clock; it was four in the afternoon. It looked like the boss had started on the whiskey earlier than usual. "Well, sir. Landewedock seems to have a proclivity for young mistresses," The Fixer replied, waiting for a follow-up question. When no response happened, he continued, "And Phillack's daughter is a drug abuser. That is all I've been able to find out so far."

"That's not enough. Keep digging," Gund said, then hung up.

The Fixer stared at the phone and then said softly to himself, "And James Xavier Gund is a belligerent alcoholic."

That evening, Holmes came into the kitchen of the house that now belonged to Tyler Watson. No lights were lit, but the orange cat had no trouble seeing Watson sitting in a kitchen chair, embracing the dark. He jumped on the table and sat down next to his friend. Watson did not appear to notice. For his part, Holmes remained silent, not wanting to break Watson's contemplation.

"Do you miss England, Holmes?" Watson suddenly asked.

"England is just a place, mostly like any other. Places, for the most part, do not have a draw on me," he meowed.

"Do you miss your Mom?" Watson asked, knowing the story of her death.

"There are times I would like to talk to her. She was an outstanding cat, but very underappreciated where she lived. But as long as I remember her, she will always be with me."

"Do you miss your brother, Mycroft?" was Watson's next question.

"I miss locking horns with him. After me, he is the smartest cat I know." Watson smiled at Holmes for his ability to compliment someone while praising himself even more. Guessing at the reason for the question, Holmes asked, "Do you want me to find your sister Mary?"

Watson was silent. He knew if he asked, Holmes would find his sister; of that, there was no doubt. "No. She's had years to make contact with Mom after she left. I don't even know where you would begin to look."

"You doubt my abilities, sir?" Holmes asked, trying to make Watson smile again.

Watson shook his head in the dark, then stood up. "I'm going to bed. I have to make arrangements tomorrow." However, before he left the kitchen, he turned back to Holmes and said, "I'm glad you're here, Holmes."

Holmes watched Tyler leave but continued to sit in the dark kitchen and think. A work from a fifteenth-century poet came back to him:

> *Why does an event so common as death*
> *seem so severe to whomever it wounds?*
> *Why at times does man's reason retreat*
> *and the passions muster all their power?*
> *God, compassionate, just, seems cruel to us,*
> *Our understanding so is greatly perplexed;*
> *the pain abates, and faith at once returns,*
> *but firm understanding lies beyond our power.*

Ausiàs March, the Valencian poet, certainly didn't have all the answers when he wrote about the death of his wife six hundred years ago. Holmes wondered if March would be disappointed that humans have added so little to the subject other than the biological processes involved. Sitting there in Watson's kitchen, Holmes came to a decision, but even the genius detective couldn't foresee all the ramifications.

After the initial squeal, "Ahh! Cold hands!" Cassidy was able to relax as Isabella massaged her neck and back with expert skill. When she arrived home in West Hartford, Cass dramatically flopped onto their bed and announced how tired she was.

"Take your shirt off and turn over," Izzy instructed her fiancée. Izzy straddled her fiancé and began using her strong fingers to find the knotted muscles in Cassidy's shoulders and back. Then, using gentle pressure and stretching, Izzabella kneaded them to let the tension out.

"I don't deserve you," Cass mumbled, relaxing completely.

"No, you don't," Izzy teased. "Do you think a boyfriend would do this for you?"

"How would I know? I'm gay."

"Didn't you tell me that you had a crush on a boy in school?" Izzy asked.

"Yeah, but that was a long time ago," Cassidy admitted. "But that crush changed when I saw his girlfriend, and I got a bigger crush on her," she said, which made Izzy giggle.

"You're tense," Izzy remarked as her hands moved around Cass's back, seeking more problem spots. "This one feels like a marble," she commented, finding one below the right shoulder.

"Oh, yes. Right…right there," Cass murmured, guiding Izzy, and then gave a moan of pleasure.

"Can I ask you something?" Izzy began.

"Ask me anything. Just don't stop," Cass begged.

"Do you think about death?"

"That didn't take long to come up."

"Our friend's mother just died. It's a natural conversation to have." Izzy replied.

"I guess I do think about it," Cass admitted. "I have been a part of some really weird stuff, with the cats I know and all. But I'm not afraid of it. If you ask my old cat, Mittens, after this existence, there's the Infinite."

"What's that?" Izzy asked, moving from one shoulder to the other.

"I think it is Cat heaven. Mittens is a little vague about it, but she sounds very sure."

Changing the subject, Isabella asked, "Remember when we talked about having kids?" Because Izzy had found a good spot on her back, Cassidy could only grunt in the affirmative. "In a few years, I think we should adopt a two or three-year-old."

"I think I know, but why in particular?" Cass asked.

"When I was cleaning up, I found some of the old files I used to prepare for my undercover. The stories about the girls caught up in human trafficking gave me nightmares when I had to study them last year." Isabella paused, remembering the statistics she had learned. "Trafficked girls can be any age, from one year on up. Once the girls are lost in that world, they're gone. The families almost never find them."

"It sounds horrible," Cassidy agreed.

"It is," Izzy confirmed. It's easy to put a baby up for adoption, but once they get to two, three, or older, the ability to find adoptive parents really goes down. That is when the human traffickers come in and exploit the situation. It made me almost ill to read about it. I never knew it was that bad." Izzy finished.

Turning over to face Izzy, Cass asked, "So, you would like to adopt a two or three-year-old and give them a safe home and family?" She watched as Izzy nodded, and then she asked, "What about having one of our own through artificial insemination?"

"We should look into all options when we're ready to begin a family," Izzy remarked. "What do you think?"

"I think I love you even more, Isabella DeLeón," Cass replied as she sat up to kiss Izzy and hug her. "I think you will be a great mom." Both women held onto each other until Izzy said, "Okay, I will."

"Okay, what?" Cass asked.

"You just said for me to lie back; it was my turn for a massage," Izzy replied.

"I didn't say that out loud. I was thinking it, but I didn't say it," Cass explained, a faraway look on her face.

"I swear I heard you?" Izzy said, confused.

"This is weird. Years ago, I projected my thoughts onto the cats a couple of times. One instance was when I was stuck in a tree and very frightened. But the ability seemed to go away."

"You always said you were very close to the cats growing up, maybe it happened again because of how close we are?" Izzy suggested looking for a reason.

"Perhaps. Let me try again," Cass said, then appeared to concentrate.

"I got nothing," Izzy confirmed after a minute.

"Well, I'm too tired to keep trying this. Let's mark this up as another example of how weird your wife-to-be is, and let it go for tonight," Cassidy replied lightheartedly, and then began massaging her fiancé. Lying face down, Izzy couldn't see Cass's expression of worry, wondering what in the world was going on now.

CHAPTER X

Services

The pastor stood over the casket at the cemetery, extolling the special relationship between mothers and sons and how hard it was on the survivors when one of them was called on to their reward. Watson was sitting in the front row in a black suit with Holmes on one side and Izzy and Cassidy on the other. Behind them, quite a few of the chairs were filled with friends, and Watson was grateful to each one of them. The DeLeóns were there, and so were the Macgregors. Anne Gaumont was sitting next to Mrs. Barnes, the neighborhood busybody who had known Tyler Watson Baumann all of his life, as well as a significant portion of Mrs. Baumann's church group. All in all, it was a fascinating collection of people: a couple of millionaires, a couple of academics, a retired Chief of Detectives, and quite a few of the hoi polloi of Torrington. In Holmes's opinion, those people were more interesting than the affluent.

The pastor reached a point where he asked if anyone wanted to say anything. There was silence until Holmes gave a long meow. All eyes turned to the orange tabby in the first row, but it was Cassidy, pretending they were her thoughts, who translated what was said to those in attendance: "Mrs. Baumann was a strong, smart woman. The world was better for her being in it." Watson began sobbing, put his hand on Holmes's back, and patted it.

A few more people said some very kind things about Tyler's mom, and then the service ended. Cass and Izzy watched as Tyler stood up, walked forward, laid his hand on the coffin, and bent his head with his eyes closed. A moment later, he turned and left the gravesite.

A small gathering was scheduled immediately following the service at Watson's house. A half-hour later, a number of people were milling about, sipping coffee, tea, or a beer, and telling Watson how sorry they were. The refrigerator and freezer were now full of casseroles brought by half of those attending. At one point, Cassidy, Izzy, Anne Gaumont, and Holmes found themselves together. "As soon as this is over, I need to speak to all of you about the plot against Izzy and the missing art case. We may have a break," Holmes meowed. "Where's Watson?"

Anne looked around the room and pointed, "He's over there talking to a guest." All three of them watched as an attractive woman reached out her hand and lightly touched Watson's forearm, then she leaned in to put her head closer to Watson, never breaking eye contact.

"Wow. She's really into him," Cassidy announced. "Her body language couldn't be more obvious."

The mystery woman drew Watson into a hug and gave him a peck on the cheek, then left through the front door. Watson watched her go, then turned to see that he was being watched by three women with wide grins. Casually, he walked over to the group and asked, "What's up?"

"Who was that?" Cassidy asked, still smiling.

"Her?" Watson asked, pointing at the front door with his thumb. "That was Davina Cassock, an old friend. We went to school together before I got into trouble."

"She really likes you," Anne remarked, also smiling.

"What, Davina? No. We've been friends for ages. Besides, she's probably married."

"There was no wedding ring on the hand brushing your forearm," Holmes casually meowed.

"You should ask her out," Izzy suggested.

"You four," Watson said, gesturing to all of them, "are imagining things."

Holmes let off a deep sigh and meowed, "We need to talk about the Art case and the plot against Izzy after everyone is gone. In the meantime, Captain Oblivious, you should get back to your guests.

By four in the afternoon, the wake had broken up, leaving only the employees of Holmes & Watson and Isabella. Since the attempt on Izzy's life was the reason for this investigation, Holmes thought she should stay on and be aware of how the case was progressing.

Izzy and Cassidy sat on the couch under the front windows. Anne Gaumont was in the chair on the left, and Watson was in his chair on the right. Holmes sat on the coffee table and began by giving an overview. "As you all know, when Isabella's undercover went sideways, it interfered with Xavier Gund's plans to put his man, Gable Finch, into the Senate. Gund's response to this was the subsequent attempt on Isabella's life. Since that time, and based on the initial information I was able to gather from the Assassin's crypt, I was able to locate Gund and his home in East Texas." Everyone nodded, so Holmes continued.

"Gund's estate is massive, with both automated and human security elements guarding it. A standard blitz to gain entry and collect intelligence will not be possible. Furthermore, I believe that if Gund realized we were investigating him, it would put our lives in danger. What we need to do is disguise our true intentions when approaching this quarry. Fortunately, the Philadelphia Art case that Cassidy and I went on last week will provide that means."

"How so?" Watson wanted to know.

"Cynthia Delacourt of Philadelphia is descended from the Gundisalvus family. In the early 1800s, there were twins, a boy and a girl. The girl stayed in Philadelphia, married, and became a Delacourt. The boy, Andrés Ulysses Gundisalvus, moved to Texas as a young man to establish a farm. Eventually, they changed the family name to Gund, the very same Gund that initiated the attempt on Isabella."

"You think this Gund character is behind the missing painting?" Anne shrewdly guessed.

"Yes, I do," Holmes meowed.

"Why?" Cassidy asked.

"Because whoever took this painting wasn't in it for monetary gain. The theft of this painting was for personal reasons."

"Why do you say that?" Watson wanted to know.

Holmes turned to him and meowed, "You have not seen this house. Therefore, I will explain. Art, far more valuable and easily accessible, was available on the first floor; yet, the thief went to a second-floor sitting room, took one painting, and then rearranged other paintings to cover the space. This was a contracted job."

"Okay. I'll buy that. But why did Gund contract to steal the painting? Why not ask for it?"

"From everything I have been able to learn, the Gunds are fantastically arrogant and entitled. They would want an original painting of their founding ancestor to be with them, not in a cousin's parlor in Philadelphia. Furthermore, from what I have learned, James Gund doesn't ask. He takes. He thinks he is untouchable."

"Okay, let's say your guesses are correct," Cassidy began. "How do we use it to our advantage for the art case and the attempt on Izzy's life?" When she finished speaking, she reached over and took the hand of her fiancée.

"I do not guess," Holmes meowed. "I process data and observations to create deductions."

"Fine. You don't guess. That still does not answer my question," Cass replied.

"We are going to use this missing art as a pretext to gain entrance to Gund's world. However, before that attempt is made, I want us to do our due diligence. When we return to Philadelphia to re-interview Ms. Delacourt, we must be able to convince her that the answer to the missing art lies with her cousin in Texas." Holmes finished and looked around, and various heads nodded. "We need access to Gund and his world."

"Do you think we will be able to gain access?" Watson asked.

"Of course. It's elementary," the orange detective purred.

That night, after Watson was asleep and the house was quiet, Holmes left and made the trek to talk to one of the few creatures he truly admired. Once he got to Mittens' home, he followed the Protector's way in, which hadn't changed over the years. Creeping up from the basement, he found her on her pillow in the front room; as usual, her arthritis prevented the climb to the second floor, so the family had made her a comfortable nest on the first floor by the radiator. The glow of the full moon gave a bluish cast to the room as Holmes sat at attention; if the old Protector awoke, they would speak. However, he would not disturb her otherwise.

The impact of this particular cat could fill volumes, and the number of people she had helped could not be accurately determined. For a cat like Holmes, who considered pomp, ceremony, or hero worship to be bollocks, standing in Mittens' presence was a decided privilege.

After a number of minutes, Mittens opened her good eye and saw the detective watching her. She lifted her head and softly meowed, "Yes, Holmes?" in a tone that brooked no surprise.

"I have come to seek guidance."

"I assume that even you understand the concept of retirement? Belle is the Protector now."

Holmes nodded. "The young Protector is brilliant. But you have the wisdom and empathy I require." He watched the old Protector and was conscious of the fragility that was before him. *Damn age, altogether,* he thought.

"What do you want to know?" Mittens asked.

Holmes delved into everything he had learned about the case concerning Isabella, the art case, and finally even brought up Ms. Adler. He finished his recitation with, "Do we pursue this or walk away?"

"Holmes, you already know what you intend to do. What you seek from me is absolution, and that is not mine to give," Mittens replied. "I am not your Confessor. Do your friends know the risks? Have you told them?"

"Yes, of course. But Cassidy and Watson will follow me because they trust me. What if I am wrong and someone gets hurt again?" Foremost in Holmes's mind was the near-fatal attack on Cassidy the year before. Nobody but Holmes realized how much that had affected him.

"That is a risk that all leaders take, the responsibility of others under them." Then, the old Protector changed the topic. "Who will you turn to with these questions when I'm gone, Holmes?" The detective was caught off guard by Mittens's question and didn't answer.

Mittens nodded her head and replied, "For you, justice is like a narcotic that you have become dependent on; you cannot exist without it. You cannot tolerate those who break the law. Likewise, you want to provide a remedy to those who have become victims. You never worried about your personal safety when it was just you. However, now you are hamstrung to the point of inaction, contemplating the danger to those who have breached your independence with their friendship."

After a moment, Holmes merely nodded, unable to speak. "Holmes, on this path, you must make your own decisions. If it helps, I think you will make the right choice. Now, shoo. I'm tired and need my rest."

Holmes watched as the Protector lay her head down and closed her eyes. Bowing his head to the Protector, he left as silently as he came.

Three days later, at 2:00 a.m., all the cats were standing in a silent vigil around the old Protector. Giblet and Belle, with Lily by her side, Hamilton, and Holly Bear were in a rough semicircle around Mittens. None of the cats could prevent themselves from hearing Mittens as her labored breaths grew increasingly shallow. Belle, tears streaming down her face and whiskers, stood at attention, determined not to show weakness.

The old Protector's eyes opened one more time, and in an almost inaudible whisper, she meowed, "Take care of each other." Her eyes closed for the last time as her last breath left her body.

Above them all, a multicolored glitter began to swirl softly, gradually forming a vortex. In complete silence, the vortex created an empty center where a cat's face appeared; Belle recognized Mackayla, a family cat that passed on years before, and seemed to be the ethereal guide for their clowder. Lily moved between her mother's legs, shaking with fear. Belle, Giblet, and Hamilton had witnessed this before; a doorway to the Infinite had opened to accept another cat soul. Another face formed next to MacKayla. It was Mittens looking like she did years ago when she was in her prime. The spirit of Mittens looked at her family and smiled, then the doorway closed, and the vortex faded into the night.

"Bye-bye, Grandma Mittens," Lily meowed in a soft voice.

Now, all the cats began to move closer together to support each other and share this moment. After all the tears stopped and were dried, Belle looked down at Lily and told her she needed to go home and get to bed. "I'll make sure she gets back to Anne's safe," Giblet meowed. "Come on, squirt." Belle licked her daughter's head as she turned and followed Giblet out.

All the cats knew that Belle would not leave Mittens's side until their people came in the morning to bury the old Protector. It was the least she could do for a cat that she loved, who had been like a mother to her and meant so much to so many others.

CHAPTER XI

Philadelphia, Part II

Two weeks later, Cassidy, Watson, and Holmes were on their way back to the Delacourts' home, having secured another interview. In the interval, Holmes had scoured the dark web for any sign that the painting had been offered for sale. He also had Cassidy make several quiet inquiries to known art fences, seeing if they had heard anything about this missing painting. Holmes did not actually expect to find the painting that way; he firmly believed that Gund had taken the painting. "Still, we will file away these inquiries under the auspices of being thorough," He meowed to his partners.

Both Cassidy and Holmes were still feeling the effects of Mittens' passing. For Cassidy, Mittens represented a presence who had been there for her as long as she could remember. For Holmes, it meant the loss of a counselor and a cat he venerated.

For his part, Watson spent a considerable amount of time going through his mother's belongings and sorting them out. One pile was comprised of items destined for the local charity. The second pile consisted of things he planned to give to friends so they could remember his mother. And the final pile was the things that he intended to keep. One of those items was the Art Deco wedding ring his grandmother wore. The question of how his grandfather was able to buy such a ring was always a source of speculation at the few family gatherings they had.

When Watson showed the ring to Cassidy and Holmes, she teased, "That would be a lovely engagement ring."

"Why do married and engaged people always try to set up their friends?" Watson wondered aloud to Holmes.

"Perhaps, in your case, it is because you have gone out with Ms. Cassock twice since the wake. Or, perhaps it is because Cassidy has the latent genes of a *shadchan* in her." Holmes waited a moment and then added, "That is a Jewish matchmaker, in case you are interested." All Watson could do was roll his eyes.

There were multiple discussions on how they were going to approach the meeting with Ms. Delacourt. While they were driving, Holmes had caught Watson up on Cynthia's cat, Ms. Irene Adler. "I don't know what her angle is, but *That Female* is not to be trusted," Holmes said for the third time.

"She's really rattled you, hasn't she?" Watson suggested.

"Nothing of the kind," Holmes insisted. "When you meet *That Female,* you will find her insouciance frustrating. However, that is a misdirection. She is plotting something, and I do not intend to be caught off guard. I will question *That Female* while you and Cassidy confront Cynthia Delacourt."

Watson and Cass both nodded, and then she brought up a new topic, "On a completely different matter," Cassidy began while watching the road. "Izzy and I have picked a wedding date. It will be on Saturday, September 2nd, in Torrington. Make sure you both don't make other plans."

"I don't think you will let us forget," Watson said, smiling as Cassidy pulled to a stop in front of the Delacourt house in Society Hill.

Sinkson, the butler, once again met them at the door and directed the trio to the front parlor. "Ms. Delacourt would join you momentarily. May I bring anyone coffee or tea?" he asked. Both Watson and Cass gave their orders, and Sinkson inclined his head as he closed the pocket doors and left.

Holmes and Cassidy sat together on the couch while Watson commented on the artwork and toured the room. "They really have a nice collection here," he commented.

"It's like this throughout the whole house," Cassidy admitted.

The pocket doors opened, and Cynthia came in, followed by her cat, Ms. Adler. "Welcome back, welcome back. I see you brought a new person. How marvelous," Ms Delacourt said to them, walking up to Watson and extending her hand. "Hello, I'm Cynthia Delacourt."

Watson took her hand and introduced himself, "Tyler Watson. A pleasure to meet you."

"We want to update you on our investigation and discuss a couple of ideas," Cassidy informed their client.

While the humans were talking, Ms. Adler got up, stretched, and began a lazy saunter toward the door. However, before she left, she made a point of turning back, catching Holmes' eye, and giving the detective a come-hither flick of her tail. A moment later, Holmes got to his feet and followed her out into the hallway. Once there, the white cat climbed the stairs to the second floor, with Holmes following.

At the top landing, Ms. Adler turned and went into the sitting room where the missing painting used to hang. When Holmes arrived, she meowed, "This is a good place where we won't be interrupted. You seemed a bit bewildered the last time we met." Smiling, she asked, "But now, I think we can have a good talk. How've you been? It's been some time since Chinatown." Holmes stared at the white cat and waited for her to get to the point.

Not put off by the detective's laconic nature, she continued, "I see you have new friends. Tell me, do they know your background, hmm?" she purred.

"I have been honest with my partners. Can you say the same for your human? What happened to your previous associate, the leader of the Triads?" Holmes asked, genuinely curious.

"Oh, him. I think he will be out of prison in about ten to fifteen more years," Ms. Adler replied. "He didn't want to listen to me, and I'm not the type to wait around."

"What are you doing in Philadelphia?" Holmes asked, getting to the point.

"Would you believe me that I am just a house cat enjoying the company of a nice woman?" Ms Adler asked Holmes.

For his part, Holmes simply stared at the white cat, an incredulous look on his face, then asked, "I don't suppose you intend to tell me who took the painting."

"You're not here about the painting, Holmes. I saw your reaction when Cynthia told you about her family. Why are you after James Gund? If you make it worthwhile, perhaps I could ask around on your behalf. I've always fancied a warmer climate…say Florida or Southern California. You help me move there, and I will be your cat on the inside."

"Believe me when I tell you, you don't want any part of James Gund. He is very dangerous." As Holmes was meowing, his excellent hearing picked up someone knocking on the front door, followed by the front door opening.

"Oh, you're worried about my safety," she smiled as she purred. "How sweet. You don't think I can take care of myself? Maybe you should teach me," she meowed seductively as she rubbed her head against Holmes's head.

"Teaching you to take care of yourself would be as redundant as teaching a duck to swim. However, Gund is a whole new level of evil, one that even you are not prepared to deal with."

"Oh, dear," Ms. Adler exclaimed. "Then perhaps we should go downstairs and make sure your friends are okay, then. That was Gund who came to the front door."

Holmes was frozen for a moment, not comprehending what she meant. When he realized what was going on, the detective took off at a full run, heading downstairs to the front room.

Cassidy chose tea, while Watson had a perfect cup of coffee brought by the butler. Ms. Delacourt, Cass, and Watson were engaged in chit-chat, a preamble to their meeting, when the front door knocker sounded. "Oh, excellent," Mrs. Delacourt announced. "That is our special guest. Sinkson, please let the gentleman in," she called out.

Watson and Cass heard someone come in the door, and a moment later, he was standing in the doorway of the parlor. The man was of average height, with a touch of gray at the temples. He was wearing a camel hair sport coat over a white Oxford shirt and pressed blue jeans that came from Neiman Marcus. His shoes appeared to be Lucchese cowboy boots, but most of the boots disappeared under the jeans.

Cynthia stood up and gave the man a hug, then turned and said, "You got here right on time, James. Let me introduce Mr. Tyler Watson and Ms. Cassidy Macgregor; this is my cousin, James Gund, from Texas." In a testament to their professionalism, neither Cass nor Watson reacted to the introduction.

James Gund walked towards the two detectives, smiled, and extended a soft, pink hand adorned with a class ring from a private military academy in Texas. First, he said to Cassidy, "Please call me Jim," taking her hand gently in his. Cass gave off her best smile and used the opportunity to do a quick scan. Then he shook Watson's hand in a much more aggressive manner.

"I called James about the missing painting after our last meeting," Cynthia reported. "When I told him I had called in detectives, he insisted on coming to Philadelphia to see us."

When everyone was seated again, Jim Gund said, "I'm sorry that you were called in for this missing painting. I have it." Then, turning to Ms. Delacourt, he said, "Did you forget? You told me I could take that painting back to my house in Texas.

"I don't remember that, James. When did you ask me?" Cynthia questioned.

"Last Christmas, during my visit," was Gund's smooth reply. Turning to the detectives, he added, "When I was called last week about the missing picture, I knew my Cousin must have forgotten. I'm sorry you were brought in on an obvious misunderstanding."

Before anyone could say anything else, Holmes came bounding into the room and skidded to a stop on the hardwood floor. Looking up, he had no trouble seeing the same man from his reconnaissance in Texas last year. For his part, Gund stopped talking and stared at the orange cat, a look of puzzlement on his face.

Sensing the danger in the situation, Watson quickly said, "And there's our company mascot, Holmes." Taking a cue from Watson, Holmes promptly sat down and began grooming himself, attempting to act like any other cat would in the presence of humans.

Cassidy, attempting to switch the conversation back to painting, asked Ms. Delacourt, "Since the painting has been located, I guess we will bill you for our time to this point, and you can work it out with your cousin on getting the painting back?"

"I want you to go down to Texas and bring my painting back," Cynthia protested to Cassidy. Then, turning to her cousin, she said, "James, when can these nice people pick up my painting?"

There was an awkward silence in the parlor as Gund struggled to find a response in the presence of outsiders. Everyone could see by the red rising from his collar that James Gund was searching for a way to keep the Holmes & Watson agency out of Texas and away from his home. However, what eventually came out of his mouth bore little similarity to his first instinct, "Okay, Cynthia. Let's talk it over. But I think we should let your guests get about their work while we work out the details." Turning to Watson, he said, "We won't take any more of your time. Thank you for coming." His words came out in a conversational and polite tone, but the look in his eyes left no room for debate. This visit was over for them.

Watson got to his feet while Cassidy scooped up Holmes, who by now was playing with his tail. Smiling, Watson said, "Please call us, Ms. Delacourt, if we can help you with anything more. Thanks for the coffee." Looking Gund in the eye, Watson added, "A pleasure to meet you, Jim. I hope we meet again," Cassidy nodded her head at the two of them and followed Watson out of the room.

Watson, Cassidy, and Holmes were exiting the front door when they encountered two formidable-looking security personnel, undoubtedly personal protection for Gund. Cassidy once again gave her best disarming smile to the bodyguards, but its effect, if any, was hidden by the dark sunglasses they both wore, which also prevented her from reading their minds. Holmes watched as one of the guards took several pictures of Cassidy's car as she drove away.

Once they turned the corner, Watson reached into the glove compartment and removed a small but excellent RF signal detector, scanning the car. Throughout the scan, the detector's light remained green, revealing no listening devices. Visibly relaxed and leaned back against the car seat. "It's clear, we can talk. That was close," he admitted to his partners. Then he asked Holmes, "Do you think he recognized you?"

"I don't think so. When we met Gund at his home in Texas last year, I simply watched him. When he saw me today, I was mimicking the behavior of my species."

"Let's hope you're right," Watson conceded. "Were you able to scan him?"

"Yes," Cassidy admitted. "He's full of rage. He was furious at his cousin for calling us in to investigate the missing painting."

"Anything else?" Holmes asked.

"Yeah. That man scares the hell out of me," Cassidy confessed.

They drove in quiet for a while, each lost in their own thoughts. Finally, Watson asked Holmes, "What did you learn from that white cat?"

"She's looking to improve her station in life, preferably in a warmer climate, which is bollocks. I am not sure what her angle really is, only that she is mercenary by trade. She will honor an agreement only until a better one, in her view, comes along. She is well aware of what kind of man James Gund is."

"Looks like the investigation is over then," Cassidy guessed.

"Nonsense. We will be called, and soon. Gund wants to know what we found out about him and his business and what Cynthia Delacourt might have told him." Holmes added, "This is far from over."

CHAPTER XII

Escalation

James Gund returned to Texas in an ugly mood. When his cousin Cynthia left him a message saying the Gundisalvus children's painting had gone missing and that she had hired private detectives to find it, he knew he would have to travel to Philadelphia to sort out the details. It was well-known in the family that the commissioned portrait of his ancestor, Andrés Ulysses Gundisalvus, and his sister, Adelaide, was in the possession of the northern branch of the family. They had maintained ownership for almost two hundred years.

Several things about this arrangement had always annoyed the man from Texas, not least of which was that Andrés, not the sister, had put the family on the trajectory for greatness. Second, Cynthia was childless, and the northern branch of the family would come to an end with Cynthia's passing. He did not trust her not to bequeath the painting to the Philadelphia Museum of Art. James Gund had a son who was presently away at military school, and he wanted the painting so that he could pass it on to him, thereby keeping it in the family.

It was last Christmas, during a visit to Philadelphia, that James Gund rectified the status of the portrait. While he and his cousin were visiting that evening, one of his bodyguards had collected the painting, rearranged the remaining portraits to cover the empty space, and loaded the painting into their car. The painting was now hanging in his private study, as it always should have been. Gund never thought the old bat would discover it missing.

During his flight back to his ranch, he began a cursory investigation of Holmes & Watson on his laptop. They appeared to be a small, moderately successful investigative firm based out of Connecticut. Still, it would not do for them to be looking into his businesses. He wondered if he should have The Fixer look into the detectives, but decided against it. The project he had The Fixer working on was more important. He could handle this. Arriving back at his study, he made himself a double whiskey and fumed. As his level of inebriation rose, two plans, both independent of each other, but with far-reaching implications, came to mind. And unsurprisingly, Gund talked himself into pursuing both despite the potential for serious consequences.

"I'm sorry, sir. What did you do?" The Fixer asked his boss over the phone.

"I am taking care of the Landewedock problem," Gund happily replied on the evening encrypted status call from The Fixer. It had been a month since his return to Texas, and the idea concerning Ladewedock that had begun on his trip home was now ready to be put into action. "I also have another plan, but this one is personal."

"What are you going to do concerning Landewedock, sir?"

"I sent a couple of my guys over to create a little scandal. This should eliminate Landewedock from the Circle," Gund said cheerily. "The bastard will never survive this."

"I thought you wanted research into the Circle in case of a problem in the future. What's changed?" The Fixer asked.

Gund ignored the questions and instead asked, "Getting squeamish? That hasn't been your style." The line was silent for a second while Gund took another swallow of whiskey. "You need to finish the report on the other members of the Circle," he barked over the phone.

"I am, sir. But I have to tread carefully, or they will know what we are doing," The Fixer explained.

Gund frowned. Why did his Fixer keep trying to ruin his mood? "Just keep watching the news. It should be all over the place by sometime tomorrow."

"You said two plans. What is the second one?" The Fixer asked. "Sir, I have to know what you have planned if I am going to protect you," but there was no response; Gund had hung up as soon as he finished talking. The Fixer sat and wondered exactly what his boss had done and what the repercussions from that would be. But with nothing to go on, all he could do was wait and worry.

Prescott Landewedock was on his way to his latest mistress and feeling pretty good at the moment. This young woman, a twenty-five-year-old redhead, seemed like a lot of fun. They had met at some dumb charity event Prescott couldn't be troubled to remember. He picked her out of the crowd and began the seduction, a skill that he was pretty good at if he did say so himself. He would tell the woman that he and his wife were no longer close. That much was true. To his horror, after Prescott wed Annabelle, he found out that she only believed in sex for procreation. After the two children were born, she wouldn't let him touch her. She contented herself with her church group and left running businesses to her husband.

Then Prescott would tell the girl that he and his wife were separating and on their way to a divorce. That was a flagrant lie. He had no intention of leaving his wife. Her majority ownership in one of the largest health insurance companies in the country, coupled with his majority shares in the other, meant Prescott Landewedock controlled access to healthcare for more than half the nation. Under his careful administration, the revenue increased, and payouts for life-saving procedures decreased significantly. Turns out, if you keep delaying the approval for needed medical procedures long enough, about half of the people will die—problem solved.

Finally, a couple of moderately expensive presents were sent to her home, along with a couple of nice meals at expensive restaurants, and the girl would be willing. He didn't know how long any particular affair would last. If the girl continued to surprise him, then it might go on for a while. If she were boring, then Prescott would move on.

As he drove to tonight's dalliance, he thought back on the number of conquests. Prescott gave up after counting to twelve. However, out of those dozen, only two were problematic when he decided to call off the affair. One made a fuss until Prescott had her aged parents' health insurance frozen. The other girl left when he pointed out that with one phone call, he could have her apartment lease canceled, and she would be listed as a problem renter, so nobody else would offer her a lease. In the end, both women acquiesced, and Prescott never gave them another thought.

Prescott pulled into the apartment complex and walked up to the door. He knocked twice and tried the doorknob; it was open. Walking in, he saw her on the couch, but the scene was all wrong. She was gagged, her hands were tied together, and she was crying. Landewedock didn't have time to sort out what was going on when something cold was pressed against his neck, and then he knew nothing more.

While Prescott Landewedock was driving to his mistress, Watson was in the office going over some paperwork. He was working late because there was no reason to rush home anymore. Holmes was also with him, providing companionship and rereading *Agamemnon,* a tragedy by Aeschylus, in the original Greek. Watson looked up and watched as the cat reached down with a paw, extended one claw, hooked the page, and gently turned it over. "You know, there are a lot of good books out there that aren't twenty-five hundred years old. You might think about reading one of them," Watson suggested.

"All modern literature can be traced to archetypes the Greeks explored. Why not read the original? This one deals with hubris and malignant pride. A lesson that many people today need to learn," Holmes meowed.

Watson was saved from responding when the phone rang. Pressing the speakerphone option, he answered, "Holmes & Watson."

"Mr. Watson? Cynthia Delacourt. How are you? I hope I am not calling too late." At the sound of Cynthia's voice, Holmes walked over and jumped on the desk to listen.

"Hi, Ms. Delacourt. No, it's not too late at all. And how are you?"

"I'm doing okay. I have some good news. My cousin Jim Gund has said that he wants to send my painting back."

"That's wonderful, Ms. Delacourt. I'm happy you have a resolution." Watson replied while raising an eyebrow at Holmes.

"He said he didn't want to trust it to a shipping company. So, he wants to send his jet so that you and Ms. Cassidy can come down and bring it back to me." Cynthia said, sounding pleased.

"Do you know when he wants to do this?" Watson asked.

"Jim said whenever your schedule works."

Watson looked at Holmes, who made a slashing motion with his paw. "Ms. Delacourt, can you hold a moment? I need to check my schedule." Watson pressed hold on the phone and turned to his partner. "What do you think?"

Holmes gave a look of satisfaction on his face and said, "I told you he would want to see how much we have learned about him. This is excellent. Tell her you can do it in two weeks."

"Why two weeks?" Watson asked.

Holmes shook his head and said, "Tell her. I will explain after you hang up."

Watson pressed the hold button and said, "I think we have some free time in about two weeks. Is that okay?"

"That's fine, Mr. Watson. Thank you so much. I will let you know when Jim gives me the arrangements. Goodbye," and the call ended.

"Want to tell me now what you couldn't a moment ago?" Watson asked.

"We will go over everything with you and Cassidy when the three of us drive to New York tomorrow," Holmes said, barely concealing his glee.

Izzy and Cass returned to their condo with the week's worth of groceries, thankful that their unit was located at the end of the group of attached units, where parking was much easier to find. In fact, they usually could park right in front of their door, which was great in bad weather. Each woman had several bags in their hands as they approached their front door, where Izzy saw a package on the welcome mat. "Looks like we have a delivery," she said as she unlocked the door and stepped over the box.

"I'll get it after I put these bags down," Cass replied.

Both women went to the kitchen to deposit their bags. Izzy started putting things away while Cass went back to collect the mail and the package on their welcome mat. Out of habit, she glanced back at the parking lot, but there was nobody about, and she recognized the cars as belonging to her neighbors, all except for a white plumber's van. Thankful that they didn't have any plumbing issues, Cassidy stepped back into her home and locked the door.

"Just junk mail," she reported, looking over the three pieces of mail. "And the package is addressed to you."

Izzy finished putting away the groceries and picked up the mystery box. It weighed very little for its size. In fact, it could have been empty except when Izzy shook the parcel, something inside sounded like it was moving around. Using scissors, she cut the tape and opened the shipping box to reveal a second package inside from a bridal shop in Bogotà, Colombia. Opening the second box, she saw a small ivory envelope on top of something carefully wrapped in tissue paper. Removing it, Isabella saw what it was.

"What is it?" Cassidy asked, looking at the white lace scarf.

"This is a traditional Colombian mantilla. A head scarf for the bride at her wedding." Holding it up, she saw the delicate lace pattern and marveled at the craftsmanship it took to make it. "I think this one is handmade."

"That would be expensive," Cassidy guessed. "Who sent it? Was there a card?" Opening the envelope, Isabella saw a handwritten note in Spanish:

> *Mi queridísimo corazón,*
> *Me he enterado de tu compromiso y me alegro mucho por ti.*
> *Por favor, acepta este sencillo regalo y llévalo el día de tu boda.*
> *Serás una novia preciosa. Por favor, dale mis mejores deseos a*
> *tu prometida, Cassidy. Me cae bien. Por favor, dile que estoy*
> *agradecida por protegerte el año pasado.*
> *Abuela.*

"It's from my Grandmother," Izzy reported, raising her eyebrow.

"What's it say?" Cass asked.

"Well. The mantilla is a wedding gift from her to me. She says that she heard about our engagement and that she is happy for us." Reading on, Izzy added, "She also mentioned you, and that she was grateful for your help to me last year. Grandma says she likes you."

"The head of one of the biggest cartels in Colombia likes me," Cassidy acknowledged. "That's something not many people can claim. How did she find out about our wedding?"

"It must have been when Dad put an engagement announcement in the paper. You know what a traditionalist he is. Somehow, it got back to Abuela in Colombia."

"Are you going to tell your Dad about it?" Cassidy asked in an unambiguous tone, conveying that she thought she shouldn't.

"Are you kidding? No way. Dad would have a fit." Izzy put the mantilla on her head and wrapped it around her shoulders. "It is pretty, though. Do you like it?"

"It's lovely," Cassidy admitted, moving to stand in front of her love. "You should wear it. You will be a beautiful bride."

"I don't think you should tell your parents, either. No sense in making them worried about a veil," Izzy suggested.

"You know, girl," Cass said, running her fingers lightly along the mantilla and smiling. "When you're right, you're right."

CHAPTER XIII

New York

Watson picked Cassidy up at 7:30 in the morning, then set his maps program for New York City. "Now that we are all here, mind telling us why we're going to New York? Watson asked.

"Simple," Holmes replied. "Being invited down to Gund's home, the belly of the beast, as it were, gives us a unique opportunity to gather evidence of his crimes. There is a man in the city who is an expert in custom-built listening devices. He's brilliant. I propose we plant a device in Gund's house and see what we can learn." The detective finished and waited for the inevitable questions to begin.

Both Cassidy and Watson were quiet. Finally, it was Watson who broke the silence, "If Gund is as paranoid about his security as you have indicated, how do you propose we plant a listening device?"

"I am going to teach you how to plant the device without anyone realizing what you are doing," Holmes meowed confidently.

"How do you know they won't search us on the way into the house?" Watson wanted to know.

"The device will be concealed before you travel in such a way that nobody will find it before you are ready to plant it," Holmes answered with assurance.

"Don't you think Gund will sweep the house the moment we leave? The device will be found," Watson said with certainty.

"The instrument I envision will have a twenty-four-hour delay before it self-activates. We can even set it to wait forty-eight hours if needed. When they scan the room after you leave, nothing will show up because there won't be a signal," Holmes meowed. Then, turning to Cassidy, he waited for her next question.

"You are forgetting one thing, Holmes. If the bug is found, Gund will know precisely who placed it there. He had the Assassin killed in a federal lockup. Aren't you worried about blowback against us or our families?" Cassidy asked, thinking of Izzy and both of their families, and subconsciously reaching down to rub the scar on her abdomen where she was stabbed last year.

"A bridge too far," Watson said softly, staring at Holmes.

Cassidy had a questioning look on her face and asked, "What's that?"

Holmes looked at Cassidy and said, "During World War II, the Allies had a plan for securing five bridges through the Netherlands and establishing a pathway into Northern Germany for the 2nd Army, effectively cutting off the industrial heart of the German war machine and ending the war sooner. Although the Allies were initially victorious, they were halted at Arnhem, the last bridge over the Rhine. An Irish journalist, Cornelius Ryan, coined the term A Bridge Too Far to mean a plan whose goals exceed their grasp."

"Or too reckless," Watson added.

"I don't undertake this lightly. I am aware of the dangers. But I am also aware that it was on this man's order that an assassin came after Isabella. I want to make sure that does not happen again."

Holmes paused and then began again, "Picture a man, unstable, fabulously wealthy, and drunk on his own power. A man who thinks he is above the law. I think the greater danger is to do nothing."

Cassidy and Watson looked at each other but were silent. Neither was convinced that this was the correct approach, but neither had a sound alternative to offer. The rest of the journey was traveled in silence.

HOUSTON–1996: It had been eight years since Joe Goebel had taken the job offered by Kerwin Gund and become the Gund family's Fixer. In those years, he had learned the extent of the Circle's reach into the workings of the United States, how the four families divided the tasks among themselves, and how ruthlessly they dealt with what they considered non-compliance. The Fixer had called on Judges, Congresspeople, and Senators. For the most part, these people were more than willing to sell their convictions without a second thought. Rare was the one who actually tried to stand up to the Circle. "Find the right pressure point, and even the strongest will yield," Kerwin told his new Fixer. It was almost cliché, but it worked.

For Joseph Goebel, it was the ideal occupation. He got to manipulate people and events with impunity. Over the last ten years, there were two occasions when he met with frustration. First, he was never able to track down his father after the latter's brief appearance in his life. Once again, the man disappeared as if he never existed. The Fixer was certain that Kerwin Gund knew something about his father, but he refused to divulge anything, telling him, "Don't worry about it." The last time, however, The Fixer was warned not to revisit the subject. That was the kind of warning a person didn't disobey.

The second peeve had to do with Kerwin Gund's son and heir. The Fixer found that he spent an inordinate amount of time cleaning up the messes that James Xavier Gund, also known as Jim to his friends, managed to get into. The younger Gund had gone from a precocious child to an aggravating teenager, then to an incalcitrant college student.

At each stage, the young Jim Gund tested his father's limits, requiring The Fixer to bail him out of trouble. The Fixer knew that his future was tied to this petulant young man. All Joe Goebel could do was hope that maturity and a little sober effort could keep James Xavier Gund from mucking it up too severely.

PRESENT DAY: The Fixer was watching the feed from a cable news program, and the story was the same as it had been on the other two channels; Prescott Landewedock and his mistress were dead in an apparent murder/suicide at the young woman's apartment. Detectives were very early in the investigation, but it appears that the young woman was strangled, and then Prescott hanged himself. Mrs. Landewedock hasn't issued any statement, and the family asked for privacy at this time.

"Gund, you idiot," The Fixer said softly, watching the TV. On the screen, the reporter began discussing the Landewedock family, old money, and their controlling interest in two of the most significant health insurance companies in the United States. Neither company has issued a statement, the reporter said.

The Fixer shut off the TV and reached for his phone. He needed to talk to his boss and fast. This was going to be a mess of epic proportions. On the third ring, Gund answered the encrypted line. "You see it?" was his way of saying hello.

"Yes, sir. I thought you were going to extort Landewedock for concessions, not remove him and his mistress?" The Fixer asked, seeking a reason.

"It was only supposed to be the girl, but things got out of hand when Prescott woke up too soon after being drugged," Gund replied matter-of-factly. "The men made the suicide look convincing."

"Sir, the police are going to do a thorough investigation. Mrs. Landewedock will insist on it." What he didn't say was that Mrs. Landewedock didn't need to depend on the competency of the local police force. She had more than enough money to hire the best forensic investigators and provide them with unlimited resources to find the truth. Then The Fixer asked, "Are you sure your men cleaned the scene sufficiently? Nothing that can be linked back to you?"

"If you think it's a problem, you can take care of the men who did it. No loose ends," was Gund's favorite answer to most things. Then he asked, "When are you going to have the information on Camborne and Phillack?"

"I hope soon, sir," The Fixer answered. Then he heard the click and saw that Gund had hung up on him once again. Swearing, The Fixer set his phone down. The two men who did the job on Prescott Landewedock would have to be removed. He didn't trust them not to leave evidence behind, and they would roll on Gund if the cops caught them. Once they arrived back in Texas from California, he would send them down to Mexico under the pretense of another job, but in this case, they would not be coming back.

Why did James Gund make such a rash move against a member of the Circle? Part of the problem was, of course, the father-complex James Gund had, and the inadequacies that he felt when people compared him to Kerwin, as the members of the Circle did, relentlessly, when James took over. James was aching for a win, one that he could claim, totally on his own. It's no wonder that the son was investigating the Circle. Eventually, he wants to get even with them.

The problem with Gund and the Circle was that they each believed in their own invincibility. The Fixer knew better. In 1890, when the Circle was formed, you could quite easily get away with murder. There were no forensic experts to speak of, and formal forensic training was still about three decades in the future. Furthermore, the job of a law enforcement officer was often bestowed as a patronage job, rather than being given to the most qualified. Nowadays, The Fixer knew if he looked, he could find traffic-cam images of those two men around the apartment where the murders took place. That's how it always starts. One piece of evidence leads to the next, and pretty soon, the cops are knocking on your door, asking questions, and your alibi unravels in real-time.

He picked up the phone to make a plane reservation for Mexico City for the next day. He needed to meet a contact he had used before to clean up Gund's most recent mess.

Hasim Bashir

Until a year ago, Hasim Bashir was frequently mistaken for a high school student. Everywhere he went, it seemed that the twenty-seven-year-old M.I.T. graduate and electronics shop owner had to pull out his ID to prove he wasn't fifteen. Of course, part of the problem was his height and build. The Bashir family male line was consistently thin and vertically challenged. Five-foot-five might be okay for a high school freshman, but it was a lot more annoying when you were an adult and trying to order a glass of wine. The second issue was Hasim's boyish face. While there was nothing that could be done to make him sprout another five inches, he was able, after a whole year, to grow an acceptable beard. Finally, the carding ceased while he was on dates. In addition, Hasim found his solace in the fact that he could still shop in the young men's section of the department store, where the clothes were less expensive.

When Hasim graduated summa cum laude from M.I.T., his family was justifiably proud. A dozen companies offered Hasim jobs based on his grades and the praise of his professors. But to everyone's astonishment, the new graduate didn't take any of those offers. Instead, he leased a small storefront property in the Flatiron District of New York and put up a sign that read "Bashir Electronics." What his parents and grandmother failed to understand was that Hasim Bashir was a tinkerer and inventor at heart. He was happiest when someone challenged him to create something new that everyone else said couldn't be done. Saying that to Hasim was akin to waving the red cape at a bull. Not only would Hasim say that it could be done, but he would also extemporaneously outline how he was going to do it, and then he would actually build the darn thing.

On two occasions, Mr. Bashir's electronic inventions, along with their corresponding drawings and patents, were seized by the U.S. Government on the grounds of national security. One of the seized items was a high-speed electronic switch device. The problem was that Hasim's invention, while benign for the purpose for which he designed it, could be altered to become the principal switching device for setting off a nuclear bomb. When the Federal agents left his shop with all his drawings and the working model of the switch, Hasim said to the agents, "You know, I only got a B+ in Signal Processing," referring to the MIT course that greatly influenced his ability to create the switch. "What are you going to do about all the people who made A's? Especially if they are angry?"

This morning, Hasim was in his shop, fiddling with a clock radio that was at least five decades old if it was a day. *At least it doesn't have tubes;* he thanked the universe for small favors. When his grandmother asked him to repair this antique, he begged her to let him put in a new AI virtual assistant in her apartment. "Please, Grandmother, let me give you this AI assistant," setting a black cone that was about six inches tall on the countertop. "All you have to do is ask it what you want."

Hasim cleared his throat and asked aloud, "Carson, what time is it?" A moment later, the top portion of the black cone blinked and said, "The time is 10:30 a.m." with a crisp British accent. Smiling at his grandmother, Hasim then asked, "Carson, what is the temperature outside?" The black cone blinked and said again, "The time is 10:31 a.m." Looking embarrassed, Hasim repeated, "No. Carson, what is the temperature outside?" The black cone blinked yet again and replied, "The forecast today is for sunny weather and a high of 83°."

Hasim's grandmother smiled at her grandson, as if he were still ten years old, and said, "When can I pick up my clock radio?" That was a day ago, and he was no closer to repairing the device because there were no parts available for something this old. He was about to go online to see if he could find a different clock radio for sale when the bell on his front door drew him away from that problem. Glancing up, he saw a man and a woman entering his shop. They weaved around display cases containing various electronic gadgets and stopped at the back counter where Hasim was sitting.

Smiling, Hasim got to his feet to greet his customers when an orange cat jumped onto the display case and stared at him. "You?" he spluttered, taking a step back, his smile immediately being replaced with a look of alarm. "What are you doing back? I thought you left town. I hoped you left town." Then, looking at Watson and Cassidy, he sputtered, "I barely survived the last time I worked for him."

"That's being a tad dramatic, Hasim," Holmes meowed, with Cassidy translating. "The situation was never out of my control."

"Situation?" Hasim sputtered. "I had a gun pointed at my head while the head of the gang demanded to know who I sold the bug to! What was I going to tell him? That an orange cat asked me for a favor?"

"Didn't the police show up in time, just like I planned?" Holmes reminded him. "Don't be such a fusspot. Anyway, now you know that you can't leave any identifying marks on your product, like 'Bashir Electronics' was on the last device you made for me."

Wary suspicion replaced the look of alarm as Hasim asked, "Why are you here?"

It was Watson who answered this question: "We need a bug. There needs to be a time delay before activation, like 24–48 hours after we plant it. The device must automatically locate and access the nearest

Wi-Fi network, so that it can transmit the conversations it picks up to a private internet account where we can retrieve them. The bug needs to be voice-activated, and it needs to be small enough that it won't be found if we get searched."

"And your name really *shouldn't* be on it," Cassidy replied with a helpful smile.

"Anything else? Perhaps some spotted dick with your tea while you wait?" Hasim replied sarcastically to the group.

"Hasim," Holmes meowed. "You are a genius with electronics. If there was anyone I would trust to build this device, it would be you." Holmes let that sink in for a moment, then added, "I am sorry for the distress last time. But as I remember, that gang was also terrorizing your family as well. That's why we met and you helped me."

"Hasim, this is very important," Cassidy added. "The person we are trying to collect evidence on tried to have my fiancé killed last year."

The young man remained quiet and stared at the ceiling of his shop, ignoring Holmes, Watson, and Cassidy when Watson said, "It's alright if you can't do it. I didn't think a bug with this set of parameters was possible anyway."

"Quiet," he snapped at Watson. "I would have to buy the parts for the bug in a way that they could not be traced back to me," Hasim began, visualizing the instrument. "Then there are the unique qualities, the delayed activation, and the ability to find and tether a wi-fi network…" his voice trailed off as he went deeper into thought. After a moment, he turned his head to look at his customers. "Describe the room where you are going to place the device?" Hasim asked Watson and Cassidy, sure that Holmes wouldn't be doing the job.

Watson shrugged his shoulders and shook his head. "I deduce that my cohorts will meet in the man's private office in his home. But, as to the mise-en-scéne, we have no idea," Holmes answered.

"A bug with these specs for a room we know nothing about. This is going to be expensive." Hasim calculated.

Watson was about to ask how expensive it was when Holmes overrode him by meowing, "How long will it be until it's ready?"

"Two to three weeks," Hasim replied distractedly.

"Get started," Holmes replied. "Watson, give the man a deposit."

Watson gave Holmes a sour look concerning his generosity with the Firm's funds, then asked Hasim, "How much do you need to get going?" However, the young electronics wizard didn't answer. He was lost in thought as he went back to visualizing the device.

"Is a couple of hundred okay?" Watson persisted. Hasim blinked his eyes, finally realizing he was being addressed. He didn't answer but did manage to nod.

Cassidy reached into her wallet first and removed a company credit card. Handing it over, she said. "Thank you for this," she said, smiling again.

"When shall we come back?" Holmes meowed.

"Two to three weeks, maybe more, depending on the availability of the parts," Hasim replied while running the card for the deposit. "I'll call you."

"Thank you," Watson said, leaving his business card. "Call us if you have any questions." Then, the three investigators turned and left the shop.

2003–GUND RANCH: The Fixer made the long six-hour drive from his home outside Houston to the Gund family ranch called Perpetuus. Even though he had been working for the family for fifteen years, this was the first time he was told to meet at the ancestral home of the Gund family. Kerwin Gund always preferred conducting business from his office in Houston. But now he was dead at 88 years old, and the son was finally in charge.

The instructions for their meeting were quite specific. The Fixer was to arrive at 2:00 p.m. and give the guard at the gate his name. He was then supposed to park in the employees' parking area, walk around the right side of the house to the exterior door of James Gund's office, and knock. Under no circumstances was he to come in the front door of the home; that was for family and friends. Not employees.

The Fixer followed the instructions to the letter, and at 2:00 p.m., he knocked on the office door and was let in by the new de facto leader of the Gund family. The son directed The Fixer to one of the chairs in front of the large wooden desk, while he took his seat behind it. "Now that my father's dead, I'm going to make some changes to our business," the son began.

The Fixer nodded but remained silent. This was to be expected. Each subsequent generation felt the need to reshape the business and put its stamp on it. To say that Kerwin Gund's son had been anxious to take over was an understatement. For the last five years, he had been assuming a larger leadership role within the family and, at times, contradicting his elderly father in meetings that The Fixer attended, making all those present uncomfortable witnesses. However, the rules of the Circle, established by the founders, stipulated that each family was to be led by the oldest male relative. Such was the male-dominated world of the late 1800s that Agnatic Primogeniture was considered to be a perfectly viable succession plan.

Interestingly, the original Circle bylaw requiring the oldest male to rule was suspended fifteen years ago when one family was rendered leaderless when Justine Camborne, the man in charge, unexpectedly died from a heart attack before his son was old enough to take over. The Circle's solution was to have the mother, acting as a sort of Regent, take over running things during the son's minority. The only problem was that the Mother never surrendered her power, even after the son grew up. The Circle's solution was to quietly do away with the oldest male rule rather than have an open conflict with the Camborne family's real-world version of Lady Macbeth. Nevertheless, the Gund men believed in that tradition. Therefore, James Gund's older sister, Lilith, was passed over in favor of James Xavier Gund taking over the family.

"I'm closing the office in Houston, and I will be working out of here. You are going to find a place nearby for when I need to see you," James Gund began, outlining how he was going to run things.

The Fixer was annoyed at this news but didn't say anything. Over the last two decades, Joe Goebel had grown to enjoy Houston. Its International Airport afforded him quick access to travel around the country and around the world for Circle business. Living here, in Central Texas, he would have to drive hours to reach a decent airport in either Dallas or Austin.

James Gund didn't miss seeing The Fixer's eyes narrow at the news. "Don't worry about it. You don't have to live here full-time. I'm sending you to Washington, D.C. We're going to expand our influence with the new Administration, and I want you there."

The Fixer nodded, and Gund went on with his meeting. After an hour, he dismissed The Fixer and, alone in his office, poured himself a generous portion of Pappy Van Winkle Family Reserve, a twenty-year-old bourbon. Gund had already decided that The Fixer would handle the political side of the family business, while he explored new markets and opportunities. His rationale for keeping The Fixer in the dark was fifty percent generational; James didn't think The Fixer had the belly for the kind of businesses he had in mind. The other fifty percent was trust, and he didn't trust the loyalty of the man who worked for his father.

CHAPTER XV

Progress

The wedding was a mere two months away as Izzy sat on the floor of their townhouse in front of the coffee table, going over guest lists. Cassidy was lying on the couch behind her, ready to help, but knowing that this was the kind of task Izzy loved to do. According to etiquette, invitations needed to be mailed six weeks before the event, and all the essential dates for their marriage ceremony were on Izzy's calendar, circled in red. "Are you sure I can't help?" Cassidy asked again.

"You *are* helping," Izzy insisted, going over the names on her mother's list. "You're helping me cut down this guest list."

To Cassidy, it seemed like every evening that they were together was taken up with some facet of wedding planning or a decision about their lives after marriage. Just the other day, they decided to hyphenate both of their last names after marriage. This would be particularly helpful when they had children to raise. "I put the deposit down at the hotel in Martinique," Cassidy informed her fiancée. Martinique was chosen for the honeymoon because it was expected to be beautiful, and the island had a welcoming attitude towards LGBTQ+ guests.

Izzy nodded her head to let Cass know she heard her. "We'd better bring a fire extinguisher along when we plan on lying out on the beach," Izzy said while she studied the lists in front of her. Even though her father was from Colombia, Izzy inherited her mother's complexion, including her porcelain skin and strawberry-blond hair. Neither trait was an asset in the strong Caribbean sunlight they were likely to encounter, "But that is what sunblock was made for, I guess. What I want to see is you in that black bikini you bought," Izzy said naughtily.

"You're such a pervert sometimes," Cass said playfully. "What's our guest count now?" she asked. The venue the two women picked for their wedding and reception was perfect. It was called the Cider Haus, and they both knew how incredibly lucky they were to get it on less than a year's notice.

The Cider Haus was originally a family apple farm in rural Burlington, Connecticut. The property dated back to the late 1700s, and the first owner was a German man named Helmut Jobst, a Hessian mercenary who came to the Colonies to fight for the Crown. However, once here, Jobst fell in love with a woman from New London, Anne Dallow, who could speak to him in his native language. She told Helmut what the colonies were fighting for, and it was the young Ms. Dallow who convinced him to change sides.

Offered a commission in the Continental Army due to his formal military training, Jobst was soon commanding a company of Continental Regulars, with his wife by his side, translating many of his orders into English. By the end of the war, Helmut Jobst was considered a very valuable soldier for the Continentals and, upon his discharge, was granted 69 acres on which to start his family farm. Their principal crop was apples, and people all over Connecticut loved the Jobst farm cider and the apple brandy he distilled called Drachenblut. The farm stayed in the family for two hundred years until the property was divided and sold by the last Jobst descendant, who had no children.

One of the original buildings on the Jobst Farm was a stone and wood timber barn where the Jobst family processed their cider and brandy. When the property was purchased, the new owners decided to convert the original barn into a wedding and meeting venue, naming it the Cider Haus in recognition of the barn's original purpose. After the extensive remodel, the barn's entrance became a wall of glass with two sets of French doors that opened onto an English garden.

It was not quite as formal or stuffy as a French-sculpted garden; the English garden had red brick paths around fountains, shrubs, and other water features. The wide variety of greenery, flowers, and other native flora was, beyond doubt, beautiful. At night, discreet lighting gave the garden an otherworldly feel. When Isabella called the venue to ask about using it for their wedding, the woman who answered the phone told her that they had a cancellation, "But if you want to reserve the Cider Haus for September 2nd, we need to do that today. Otherwise, it is 14 months before we have another open reservation."

A frantic call to Cassidy, followed by an immediate, unplanned road trip to the venue, resulted in a change of date of their wedding to September 2nd. When Cass and Izzy saw the Cider Haus, they fell in love with the place at first sight. The only problem was that the occupancy for the Cider Haus was capped at 120 souls.

"Your parents have 38 couples, including neighbors, relatives, and faculty from their work. My mom and dad have 42 couples. When I add the friends we have, we are at a hundred and forty people," Izzy answered, tapping her pencil on the paper. "That is too many for the location we have." Both sets of parents agreed to split the wedding costs, so a larger setting could have been picked, but Isabella and Cassidy didn't want a large wedding.

"Hand me my parents' list," Cass asked. Scanning "Well, no wonder. I think they've invited the entire English and history departments' faculty from the university."

"My parents are no better," Izzy admitted. "There are people from mom's side of the family I haven't seen since I was five." What was left unsaid was that there were no invitees from Dad's side. The only way the Colombian side of the family would be coming to the US would be in cuffs and on an extradition flight.

"What if we told both sides that they could only invite immediate family and a few close friends?" Cass asked.

"I'm game if you are," Izzy agreed. "Just a small wedding and reception with only people we really know." A moment later, Izzy felt Cassidy's nose nuzzling her and then felt soft kisses on the nape of her neck. A spontaneous, low groan of pleasure came from the back of Izzy's throat before she murmured, "This isn't going to help us finish these wedding lists," she reminded her partner as her breathing quickened.

"Maybe I'm a pervert as well," Cass whispered. "We need a break tonight, I think?" she said seductively, her kisses moving around to the side of Izzy's neck, and at the same time, she reached around to cup her fiancé's right breast.

"You're right. Work will keep," Izzy softly agreed, surrendering to the moment.

Two weeks after their first meeting, Hasim Bashir left a message for Watson; the bug was ready. Once again, the full complement of the Holmes & Watson firm made the two-and-a-half-hour drive from Torrington to Bashir Electronics in New York. Along the way, Cassidy reminded Watson of his Tuxedo fitting. "I know. I'll do it before the end of the week," he promised."

"And you," Cassidy began, looking at Holmes.

"And me, what?" the orange cat asked.

"I have the cutest little black bowtie for you," Cassidy said with a big smile. "But, you know what? They sell a wide range of clothes and accessories for cats online. Maybe I can get you a little cat tuxedo."

Holmes's ears went flat, and his glare was colder than the surface of Europa. "I hope for your sake you're being funny, Macgregor,"

Cassidy began laughing and replied, "You have no sense of humor."

Two hours later, they arrived at their destination. Hasim was at his desk and rose to greet his customers. "You made good time," he said, looking at his watch.

"We're excited to see what you came up with," Cassidy responded as Holmes jumped up onto the counter.

Hasim smiled and set two objects on the counter. The first was the size of a quarter and was flat black. The second item was also black and was about four and a half inches long, or the size of two double-A batteries, set end to end. Everyone looked at the items, and finally, Watson asked, "Which is the bug?"

"They are two parts of the same instrument," Hasim replied. "Here is our dilemma. How do you design a bug for an office or study that none of us has ever seen? We can't use the old standby of making it a pen. We don't know what he uses to write with. A mystery pen would stand out like a sore thumb. We can't be sure what kind of chair is in the room; there may be no way to reach under and stick the bug." Hasim stopped to see if everyone was following his logic.

It was Holmes who came up with the answer, "So you made the device into components. The actual listening device is this small, flat black disk," he said, pointing. "And the transmitter is the four-inch black rod."

"Exactly," Hasim replied, feeling very proud of himself. "As long as the two are within twenty to twenty-five feet of one another, it will work. One of you can excuse yourself and go to the restroom and plant this part of the unit," he said, holding up the small black rod. "One side of the transmitter has an adhesive on it and should stick to almost anything. My suggestion would be to place it inside the vanity or behind the toilet tank. And the actual listening component is small enough to go almost anywhere. It has the most sensitive microphone available. Anyplace in the room should work."

"How long will it run?" Holmes questioned.

"Probably a month, more or less. I have the highest purity lithium batteries powering the device. Once it is activated, any sound will be collected and transmitted. If the room is quiet, the bug goes into standby mode."

"How do we start the timer?" Watson asked.

"Press this," Hasim said, pointing at the end of the small black rod. "That activates the timer, and in thirty-six hours, the bug is live. Until that time, the device is essentially off." Hasim handed Watson a business card; the detective turned it over and saw a web address printed on it. "This is the online account where everything will be recorded. The account was opened under a fictitious name, and the server is located in Belarus. Just use a VPN when you log on to the site, and they should not be able to backtrack to you."

"And your name isn't on any of it?" Cassidy said with a smile. Hasim grinned and nodded his head.

"No. My name isn't on it," Hasim assured everyone.

"This is brilliant," Holmes replied. "This should work quite nicely."

The Fixer got the email he was expecting, reminding him to pick up the dry cleaning. That simple phrase told him that the two men that Gund had used to kill Landewedock were dead and that their bodies were so thoroughly destroyed that no identification was possible. Even the car the two men used was expertly disposed of; first, it was crushed by a car crusher, followed by a metal shredding machine. The remnants were probably already melted down into scrap metal. This was the easy part. The hard part was going to be guessing what Landewedock's family was going to do now that their namesake was dead. In The Fixer's opinion, Gund had seriously erred when he ordered the action against Landewedock. It would have been better to collect information and hold it until it was needed.

Landewedock's family had ordered a private autopsy by a very competent forensic doctor. The family now had the final report, and The Fixer was desperate to see a copy to find out what they might have uncovered. It was his job to head off any blowback against his employer, but so far, every avenue to gain access had been stymied. He even thought about approaching the doctor, but that would be counterproductive. Any action against the doctor would only prove that there were parties worried about what might have been uncovered. "No. We can't threaten the doctor," The Fixer said to himself. So what was left? The answer was eluding him. Further reflection on that topic was halted when his phone rang, and he recognized the caller.

"Yes, sir," The Fixer said by way of answering.

"I want you here Monday afternoon," was all that Gund said, and then the line went dead.

The Fixer gave a deep sigh. *What on earth was Gund doing now,* he wondered.

"I just got off the phone with Ms. Delacourt. She wants us to be at her place by seven in the morning on Monday," Cassidy announced to her partners. "She wants us to escort a new painting she's giving to her cousin, and we will be responsible for bringing the Thornhill painting back to Philadelphia. Gund is sending his personal jet to pick us up."

"Excellent," Holmes meowed. For the past three days, both Watson and Cassidy had practiced planting the device and the transmitter with a sleight of hand so that even if they were being watched, the onlooker wouldn't know what they were doing. For the last run-through, Cassidy was placed in a pitch-black bathroom and had to set the transmitter by feel. They were as ready as they would ever be. "Go home and get a good night's sleep, and we will set out in the morning."

"You're coming along?" Watson asked the orange tabby.

"Of course. I will stay at the Delacourts until you return with her painting. It will give me time to question Irene Adler at greater length."

Both Watson and Cassidy looked skeptical at Holmes' plan but remained quiet. Unfortunately, Isabella was not so understanding.

"You're going down to the home of the man who ordered my death?" she said, raising her voice. "Are you crazy?"

"Izzy, he won't do anything to Watson or me. Too many people know we're going down there. Gund won't risk that kind of publicity."

"Somebody that rich and convinced of his power might just crash the plane you're on. Have you thought about that?" Izzy asked, with fear in her voice.

"Again, too many people know what we are doing. Gund is crazy but not suicidal." Cass looked into her lover's eyes. "I bet I would have said the exact same thing if we had known each other, and you said you were going into an undercover involving a notorious drug cartel." Cass waited a beat, then added, "And I bet you would have said to trust you."

Isabella looked at Cassidy, knowing she was right. All the things she wanted to say were pushed aside, and instead, Izzy begged, "Hold me."

Cassidy wrapped her arms around the woman she loved and whispered, "It will be alright. I will be home tomorrow night." Isabella returned the embrace as though it were a lifeline, keeping her and Cassidy safe. But, in her mind, she promised the universe that if Cassidy Macgregor was hurt or killed, she would kill James Xavier Gund, and no power in heaven or Earth would stop her.

CHAPTER XVI

Texas

The drive to Philadelphia was quiet as the sun rose; the day promised to be warm and clear. Watson was wearing a sports coat over his white shirt and khakis, his shoulder holster concealed under the jacket. Keeping with the business casual look, Cassidy had a white jacket over a blue blouse and nice jeans. However, she also added a leather cross-body satchel as a final accessory to carry a few personal items. Each member of the Holmes & Watson firm was lost in their own thoughts. This morning, when Izzy kissed her goodbye, Cassidy accidentally began reading her but quickly closed her eyes to stop. The smile on Izzy's face was a mask; the feelings behind it held anger, confusion, and fury. Izzy was angry at Cassidy; she shouldn't be putting herself at risk. And worse, there was a darkness in Izzy's mind of what she would do if today didn't go as planned or if Cass got hurt. Today had to go well, if for no other reason than Cassidy had to keep Izzy from ruining her life with revenge.

For the first time, it really sank in for Cassidy Macgregor that she wasn't alone anymore. She always cared about the people and animals in her life. After reading Izzy's mind, it was clear that her actions, for better or worse, would have severe ramifications for the woman she intended to marry and the people who were important to her.

As they approached the Delacourt house, Holmes meowed his final instructions, "Don't deviate from the plan. Pick up the painting, plant the device, and come home. Do not challenge or confront Gund in any way. I trust you both not to do anything that would be an unwarranted risk."

"You mean a risk like planting a bug in the home of a lawless oligarch that has had people murdered?" Watson quipped.

Holmes ignored the sarcasm and said, "Macgregor, read Gund if you can. If you think it is unsafe, abort the mission. I won't second-guess you." Holmes wasn't in the least telepathic, but his ability to read body language was unparalleled. He knew that Cassidy was really struggling with this assignment. The woman who was totally at ease while working with a deadly pathogen was terrified this morning, and it wasn't hard to guess why.

Holmes never worried about his own life. If he were to die on a case, well, that would be that. However, now, despite his best efforts, the lives of his partners were affecting his decisions. Damn it all to hell. Try as he might, he could not separate the lives of his comrades from the mission and the decisions he had to make. Holmes really wished Mittens were still around to talk to.

"We're here," Watson said as he pulled into a parking spot on the street, causing all musings to cease.

When they were welcomed into the house by the butler, they found two people from the Gund organization were already there. Even though both men wore suits, they had the air of professionally trained brutality about them. Cynthia was directing the loading of the painting destined for her cousin James Gund, and her cat, Ms. Adler, was watching the proceedings. As soon as the white cat saw Holmes, a feline smile spread across her face.

As it turned out, it was the Thomas Cole painting of André Gundisalvus' homestead in Texas. "I think Jim is going to love this painting," Cynthia remarked as the painting was put in the padded art crate and sealed.

"Is it okay if we leave Holmes here until we get back?" Cassidy asked. "I didn't want to let him home alone all day."

"Of course," Cynthia replied without hesitation. "He'll have fun playing with Ms. Adler."

"Thank you, Ms. Delacourt. We'll see you late this afternoon," Watson said, looking at Holmes, who nodded back. Then, he and Cassidy followed the security men out of the house.

As soon as the door closed, Irene Adler meowed at Holmes, "We are going to have such fun today."

Cassidy and Watson rode in silence in the back of the black SUV. Both knew that any conversation they had would likely be recorded. Their destination was a small private airport in Philadelphia, where numerous corporate jets were parked. The driver pulled up to the gate and rolled down his window to hand the Guard his pass. The guard glanced at the paper and then waved them through. Two hundred yards later, they pulled up to a white Gulfstream. The pilot was walking around the aircraft, completing his pre-flight check.

The two investigators watched as the two security men removed the painting from the SUV and carried it into the jet. A moment later, they came back to the cabin doorway and climbed down onto the tarmac. "Mr. Watson," the taller security guard said. "It is Mr. Gund's policy that guests cannot be armed on his plane." He paused a moment, then went on, "It's for safety."

The shorter security guard stepped forward and opened a black metal gun case with a combination lock built into the lid. "Please put your sidearm in here. It will be returned to you as soon as we return to Philadelphia."

Watson had actually been expecting this. The night before, Holmes had meowed, "They will relieve you of your sidearm before they let you on the plane. Don't object. Simply smile and comply with their orders."

"Should I have my backup in the ankle holster?" Watson asked.

"No. Don't even bring it along. I don't want you to give them any reason to distrust you," the detective instructed. "And you know what to do for your part?" he asked, turning to Cassidy, who nodded at the question.

Back on the tarmac, Watson opened his jacket and slowly removed his 38 Special. He gently set it down in the portable gun safe. "There you go. Happy to comply," he said, smiling at the man. The shorter guard, who had remained silent throughout, closed the gun case and spun the combination.

The taller security guard asked, "Can you please pull up both pants legs?"

Watson complied without questioning and, still smiling, told the guard, "I don't have a backup gun."

"Thank you for your cooperation, sir." The taller guard replied, then retrieved a wand from the car and approached Cassidy, "Miss, can I check you for weapons?"

"Of course," Cass said, and held out her arms, and the guard passed the metal detector over her body, but no weapons were found.

"Can I see in your purse, miss?" the same guard asked. Cass didn't hesitate. She handed her satchel purse to the man and waited while he examined it. Inside, he saw a wallet, a tampon container, a brush, and car keys. Closing the purse, he returned it to Cassidy with a perfunctory thank you and said, "Please step on board, and we will be off."

Watson gestured to Cassidy that she should go first, and as soon as she was in the cabin, he followed. Then, both security men climbed on board, and the door was shut. Almost immediately, the engines revved up, and they began slowly taxiing. The two security guards had picked seats at the front of the plane, leaving Cass and Watson to themselves in the back. When the aircraft made the turn onto the runway for take-off, Cass closed her eyes and had a death grip on the armrests of her seat. Five minutes later, they were airborne, and ten minutes after that, the plane leveled off.

The pilot came on the intercom and said, "Ladies and gentlemen, the weather is clear between Philadelphia and our destination in central Texas. The estimated flight time is four hours and fifteen minutes. Enjoy your flight. Thank you."

A single hostess greeted Watson and Cassidy, asking if either of them would like something to drink. Cassidy shook her head, but Watson asked for a cup of coffee. The hostess went to a tiny galley in the back and returned with a cup of coffee in a china cup. "Cream? Sugar?" she asked.

"No, thank you," Watson replied, and the hostess went to sit with the security guards. Looking over at Cass, Watson tried to start a conversation with Cassidy several times, but Cassidy shook her head and sat back with her eyes closed. "You can take off your seat belt," he offered, but she just shook her head again.

After an hour, Watson leaned over and tapped Cass on the arm. Whispering, he asked, "What's wrong? I've never seen you this upset, and I've seen you deal with a serial killer. The job is going to go fine."

"I'm afraid of heights, and I've never flown before," Cassidy said with her eyes closed tight while still holding onto the armrests of her seat.

Watson stared at her with an incredulous look. "You're kidding me. You've never flown?"

"No, Mr. World Traveler. I've never flown. And I've been afraid of heights ever since I was a little girl and got stuck in a tree."

Watson stared at her, dumbfounded. Finally, he put his head back and laughed so hard that it drew the attention of the hostess. When she approached, she asked, "Is everything alright?"

"Sorry," Watson said, still grinning. "My friend here has never flown before, and she's a little nervous."

The stewardess nodded and said in an understanding way, "It will be okay, Miss. This is a very safe plane." Cassidy nodded her head but otherwise didn't respond. Watson watched the hostess return to her seat, where she leaned over to whisper something to the security guards. Both guards looked back at Cassidy and grinned.

The plane ride was as uneventful as promised, and once they were on the ground, Cassidy appeared to relax. Still bemused by his partner's reaction to air travel, Watson asked, "How are you going to take a seven-hour flight to Martinique for your honeymoon?" Unfastening her seat belt and standing up, Cass replied simply, "Many Margaritas."

The airfield they landed at appeared to be Gund's private strip with one outbuilding and one hangar. Though it was still morning, the heat was already oppressive; Watson and Cassidy stood and watched as the heat waves rose off the tarmac of the landing field, while the Thomas Cole was taken out of the plane and loaded into the black SUV.

"How long does it take to get to Mr. Gund's estate?" Cass asked the nearest guard.

"You're on his property now," was the guard's reply. "But the main house is about five minutes away."

When they were seated in the SUV, Cass said, "Apparently, they have a 'type' when it comes to cars," she observed, with a bemused expression on her face.

"Did you see the glass and hear the sound the door made when it was closed?" Watson asked.

"Of course. This thing is armored like a tank."

Nodding in agreement to Cassidy's remark, Watson added, "Someone is worried about security."

It actually took less than five minutes to travel down the dusty road from the landing strip before they pulled through the wrought iron gates of the Gund Main House; the name Perpetuus was emblazoned in an oval on one gate, while the outline of the state of Texas was displayed on the other. A lush, manicured lawn replaced the prairie grass as they approached the imposing main house. As the SUV rolled to a stop in front of the main doors, Watson leaned over to Cassidy and whispered, "Here we go."

After Watson and Cassidy left, Holmes jumped on the couch and settled down. He knew he didn't need to approach Irene Adler; That Female would come to him. After a couple of minutes, he was proved right when the white cat joined him. "Nice to see you, Holmes," she purred.

Holmes remained silent as he studied the white cat. The last time they met in Philadelphia, Holmes freely admitted to himself that he was shocked. This time, he carefully applied his abilities to gain insight into this cat; the years had changed Irene Adler. Despite what Holmes assumed was meticulous grooming, she appeared to have lived hard for a while. There was a kink in her tail that indicated it had been broken at one point, plus there were faint scars on her ears and abdomen, now well-healed, that suggested a vicious fight had taken place. Even her front paw on the right had a claw missing. "How long were you on your own after you left the Triads?" Holmes asked.

"About a year," Adler said honestly. She knew better than to try to lie to this particular cat. His powers of observation were unparalleled. "New York isn't kind to stray cats."

Holmes nodded in agreement; he knew that well enough. "How long have you been with Cynthia Delacourt?"

"About six months," Irene meowed.

Holmes effortlessly did the math and asked, "So what were you doing for the other three-point-seven-five years?"

"Oh, you know," she said, smiling coyly at him. "Just surviving."

CHAPTER XVII

The Gund House

When Cassidy and Watson entered Gund's house, they were greeted not by a butler but by James Gund himself. "Hello," he said with an enthusiastic smile. Coming forward, first grasping Cassidy's hand and then Watson's hand. Their host was wearing a white Oxford shirt under a linen jacket that would be called a summer blazer. Dark denim pants and comfortable black loafers completed the ensemble. Obviously, Gund wasn't in a cowboy mood today. "Welcome to my home, Perpetuus." The two investigators were taken aback by their host's congenial attitude, but immediately went on guard. There is an old saying that a host is never more polite than when they have already decided on your fate. Both felt the situation was far more dangerous than they had planned.

The entry hall was spacious and open to the second floor. The floors were made of wood parquet, and the ceiling was a dome with an oculus in the center. A heavy wooden table with horses and cattle carved in the apron was strategically placed so that the light from the oculus shone down on the Remington sculpture that sat in the middle. On the right side of the entry foyer was a winding staircase leading to the second floor; on the left, there was an opening into a formal living room. Several closed doorways were also set into the gently curving walls.

Watson nodded and then said, "Thank you for welcoming us to your home. It really is beautiful, Mr. Gund."

"Thank you," James Gund replied. Then added, "And thank you for escorting the painting back to my cousin. But, please, call me Jim."

Cassidy smiled and asked, "Where did the name Perpetuus come from, Jim?"

"Our ancestor who first staked a claim to this land, Ulysses, used it as a word that means enduring. Their first years here were very rough. Ulysses built a home, planted crops, and worked the land. The weather, the Spanish, and the savage Indian tribes that were around were a constant reminder that they had to fight to keep their home. But, they endured."

Watson nodded politely at Gund's whitewashed version of events but wondered what the Indigenous tribes, who had been there for hundreds of years before Gund, thought of their ancestral land suddenly being taken away and sold. *Yeah, that might make anyone a little annoyed,* Watson reflected silently.

Cass looked into Gund's eyes, trying to read as much as she could. She saw flashes, images that had no context. Perhaps if she could read him more, she could get a better understanding, but she couldn't just stare at him. That was dangerous behavior.

While pleasantries were exchanged, the two security men walked past carrying the painting they had brought with them from Philadelphia. "Please follow me," Gund invited his guests as they followed the painting down the hall.

The two investigators were led to what was obviously James Gund's private study. The room was tastefully decorated in Tudor-style oak paneling and finished with a coffered ceiling. At one end of the room was a wooden desk that bore a striking resemblance to the Resolute Desk in the Oval Office of the White House. The leaded glass windows behind the desk provided an excellent view of the grounds behind the house.

Opposite the desk, taking up the far wall, was a stone fireplace framed by two cigar chairs. There was also a door that led outside, allowing Gund to walk out into the backyard if he wished.

Various artworks adorned the paneled walls, including the original Thornhill painting, which was being returned to Cynthia Delacourt. It was the first time Cassidy had been able to see the original, not just a photograph of it. However, what grabbed her attention was another Remington on a display table by the desk. A recessed light in the ceiling was focused on the cast bronze sculpture, highlighting the delicate perfection of the piece.

The taller security man began unpacking the Thomas Cole while Watson stood by and watched him. Instead of helping, the shorter security man positioned himself so he could keep both Cassidy and Watson in constant view; Watson noted this but said nothing. Cassidy, also aware of the guard's scrutiny, decided to walk over to the sculpture. "I love the Remington sculptures you have, Jim. This one is called *Coming Through the Rye,* isn't it?"

"You have a good eye," their host said, complementing Cassidy. "Yes, that is the name of this sculpture."

"It's beautiful," Cassidy replied, studying how the artist, Frederic Remington, managed to catch the four horses and their riders in motion so perfectly. Even the horse's reins conveyed movement.

"Well then, you are going to be glad you got to see it because this is the original, cast in 1903." Gund picked up the sculpture and turned it over. "See here," he said. "The foundry mark and signature? This was the first ever cast."

"Wow. I thought that one was in the Art Institute of Chicago," Cassidy admitted.

"No, they have a copy. This one is the original," Gund said proudly.

Making a decision, Watson walked over to the desk and asked, "What can you tell me about your desk?" Bending over, he admired the inlaid wood desktop. The wood was lacquered and polished to such a degree that it seemed that you could see down into the grain. "It looks like the Resolute Desk in the White House."

"It should," Gund explained. "My great-grandfather had this made as a replica. Instead of the Presidential seal on the kneehole panel, the carpenter carved the name of the estate."

Gund watched as Watson squatted down to look at the panel, holding onto the edge of the desk to steady himself. "Your woodworker did wonderful work," he complimented, running his other hand over the bas-relief.

Gund smiled and was about to tell him more of the history when the two security men interrupted. "Sir," the tall one intoned. "We're ready to swap the paintings."

"Okay, go ahead," Gund ordered. Cassidy and Watson observed the taller man remove the Thornhill from the wall as the shorter man removed the Thomas Cole from the art crate. The Thornhill was placed gently in the art crate, and the Thomas Cole was hung in the vacant space on the Study wall. The man closed the crate and sealed it for traveling back to Philadelphia.

"Excellent," Gund said, looking at the Thomas Cole on his wall. Turning back to his guests, he said, "But of course, you must stay for lunch."

"We would love to," Cassidy said, smiling. Then, looking over at Watson as he brushed his nose with his finger, added, "I'm famished. We didn't eat before we left."

Cassidy saw the signal and was impressed. She had been watching Watson closely and never saw him plant the bug. That was excellent spycraft.

"Follow me," Gund said as he led them from the Study to the dining room.

Lunch, as it turned out, was a multi-course affair served by a young Latino man in a white jacket and tie. Mrs. Gund joined them in the dining room and introduced herself. She was of average height, with shoulder-length, dirty blond hair. She wore a pair of dark slacks and a burgundy-colored blouse. A light-gray jacket and a pair of black flats completed the outfit. "Hi. I'm Patricia Gund," she said, introducing herself with a wide smile. "I am so happy to have company for lunch for a change."

When everyone was seated, the first course was served. "This is a lobster bisque with aged cognac and béchamel sauce," Patricia Gund announced to the table as the bowls were set before them. After each person had a bowl of soup in front of them, the same young man opened a bottle of white wine with a pop as the cork was removed. A small amount of wine was poured into Gund's glass for him to test. After smelling it and swirling the liquid in the glass, he took a taste. A nod of his head told the waiter to serve everyone else at the table. When the waiter was finished, he left the bottle in a silver ice bucket to stay chilled and backed away to stand against the wall.

When Cassidy looked into the eyes of the young waiter, she saw a flash of a memory from him that intrigued her, but she couldn't follow up because the young man turned his head and moved to the next person.

Watson, who had never had lobster bisque, or any bisque for that matter, tasted his soup. "This is really good, Mrs. Gund," he said, meaning it.

"I'm glad you like it. We have the lobster flown from a fish market in Massachusetts," Patricia Gund replied. "Please call me Patty."

Cassidy, whose parents occasionally took her and her brother to Boston, agreed with Watson. "You can taste that the lobster has never been frozen," she remarked. "What kind of wine is this?" she asked after a sip.

"This is a Riesling from New Zealand," Mrs. Gund replied. "I think it is even better than the wines you can get from the Rhine."

Small talk continued while they ate. When the soup bowls were cleared, a mixed green salad was served. "The dressing is an aged balsamic vinaigrette that I make myself," Patty announced. "And the new wine is Pinot Bianco from Alsace." Cass and Watson complimented her on the dressing and salad. At the same time, they both noted that Jim Gund drank two full glasses of Riesling with the soup course and was already into his second glass of Pinot when he began to steer the conversation toward his guests.

"I understand you did time," Gund said to Watson without preamble. "Assault and robbery, wasn't it?"

This was not the first time someone had conducted research on him and asked why he went to jail. However, most of the other people who asked Watson didn't do it in such an accusatory tone. "Yes, I did time. But I was later exonerated because I was innocent."

"Is that why you became a detective?" Gund questioned. "You don't trust the police?"

"No. Most police officers are honest and fair, but mistakes happen. I…we," Watson said, nodding at Cassidy, "want to make sure a person has someone to turn to if they need help." He paused, then added, "We bring a fresh set of eyes to an investigation."

Jim nodded, then said, "It's the Government behind the police you can't…" But before he could continue with his train of thought, the main course was brought in. Mrs. Gund continued to introduce the dishes, "This is a garlic, maple pork tenderloin with a sweet potato puree. I've paired it with a Pinot Noir from the Russian River Valley in California." The Pinot was served from a decanter that resembled a piece of glass sculpture more than a traditional wine vessel. The waiter began serving the wine, and because of where he started, James Gund was last to be served. When he was finished, the waiter left the decanter on the table and retook his place against the wall. Both detectives noted that Gund had the waiter pour about twice the amount of wine in his glass as the rest of them.

"The pork is so tender. I can cut it with a fork," Cassidy remarked.

"It's from our own farms," Patty said proudly.

Jim Gund noticed that Watson was eating the sweet potatoes and hadn't touched his pork yet. "You aren't one of those rag-heads who don't eat pork, are you?" he asked with a beligerant tone.

Watson knew what Gund meant by the religious slur. "No, I'm not Muslim," he replied calmly. "I just haven't had sweet potatoes in a long time. These are excellent," he told Mrs. Gund. Then, Watson deliberately took a forkful of pork and put it in his mouth. After swallowing, he reiterated Cassidy's comment about how good the meat was.

About halfway through her plate, Cassidy asked, "Can you direct me to the bathroom?"

Patty replied, "Right down the hall, on your right," she pointed.

Cassidy thanked her and left the room. The bathroom was small, holding only a white pedestal sink, a toilet, and a wicker magazine basket. Sitting on the toilet lid, Cass rummaged around in her purse for her tampon travel holder. Naturally, it had sunk to the bottom of the bag, which required her to empty most of the purse to get at it. Once the holder was in her hand, she returned everything to the purse and set it on the edge of the wicker basket. Pulling the top off the holder revealed two wrapped tampons. Selecting the right one, she tore the resealed wrapper off to reveal the second half of the bug.

Cassidy smiled at the simple camouflage Holmes had come up with to hide this portion of the bug. "No man is going to poke around a human woman's feminine hygiene product," the cat meowed, knowing human nature.

"You're right about that," Watson concurred.

Cassidy pushed the correct end of the device, starting the countdown timer to activate the bug, and then searched for the ideal place to conceal it. Only as she noted before, there wasn't a vanity sink, only a white pedestal sink, a toilet, and a small wicker magazine basket. She looked around the small room, but everywhere she looked, the device would stand out. Stymied, Cass whispered to herself, "Well, shit."

With Cassidy in the bathroom, the questioning by Jim Gund at the lunch table had grown more bad-tempered as he finished his second glass of wine. *Boy, can that man drink,* Watson thought to himself. Through it all, Watson continued to smile and answer his questions. Patty Gund remained silent but cast disapproving glances at her husband, who had built up a full head of steam. "How many laws do you break when you do your job?" Jim Gund asked.

"I can't speak for all investigators, but since the founder of our firm was a 35-year veteran police officer and detective, we stick to the rule of law."

Gund grunted his acceptance of this fact and continued to grill Watson about his other cases and his past. Then, as if a switch had been thrown, he changed subjects. "Where's your partner? Shouldn't she be back by now?"

"I don't know," Watson admitted, but before he could say anything else, Patty Gund spoke up, "I'll go check on her."

As soon as Mrs. Gund left the room and they were alone, Jim turned to Watson and barked, "Why are you investigating me?"

For her part, Cassidy was starting to panic. Three times, she tried to stick the bug controller on the back of the toilet, only to have the device fall to the floor after a few seconds. Hasim coated a sticky substance on one side of the controller, so all you had to do was press down hard on the controller for a few seconds, and it would be set. The problem was that Cassidy couldn't get her hand far enough behind the toilet to really press down on the device to make a firm seal.

"Is everything okay, dear?" Patty Gund called through the door.

"Yes, thank you. I should be out in a minute," Cassidy replied, then flushed the toilet for good measure. Sitting astride the closed toilet seat and facing the toilet tank, Cass was worried she would have to abort the mission. And that would have made this entire trip worthless to their investigation.

Turning on the seat, Cassidy looked around the small bathroom one more time to see if there was anything she had missed. Cass turned back to the pedestal sink. This time, she was looking at the sink from the side. There was a drain pipe for the sink that disappeared into the wall. Reaching over, Cass let her hand follow the pipe back to where it went into the sink pedestal. But instead of encountering the back of the china pedestal, she found that it was open. "It doesn't have a back on it?" Cassidy whispered. The logic of the construction suddenly dawned on her. There had to be a way for the plumber to install the S-bend when he installed the sink. *Well, that makes sense,* she thought.

Taking the controller, she placed her hand into the china base and pressed the bug controller firmly against the inside wall of the pedestal. After about ten seconds, she withdrew her hand and waited. It stuck and didn't fall off. "Hot, damn," Cass whispered. Then, getting up, she cleaned up after herself and flushed the toilet one more time for effect. Reaching for her purse in a hurry, Cassidy knocked it into the magazine basket. Whispering another profanity, she quickly dug her purse out of the basket and went to rejoin the lunch.

"I'm sorry," Cassidy said, retaking her seat. "I have a bit of a stomachache."

"Can I get you anything, dear?" Patty Gund asked sympathetically.

"No, thank you," Cass answered and then almost absentmindedly rubbed her nose, giving Watson the signal. Even though he saw the signal, Watson continued to frown. Apparently, there was a new level of tension around the lunch table that began while she was in the bathroom.

"As I said, Mr. Gund, we were not investigating you for this case. We were concentrating on the staff and workers who had been in the home." Watson replied in a clear and concise voice. Throughout the questioning, Watson was meticulous; he maintained eye contact, controlled his blinking, and didn't fidget, just like Holmes taught him. It was likely that Gund was not an expert in reading body language, but you could never be too sure.

Mrs. Gund was upset with her husband's confrontational tone and tried to steer the conversation to a new subject. "Would you like your plate warmed up, dear?" she asked Cassidy.

"No, thank you. I have a plane ride home," Cass answered. "This lunch was wonderful. We can't thank you enough."

The young Latino man approached Cassidy and gestured to the half-eaten lunch, silently asking if he could clear the plate. Cass nodded and then looked the young man in the eye to reread him. There was a flood of images that came from Cassidy's immediate connection to his mind. However, one picture in particular was significant to the waiter. It was of a strong, elegant older woman sitting behind a desk and smiling at the young man.

The waiter was confused by Cassidy's penetrating stare and asked, "Do you want me to take your plate, miss?"

"Ah, er, yes," Cassidy managed to say, trying to cover her lapse. The waiter nodded and removed the plate.

Gund ignored Cass's interaction with the help and continued to glare at his guests. He wanted to keep pressing Watson, but when he saw his wife getting angry, he changed his mind. "Well, I guess we'll get you back to Philadelphia," Gund announced, rising from his seat and heading for the front door. Lunch was obviously now over.

In the entry hall, Watson and Cassidy's security chaperones reappeared. Whether they had been allowed to have any lunch or had stood there over the painting the whole time, they couldn't tell. Gund nodded at the short guard, who opened the front door, and together with the other guard, they carried the painting towards the SUV.

Before the two investigators climbed into the SUV, Gund approached Watson and asked in a gruff voice, "Do you have a business card?"

Watson reached into his jacket pocket and produced the firm's card. Being so close to their host, the smell of wine on Gund's breath was overpowering. Watson said, "If we can ever be of service, don't hesitate to call." Then Watson reached out his hand. Gund seemed to hesitate before finally accepting the offer to shake hands.

As the SUV pulled away, Patty Gund stared daggers at her husband and said, "Thank you for ruining lunch," then went back into the house without another word. Once again, he had drunk too much and embarrassed her. James Gund didn't care; he wanted to find out if the Holmes & Watson firm was investigating him, but his questioning of the pair and Watson's full-throated denial did not settle that issue for him. Going back into the house, Gund went to the bathroom Cassidy used. He looked around, but nothing was amiss. The tampon wrapper in the trash can elicited a grunt of amusement and answered the question of the woman's stomachache. Giving the bathroom a final going over, he saw something out of the corner of his eye that made him stop. Reaching down, he picked up the device and examined it. This certainly wasn't here before his guests arrived. Gund left the bathroom and hustled to his office. He had to make a call and stop the plane from taking off.

Cassidy and Watson didn't talk on their way back to the airfield. Once there, they stood and watched as the two security men loaded the painting onto the plane. When they came back to the entrance of the aircraft to invite Cassidy and Watson aboard, the taller guard's phone rang. Quickly answering it, the two consulting detectives heard the guard say, "Yes, Sir," several times and then hang up. The guard whispered something to his partner, and both guards came down onto the tarmac. Unbuttoning their jackets for easier access to their guns, the taller guard said, "That was Mr. Gund. He ordered you held here. He's on his way." The shorter guard moved ten feet to the right, so Cassidy and Watson were covered from two different angles. Back in the plane, the pilot and the stewardess came to the door of the jet, wondering what was going on and why the passengers hadn't boarded yet.

Sharing a look of concern, the investigators from Holmes & Watson were left wondering if they would ever see their homes again.

CHAPTER XVIII

Trade Craft

Holmes was feigning a nap on a chair in the main hall of the Delacourt house. His eyes were closed, but his excellent hearing was picking up every sound in the old house, from the cook preparing the midday meal in the kitchen to the butler and Cynthia Delacourt having a conversation in her sitting room on the second floor. He was waiting for, no, *counting on* Irene Adler to make her move and fill in a piece of the puzzle.

His thoughts also turned to Watson and Cassidy, and how they were getting along. Calculating the travel to and from Texas, Holmes expected the pair back by six p.m. If they failed to show up, he would have to contact Anne Gaumont and get her involved. Then things would get messy. He didn't actually think Gund would harm his colleagues. Too many people knew that Cass and Watson were going to his house today, and if something befell them, the investigation would roll right up to his front door. That said, Holmes also knew that humans often did foolish things despite the consequences.

Finally, Holmes heard the flap on the pet door in the kitchen slap closed. Irene Adler was on the move. Getting up and stretching, Holmes jumped off the chair and headed to the kitchen. The cook ignored him as he went through the pet door and onto the back stoop. The small backyard of the house had one tree and was enclosed by a red brick wall with greenery across the top. The orange cat caught a glimpse of a white tail disappearing into the greenery. Still, instead of immediately following, Holmes scaled the tree to see where the white cat was going. Sure enough, he caught sight of Irene as she went up to St. Peter's Way, a pedestrian walk that passed between the houses. Instantly, he recalled the map of the neighborhood and then deduced where she was going. Climbing down the tree, Holmes hustled to get there first.

Irene Adler knew she was taking a risk, but she had to report in. She kept checking behind her for Holmes, but she saw no sign of him. That fact didn't reassure the white cat. Holmes was an expert at being invisible unless he wanted to be seen. Remembering their time together in New York, Holmes had actually changed the color of his fur with a pet-friendly temporary dye. *Now, that was a commitment to a case,* she thought.

Approaching Three Bears Park, she saw her contact exactly where he was supposed to be, quietly sitting on a bench and reading a book. The contact looked up from the book, glancing at the kid at play on the swings and seeing a white cat at the park entrance. Rubbing his eye, he went back to reading. Irene Adler saw the 'All Clear' signal and approached the man on the bench. When she jumped up to sit next to him, the man casually removed a cell phone from his pocket and set it between them. Without looking up from the book, he pushed the call button. After the third ring, a mechanical-sounding click came from the phone's speaker; the recording had started. For the next three minutes, Irene meowed into the phone. When she was done, the contact hung up the phone and put it back in his pocket. Irene jumped down and headed back to the Delacourt house.

From under a bush, Holmes thought about the behavior he witnessed by *That Female.* He was sure from the reactions and his body language that the man on the bench didn't understand cat language, so that made him a lackey. Would following him be worthwhile, or should the detective beat Irene back to her home? Quickly, he ran through a dozen scenarios and chose the one with the highest probability of future success. Committing the messenger's face to memory, Holmes turned and headed for his shortcut back to the Delacourt house.

Irene Adler came back in the pet door and rubbed against the leg of the cook, which resulted in her being lifted onto the kitchen table and given a piece of chicken from Cynthia Delacourt's lunch. Irene enjoyed the morsel, purred gratitude, and then headed into the hallway. She saw Holmes still curled up on the same chair as before, apparently asleep. Not believing it for a minute, but without a viable recourse, she headed upstairs for a nap.

Watson and Cassidy stood quietly by the front of the SUV, wondering what, if anything, they could do. Watson knew where his gun was, and he even knew the combination to the portable gun safe was 3-5-8; when he had surrendered his pistol, he made a point of glancing at the rotary dial lock before the guard closed the safe and scrambled the combination. Touching Cassidy's arm, she looked him in the eye, and he gave her instructions.

"Excuse me," she called to the security guards with a little wave. "May I go inside the plane and use the restroom? I've had a stomach ache since lunch." The two guards looked at each other, and the taller one shook his head no.

"Please. I really have to go," Cassidy appealed, giving her best smile and taking a few tentative steps towards the plane.

"I'll stay right here if that helps," Watson added, leaning against the grill on the front of the SUV.

The taller guard replied, "Sorry, miss. Our orders are to hold you right here. Please step back."

Cass turned and walked back to Watson. "Any other ideas?" she whispered.

"If the shooting starts, get into the SUV. It's bulletproof," Watson whispered back.

"We don't have the keys to start the engine," Cassidy replied, feeling she had to point out the obvious flaw in the plan.

"It's a keyless start. The big guy there has the key fob in his pocket, and as long as he is within 25 feet, the car will start, and we can drive away. We just won't be able to restart the car if we turn it off." Looking off into the distance, they saw a vehicle approaching that had to be Gund. "Get ready. Here he comes."

A well-used convertible Jeep pulled up with Gund at the wheel, the same disapproving look on his face, but now their host was sporting a Stetson hat against the strong Texas sun. Seeing Watson and Cassidy standing by the front grill of the SUV, he approached the pair while putting his hand into his pocket. "I found something in the bathroom that I think you left there," he began with a neutral tone, eyes fixed on Cassidy.

Watson felt as if his heart would burst through his chest; the adrenaline being forced into his system was giving him a bitter taste in his mouth. *Gund, I'm going to use you as a human shield,* he thought as he got ready.

As Gund's hand came slowly out of his pocket, Cassidy held her breath, knowing she was dead. "This is yours…" Gund began, then, turning over his hand, she saw a smartphone with a cat phone cover.

"That's my phone!" Cassidy exclaimed in a voice that was much louder than necessary. "How'd you get it?" she asked, trying to get a hold of her emotions.

"I found it in the magazine basket in the bathroom," Gund reported, actually smiling at Cassidy's reaction.

"My purse fell into the basket. It must have fallen out without me noticing. Thank you so much for bringing it to me."

"No problem," Gund replied. Then, turning to the guards, he said, "Let's get these people home."

Watson thanked Gund and walked shakily with Cassidy to the plane as the engines began to spool up. "Are you okay?" he asked in a soft voice, feeling unsteady on his feet.

"Yeah. But I REALLY need to use the bathroom now."

The drive back to Connecticut for the staff of Holmes & Watson was uneventful; it was just the kind of trip that everyone concerned needed. By the time the plane landed back in Philadelphia, Watson had consumed two glasses of good whiskey over ice, and even Cassidy had a glass of medicinal white wine. Dropping the painting off at Cynthia Delacourt's home went off without a hitch, and soon they were on Interstate 95, heading north, with Cassidy at the wheel. The first thing she did when they got out of Philadelphia was to call Izzy and tell her they were safe and on their way back.

Holmes noticed the fatigue on his team's faces and decided that any debrief could wait until the next day. When Cassidy came into the apartment she shared with her Fiancée, she was enveloped in a fierce hug. In fact, it seemed like Izzy was never going to let go. Burying her head into Izzy's neck, she said, "I am so glad to be home."

"Did it work? Was it successful?" Izzy asked.

"Yes. But let's talk about it tomorrow. All I want to do now is sleep."

Isabella gave her girl a kiss and led her by the hand to the safety of their bed.

CHAPTER XIX

Debriefing

SAN DIEGO, CALIFORNIA: Tristan came home from school, threw his bookbag on his bed, and sat down in front of his computer. Each day, he allowed himself a couple of hours of online gaming before his parents got home, and then he had to focus on his homework, which was not much of a chore. Tristan was precocious in every way. Being the only child of two parents who, by any measure, were high achievers, Tristan was constantly exposed to travel, music, and art that his contemporaries could only dream of. That, coupled with a thirst to learn, gave Tristan a formidable intellect.

As an elementary school student, Tristan memorized the New York City subway system while his family lived there for a year. That was the start of his affinity for maps. If you asked the ten-year-old where Andorra was, the young cartophile would immediately point to a small spot between France and Spain.

Now in middle school, Tristan was already reading at a college level and was, by his own teacher's comments, far ahead of his classmates. It was a challenge for his instructors to devise assignments that would challenge the fourteen-year-old. A case in point, while his classmates were exploring introductory algebra, Tris was taking classes in trigonometry and pre-calculus.

Before logging into his game, Tristan scanned his email. Yup, there it was. A new email and another payday. It was during an online game that Tristan heard about an easy job. All the person had to do was act as a human router, taking a .wav file from one server and sending it to the next. For that simple task, you would be paid $50.00. All of it was done online. Even the pay was sent to a digital wallet. Technically, you had to be eighteen to have a digital wallet, but those systems were easy to fool. After an email interview that consisted of twenty written questions, Tristan got the job. So far, he'd earned $650.00. When he earned enough, Tris was going to get a new gaming laptop. Wouldn't his parent be surprised?

Tristan logged onto the server to retrieve the wave file, the first part of the transfer. As always, the wave file was encrypted, so he could not listen to it. That, however, only made finding out what it was more of a challenge. The wave files always arrived with an intelligent agent embedded in the code that erased the file and the transfers from his computer. But Tris found a way to make a copy of a file before it was deleted. That was a few weeks back, and then, for the next month, Tris worked on breaking the encryption. He had to admit that the wave file was pretty well protected, but never underestimate a teenager's persistence. In the end, when he was finally able to listen to the file, it was only a cat meowing. This made no sense. Was it some kind of joke? Perhaps the real information was somehow embedded in the meows. But after dissecting the wave file, he was forced to admit it was simply cat sounds.

He really wanted to ask his mysterious employer what this was all about, but decided against it. They might be mad at him for listening to their file. Furthermore, Tristan traced the incoming and outgoing emails and found out that he was only one link in the chain; these people really wanted to protect their identity. A little sleuthing revealed that the file was sent to him from a small town in Lithuania, and when he sent the file, it was forwarded to Phuo Lanh Song Cau in Vietnam. Tris promised himself that he would visit Vietnam one day. A few years ago, his mother's work had sent her there for a few months. Her stories about the country and people made it sound very nice.

With the transfer complete, it would take twenty-four hours for Tristan to see the next $50.00 in his digital wallet. Easy money.

The day after the trio returned to Torrington, the full complement of Holmes & Watson gathered at the office to discuss what they had learned from their respective trips to Philadelphia and Texas. Cassidy was seated in one of the wingback chairs, and Watson in the other chair. Holmes was sitting on the table in between them and said, "Macgregor, you go first,

Cassidy leaned forward in the chair and reported on the problems with planting the bug controller, as well as her ultimate solution. The cat and the man nodded in admiration for her cleverness. "As far as scanning people, I got some information, but I didn't want to be obvious. I saw flashes of us and our firm when I read Gund. Apparently, he is worried about us investigating him."

"That's obvious. While you were in the bathroom, he interrogated me about the case we're on and how it involved him," Watson said.

"What else did you see?" Holmes inquired.

"When we were in his office, I scanned him and saw a memory of people on his computer screen. It looked like a video call. And there was one other face that I saw, and that was a man standing in front of him, but it's confusing."

"Why is it confusing?" Watson asked. "Was it the surroundings?"

"No. They were in Gund's study. It's what the man looked like. In Gund's mind, the man was of medium height, with dark hair and a thin face that looked pale. But then I saw him again, and I think it was the same man, but he looked different—eye and hair color, and the nose." Cass paused, then went on, "I know that he's important to Gund. If I see him again, I will recognize him."

"Anything else?"

"There are other images that I need to think about, but one thing I know is that his wife is not happy with him. Several times, I saw anger on her face when she talked to him." When she finished, Cassidy leaned back, and she and Holmes looked at Watson.

Like Cassidy, Watson began by telling them where and how he hid the bug. "I was watching you, and I literally didn't see you plant your half of the bug," Cassidy said in admiration.

Watson nodded at the compliment and stated, "Gund has a drinking problem and is paranoid," Watson began. "The more he drinks, the more belligerent he becomes. While Cassidy was in the bathroom, he interrogated me about the case. Apparently, he's had our Firm investigated. He knew specifics about all of us, including Anne," Watson said, mentioning the founder of the firm.

"Should we warn her?" Cass asked worriedly. Besides the connection to Holmes & Watson, Anne Gaumont was a much-loved grandmother to Cassidy's family.

"I'll do that this afternoon," Holmes replied. "Go on," he meowed at Watson.

"That's about it. We were kept on a very tight leash and were watched constantly. Not much opportunity to investigate and no inkling of his criminality."

Watson and Cassidy looked at Holmes sitting at the table and waited for his report. "Irene Adler is working for someone. Her being at the Delacourts is part of a larger conspiracy. Cynthia Delacourt's cat disappeared, I believe taken, and Irene Adler was put in her place as a stray needing a home."

"How did you find this out? Did she confide in you?" Cass asked.

"Not a chance. I tailed Irene Adler to a park where a contact was waiting. She made a report, speaking into the contact's phone. There was no hesitation, and their movements were well-rehearsed. This was not the first time she's reported to her handler," the orange cat concluded.

"A conspiracy…" Cass said to herself with a furrowed brow.

"Yes. Why?" Holmes meowed.

"The waiter," she exclaimed out of nowhere. "The young Latino man waiting on us at the Gunds. He's a spy!"

"How do you know?" Watson asked.

"When he looked at me, there was a flood of images. Some of them depicted him speaking into a cell phone, such as Adler making a report, and an older woman in his mind. I, er, there's something about her that's familiar. I'd bet she is his real employer."

"Any idea who she is?" Watson asked.

"No, sorry," Cassidy threw her hands in frustration.

Holmes was silent, thinking about what Cassidy said. He moved to the edge of the table, directly in front of Cassidy. "Macgregor, I want you to settle back in the chair and get comfortable. Close your eyes." When her eyes were closed, Holmes began in a calming voice, underscored by a very subtle purr, "I want you to relax. Just drift in your mind. Let your body become weightless. You're floating and have never been more comfortable or content. Now, you can see all the images from the waiter. They're like paintings on a wall. You can walk closer or adjust the angle to view the painting from a different perspective. You are all alone, able to examine every detail. Now, I want you to stand before the image of that woman." He waited, then asked, "Can you see her?" in a soft voice, the purring aiding in the hypnosis.

"Yes," was her reply.

"Is she inside or outside?"

"Inside."

"Day or night?"

"Day," Cassidy murmured.

"Can you tell if it is a house or a business?" Holmes asked.

"House, I think."

"What is behind the woman?"

"Shelves," Cass answered.

"What's on the shelves?" Holmes asked.

"There are books, pictures, and knick-knacks."

"Pick one knick-knack and tell me about it."

"It is a wooden spinning top and a short cord."

"Is the top painted?" Holmes probed.

"Yes, different Colors," Cassidy replied.

"That is very good. The top is for a game called Trompo. Look around, can you see the pictures on the shelves?"

"Yes, there is a black ribbon across the," was Cass's reply.

"Can you see the people in the pictures?" Holmes asked.

"Not clearly. They're men, I think."

"Where is the woman you see?"

"Sitting behind a desk."

"Is the desk metal or wood?" Holmes asked.

Throughout the questioning, Watson stayed very quiet and still. Holmes had used this technique on him before, when he couldn't recall important information or things he had seen but couldn't remember.

"The desk is wood."

"Is the desk old or new?" Holmes asked.

"Old, I think. There's an old-fashioned lamp on the desk."

"What color is the woman's hair?" Holmes asked gently.

"Mostly gray…"

"Can you see her eyes?"

"Yes."

"What color are they?" Holmes asked.

"Green."

"What is the woman doing?

"She's giving the man instructions. She's serious. Not smiling…" Cass described.

The questioning continued until Cassidy couldn't provide any new information. "Okay, Macgregor. Open your eyes." Holmes directed. "We're done."

"What do you think?" Watson asked, breaking his silence.

"I think we are not the only ones interested in James Xavier Gund," Holmes said matter-of-factly. "The questions are why and what is motivating them."

"What do you think?" Cassidy asked.

"I am not ready to speculate. When I know more, I will let you know. Until then, I will keep my own counsel," Holmes replied with confidence. However, inside, he wished that Mittens were still alive to challenge his reasoning.

"With the painting returned, our case with Ms. Delacourt is finished. We have no reason to go back there. How are you going to follow up with Irene Adler?" Watson wanted to know.

"Elementary, my dear Watson. We will let Irene Adler come to us."

"Do you think that's likely?" Cassidy asked. "Are you sure?"

Holmes lifted his right eyebrow and meowed, "Her reappearance is ineluctable. She will show up in Torrington within a fortnight."

CHAPTER XX

Raw Data

Right on time, the bug activated and began recording all the sounds that its sensitive microphone could pick up in Gund's office. Excitement about what they could learn from their listening device soon gave way to tedium. Many hours of what was recorded were useless or so esoteric that they had no meaning. As it turned out, the bug recorded, among other things, the maid vacuuming or Gund playing his music while he worked in his office. The music itself wasn't generally all that bad, but what made listening to it almost intolerable was Gund's penchant for singing along. The man couldn't carry a tune in a bucket, even if his life depended on it. Not to mention, half the time, he got the words wrong. As useless as most of this raw data was, Holmes and Watson were forced to listen to all of it, just in case there was something of value among all the chaff.

"The batteries will run down, and we won't have learned a thing," Watson lamented.

"Patience, Watson," was all that Holmes would say.

"I thought super-villains were supposed to monologue their plans?" Watson said with a grin.

"He must not have gotten the memo," was the reply.

The office door opening caused the two of them to look up from the computer. It was Cassidy, and she was carrying something in a garment bag. "Where have you been?" Watson asked.

"I was picking up my suit for the wedding," she said as she went to the coat closet and hung it up. "I'm keeping it here so Izzy doesn't see it. It's bad luck to see the bride's wedding outfit before the ceremony."

"More superstition?" the orange cat asked.

"In a world of talking cats, Protectors, and mind-reading, can we really say what is superstition or simply science that is yet to be discovered? Anyway, I am here to pick up the camera. We still have cases that need to be worked on."

"Where are you going?" Watson asked.

"The deadbeat dad case," she responded, going back into her lab and emerging a moment later with the camera and telephoto lens. "He says he's too poor for child support, but just bought that new car. I'm going to get a few shots of him driving that car around for the wife's lawyer."

Watson nodded. "Be safe," he reminded her as she left. Cassidy came out of the door of 221-B Baker Street and climbed into her Honda. Always fastidious, Cassidy fastened her seat belt and checked traffic before she pulled out of her parking spot. As the Honda sped up the road, another car pulled away from the curb and followed. The two men inside were determined not to lose sight of the Honda or its occupants.

While Cassidy was taking pictures in Hartford of a man who couldn't help support his son but who could afford a new Volvo, her fiancée was thirty-nine miles away in New Haven. Isabella DeLeón was trying on her wedding dress and modeling it for her mother at Ms. Aimée's bridal boutique. The small bridal shop, owned and run by one woman and employing a total of three seamstresses, was *the place* to purchase your wedding dress if you lived in New York or New England. Under normal circumstances, it could take months or even a year to get an appointment at Ms. Aimée's in New Haven, given its popularity. However, in Isabella DeLeón's case, there was no wait at all.

Twenty years ago, Aimée Auclair, fresh from Paris, arrived in New Haven, determined to open her own dress shop. For over a decade, since she was sixteen and left a lycée, she had learned clothing design. Beginning at 31 Rue Cambon, The House of Chanel, Aimée started as a floor sweeper in the atelier, where she observed the designers as they created their couturé clothes.

Gradually, she was offered more responsibility, including roles such as cutter, seamstress, and then pattern maker. At each level, the young demonstrated skill and artistry. All the while, she would save her money and sketch her own creations at night in her tiny apartment. Aimée Auclair was exposed to many different occasion-based categories for women's clothes, but in the end, it was bridal wear that she loved the most. Every extra franc went into her bank for the day she would set out on her own and make her own wedding dresses.

At twenty-eight years old, Ms. Auclair quit her job at Chanel, sold everything she owned, and made the trip to New Haven, Connecticut, to open her own shop. Figuring correctly that it would cost less to open a shop in New Haven than in New York, she set about finding an empty storefront. On Chapel Street, Aimée found the perfect place to open her shop, so she made an appointment to tour the space. The moment she walked in, she fell in love with the empty shop and its big display window overlooking the street. What a perfect place to display her wares. Standing in the middle of the empty shop, she slowly turned around, visualizing things that only she could see. The landlord and his daughter watched the young woman with smiles on their faces.

However, when Aimêe found out what was needed for a security deposit and the five-year lease, her dreams came crashing down. There was no way she could afford this place, and she told Carl DeLeón and his little daughter sadly that it was out of her price range, or so she thought.

Carl remembered all too well what it was like for a new immigrant to get started in a strange country. Instead of bidding the young woman a good day, he invited her to have coffee with him so she could tell him about her business. While little Isabella drank her chocolate milk in the cafe, Aimée talked about her shop and the wedding dresses she wanted to make. Her enthusiasm and passion won over Carl and, later, after they met, his wife, Abigail, to such an extent that they decided to invest in a start-up business. Carl would provide a low-interest loan and a rent break for her shop for three years. As it turned out, it was one of the best business decisions Carl ever made.

Within the first month of being open, Aimée used her talents to create a couturé wedding dress for a young woman who was in New Haven, day shopping with her mother. Apparently, she lived in some place outside New York City called the Hamptons. As it turned out, the young woman's family was a direct descendant of the original four hundred families that established New York society back in the 1800s. It was as if a flare was shot off in front of the little shop in New Haven. After that, you couldn't pass Ms. Aimée's shop on Chapel Street without seeing a line of chauffeur-driven cars lined up outside. Business was so good that she was able to pay off her loan a year and a half early, then she promised Carl and Abigail that if their daughter ever needed a wedding dress, it would be on the house.

Isabella turned around on the platform in front of the full-length mirrors with her mother and Aimée looking on. As far as wedding dresses go, it was elementary, as Holmes might say. It was an elegant tea-length wedding gown made with chiffon sleeves adorned with lace-trimmed cuffs. A modest V-back on the dress added a flattering touch to Isabella's silhouette. Timeless and graceful, the dress fit Isabella and her sensibilities perfectly, not to mention beautifully.

The smile on Izzy's face warmed Aimée's heart. When Abigail walked up and draped the traditional Colombian mantilla head scarf over her head, other customers in the shop stopped what they were doing and stared at the stunning bride-to-be. "You look so beautiful," Abigail said, with tears in her eyes. "That little girl with the chocolate milk mustache is all grown up," Aimêe added.

"I love it," Izzy told them, stepping down. "Thank you so much."

"It was my pleasure. Gabby will help you out of the dress, and we will deliver it this afternoon." A young assistant approached and followed Izzy to the changing room.

"Are you sure we can't pay you for the dress?" Abigail asked for the third time.

"Absolutely not," Aimée replied, shaking her head. "Your family helped me when I was first starting out. Je n'oublie pas."

"You will be at the wedding?" the mother asked.

"Of course. I want to see our girl get married," Aimée assured her.

Izzy came out of the dressing room in her jeans and sweatshirt. She got a kiss on the cheek from Aimée, and she and her mother left the shop to find a place for lunch. As the mother and daughter walked up the street, two men sitting on a bench watched from a distance. When Izzy and her Mom entered a bistro that was a popular lunch spot, the two men stood up and repositioned themselves so they could maintain visual contact. Their assignment today was Isabella and her mother, and they were extremely motivated by their Boss not to mess this up.

"Come on. You've been at that computer all day. Let's go home and have something to eat." Watson implored, rising to his feet. "If Gund says anything important, it will be recorded."

Holmes stood up on the desk and stretched, his front legs reaching out and his paws opening up to reveal very sharp claws. Then, taking a step with the front legs, he stretched out the back legs. Finished, he sat down and addressed Waton, "Fine. Let's go home. We will return in the morning and listen to see if anything useful is recorded." The orange detective jumped down and joined Watson at the door. Watson turned out the lights, and together, the partners descended the steps and exited the building. It was still quite warm this late August evening as they headed to the car. As usual, Holmes & Watson left the computer on when they left. It would go into Sleep mode in an hour, as it was programmed to do. So, no one was there when the cursor began to flash, and a large audio download began.

CHAPTER XXI

Jackpot

"Are you heading to the office?" Watson asked Holmes as he read the paper on his laptop.

"Of course. Where else would I go while the device is working?" Holmes seemed genuinely surprised at the question.

"Maybe offer to help Cassidy with the case we took?" Watson said before taking a sip of coffee. "Do you think maybe you are being a tad obsessive about Gund?"

"Nonsense. Cassidy will inform us if she encounters any difficulties. She is more than competent to perform the required surveillance." Holmes meowed defensively. "It is only logical to divide our forces to cover the largest area."

"If you say so," Watson replied, closing the laptop and standing. "I'm going to go over and see if Cass needs anything." Holmes watched his partner walk over, pour the rest of his coffee down the drain, and set the cup in the sink. "I'll see you later at the office."

Holmes watched the tall human leave and wondered why Watson questioned him. As a cat, he knew what he was doing. A moment later,

Holmes left the house and began his trek to the office. Not having to observe the rules that hampered human travel, the orange cat jumped fences, cut through yards, and made short work of the commute. When he arrived at the office and clicked the mouse to restart the computer, he saw that a large audio file had been downloaded. Clicking on the icon, the audio file began to play.

Holmes began to listen, not just to Gund's voice, but to another he also recognized. As the conversation progressed, Holmes became as excited as he ever was. This was a treasure trove of information. Over an hour later, when the file had finished playing, Holmes deliberately replayed it, wanting to ensure he had heard it correctly while committing it to memory. When it was completed for the second time, the detective began pacing, putting the pieces together in his head, and working out plans and contingencies.

Finally, Holmes sat down and looked around the empty office. He wished Mittens were here to challenge his logic. It wasn't that Watson or Cassidy couldn't provide a differential to his deductions, but they were human, and cat logic was subtly different. Belle was a possibility. The young Protector was brilliant, but her depth of experience wasn't sufficient. Give her a few more years, and she would be perfect.

Saying out loud what had been on his mind for a while, Holmes meowed, "I wish Mycroft were here."

"Thank you again for these. They're perfect," the lawyer told Cassidy, looking at the pictures of his client's ex-husband and his new car.

"No problem," she replied. "There are about two dozen pictures on the thumb drive of him, the car, and his new wife."

"Excellent. The judge will love these. What do we owe you?" the lawyer asked.

Cassidy did a double-take when she heard that. The lawyers they had worked for in the past almost unanimously never brought up what they owed you. Instead, they opt for the third notice to be sent before a bill is paid. "We'll email you an invoice for the balance," Cassidy replied. "Have a good day," she said and headed back to her car. Climbing in, she said to Watson, "Not bad. Not even lunch, and we've already had a payday."

"Good work," Watson agreed. Let's head to the office. I got an email from Holmes. Apparently, the bug picked up something interesting."

Forty-five minutes later, Cassidy and Watson came into their office and saw Holmes sitting at the desk with a frown on his face. "About bloody time," he meowed at them.

"We're here, oh great orange one," Watson said playfully. "What's up?"

"Get comfortable and listen to what our device picked up last night," the cat instructed. When Cass and Watson were seated, he pressed the Enter key, and the audio file began. Holmes watched his partners as the audio played. He saw both of them listening intently. Watson frowned at one point, but Cassidy instead raised her left eyebrow, a gesture that Holmes recognized as Macgregor's fascination with what was being said. When the audio finished, Holmes pressed Enter again to stop the playback. Silence fell over the group as each member considered what they had heard.

"The Circle?" Watson said softly. "What he said…Is that what I think it is?"

"Yes," Holmes replied. "For some time, I speculated that Gund was not alone. Now we know that there is a cabal of four extremely powerful families controlling most of what goes on in this country."

"And Gund killed one of the circle?" Cassidy asked, looking for confirmation of what she thought she heard.

"Yes, Macgregor," Holmes meowed. "Prescott Landewedock. The health care executive who died some weeks ago, in what was reported as a murder/suicide with his mistress, was on all the major news outlets. Now we know it wasn't a suicide, but a murder ordered by Gund."

"Gund called them 'pressure points' for the other families," Watson said aloud. "He wants the other man on the tape to find a way to blackmail the other families to do what he wants." He looked at Holmes for confirmation and was rewarded with a nod of his head.

"The second person on the tape didn't sound happy about what Gund was doing. I wonder if we can find that person and get them to help us?" Cassidy suggested.

"I doubt it. I deduce the second person on the recording is committed to Gund and is beyond redemption," Holmes answered, looking out the window of the office at two people walking up the street holding hands on a beautiful late August day, blissfully ignorant of the dangers of the world.

"The second voice? You know who he is, don't you?" Watson speculated based on Holmes' attitude.

"You saw him last year," the orange cat remarked, locking eyes with Watson. "He was driving that jeep that I hitched a ride on. He is also the man who sent the assassin after Isabella."

"That was The Fixer!" Cassidy said, leaning forward.

"Yes, Macgregor, right again. Full marks. I watched him make the contract with the assassin in the cemetery in Washington and order a young woman's death without the slightest hesitation. That is why I don't think turning him is a viable plan."

"Shit!" was all that Watson could come up with at the moment. "What are we going to do about this?"

"We are going to be cautious and patient," Holmes meowed. "We have the tape, but no way to prove any of it. Technically, a third party can admit a tape into evidence in Texas only if the contents can be verified as authentic. We need to verify what we heard. Until then, we have nothing."

"Gund is trying to take over the Circle. He is looking for ways to compromise the other families. There might be a way to exploit that, make them destroy each other." Cassidy suggested.

Holmes nodded. "Very astute, Macgregor. Yes, that is one possibility. But we must be sure before we act. We get one shot at this."

"When you strike at a king, you must kill him," Watson said softly.

"Emerson was correct. We need to be sure before we act," Holmes replied and looked at his colleagues for their agreement. First, Cassidy and then Watson nodded. "Let me reiterate, both of you, be aware of your surroundings. We knew Gund was dangerous, but I fear our enemies have multiplied. The other members of the Circle undoubtedly wouldn't like their business to be investigated by outsiders and would react with the same lethal intent as James Gund."

Holmes turned to Cassidy and asked, "Does Isabella still have her sidearm from her time as an FBI agent?"

"Yes. But it's put away." Cassidy answered.

"Get it out. Load it and keep it with you if you two go out," Holmes ordered. "Watson, carry your pistol with you at all times until further notice." Watson nodded somberly and looked at Cassidy. She also nodded in understanding.

"I'm supposed to be married next week," Cassidy said in a very subdued voice.

"Macgregor, you have our word," Holmes began, nodding at Watson. "You and Ms. Isabella will be married next week."

"Besides, we have to see Holmes in a bowtie," Watson added with a grin. Cassidy appreciated the way her friends were trying to reassure her. She reached out her hand to Watson, and he grasped it firmly. She reached the other hand to Holmes, who shook his head at this human sentimentality. But, ultimately, he put his paw in her hand.

The young couple that Holmes had seen from the window finished their walk down Baker Street. They looked into the shops and doorways of the street, getting a feel for the layout of the block. When they returned to their car, the woman reported in while the man kept an eye on the door to 221 B. They wouldn't leave as long as their assignment was in there. No matter how long it took.

The last Monday in August, James Gund was on his back patio, once again enjoying the Texas sunset. The blistering heat of the day was giving way to the relative cool of the evening. In a salute to the late summer heat, Gund was drinking a gin & tonic instead of his traditional whiskey. Although not as alcoholic as whiskey, Gund still managed to get rather drunk from the gin, primarily due to the fact that he mixed them at a fifty-fifty percent gin and tonic instead of the traditional one-to-four ratio that the cocktail called for.

His quiet contemplation of the sunset was interrupted by someone calling out, "Sir. I brought those papers." Turning, he saw The Fixer walking towards him with an accordion file. Gund nodded at his employee, indicating that he should come forward. The papers were from the Circle, and they insisted that they be hand-delivered.

The Fixer approached and set the file on the patio table, then walked up to look at the sunset with his boss. "It looks like you have a guest," The Fixer said after a minute.

"What?" Gund asked, confused.

The Fixer pointed at the lawn. An armadillo was sitting on the lawn, looking at them.

Gund stared at the armadillo, which was calmly looking back at him, when it suddenly triggered a memory in his gin-soaked brain. "Orange cat."

"Excuse me, sir? What do you mean, orange cat?"

Gund waved his hand at the armadillo and said, "A while ago, an orange cat was sitting in that same place, just looking at me. I tried to shoo it away, but it just watched me."

For some reason, The Fixer became agitated. "Think, sir. This is important. Have you ever seen that cat since?"

"What? No. I mean, it was just that night. The next day, it was gone. Why?"

"The day I made contact with Pelotas, an orange cat was watching us in the cemetery," The Fixer replied worriedly. "Pelotas also mentioned an orange cat after he was arrested. He said it talked to him."

"It's a cat, for Christ's sake, I don't think…Oh crap. Holmes & Watson," Gund cried out.

"The people your cousin hired for the painting? What about them?" The Fixer asked.

"When I met them in Philadelphia, they had an orange cat. I remember saying it looked familiar."

"Think. Was it the same cat?" The Fixer said in an uncharacteristic voice laced with impertinence.

Gund didn't like the attitude his *employee* was giving him. "How the hell do I know? It was a cat. And I don't like your tone." Gund replied in a dangerous, low voice of his own.

"Sir," The Fixer began in a much more deferential voice. "You had these people in your home. In your office, where we discussed very sensitive business. I am only concerned with your safety. Did you sweep the house for bugs?"

"Of course I did. As soon as they left, I scanned the whole house. Then, the following day, I scanned it all with a different detector. No bugs!" Gund said, sounding smug.

"Fine," The Fixer replied. "I'm sorry about my words; they were spoken in haste and because it is my job to guard you. Still, two orange cats behaving strangely is more than a coincidence. I'm going to look into Holmes & Watson. With your permission."

Gund nodded, accepting The Fixer's apology and also approving The Fixer's investigation. Knowing he was dismissed, The Fixer left without another word, leaving Gund to the encroaching darkness. Finishing the rest of his drink in a single gulp, Gund went back to his office and sat down. Was it the same cat? Maybe. He didn't know. But one thing he was sure of, the room was clean of listening devices. To prove it once again, Gund removed the detector, scanned the room, and watched as the needle on the detector moved from green to red. Gund looked at the detector in his hands as they began to shake. Turning it off and on, the same result. Red. There was a listening device in his office.

Gund got up and began walking slowly around the room, pointing the detector and using the needle on the meter as a divining rod; he swept the office from front to back. Move in one direction and watch what the needle does; keep following the strongest signal. Through the process of elimination, he found himself standing in front of his desk, just where that black man Watson was standing. Crawling under the front of the desk, Gund looked at the knee hole and then looked up at the underside of the desk. A small black disk, the size of a quarter, was stuck there. He peeled it off and looked at it in his hand. That wasn't big enough to be a bug? Since he was little, he had been trained about bugs, cameras, and other spyware that might be used against the Gund family. What was offered during his father's time was laughable compared to the sophisticated, and damn near invisible devices available today, so Gund had to keep current with the latest eavesdropping equipment on the market. The black disk he held in his hand couldn't be the whole thing? This made no sense, and then he remembered the girl who came with the black man.

Gund came charging out of his office, a hammer in his hand. Passing the puzzled young Latino servant in the hallway as he made his way to the bathroom that Cassidy used during their visit. As soon as he was inside the bathroom, he picked up the basket of magazines and dumped them out. Kicking the magazines around revealed nothing. Then, taking the hammer in both hands, he smashed the toilet tank and bowl. Water ran across the Spanish tile floor and sprayed from the fill valve as Gund looked around for anything that looked out of the ordinary. Finally, he began methodically destroying the bathroom sink. As soon as he broke the pedestal open, he saw it: the second half of the bug, right where Cassidy had planted it over a month before. Carefully, Gund bent over and gingerly picked up the second half of the bug, holding it in his trembling hand like it was something alive and malevolent.

For a time, Gund simply stared at it in silence, trying to recall everything he had said in his office for the last month, wondering if it was all on tape somewhere. Or, even now, being handed over to the Justice Department, a damning treatise on him and his actions. A different man might use this as an opportunity for counterintelligence, to use the bug against those who planted it. Mislead, misdirect, or even trap those who dared investigate James Xavier Gund. But Gund was not one of those strategic-thinking men, especially when he was drunk. Summoning all the rage and indignation he could muster at those inferiors who dared to judge him, he snapped the device into two pieces and pulled them apart in a savage display. Gund was relieved to see that several small wires had been pulled loose. Confident now that the bug was dead, he left the demolished bathroom.

Barreling into the hallway with a full head of steam, Gund saw a shocked servant standing in the hallway, attracted by the sounds of destruction coming from the bathroom. "Get the water turned off and clean up that mess," Gund barked at the surprised servant. The servant mumbled something at his employer, but Gund didn't slow down to listen. He marched back to his office and slammed the door. There was work to do.

Miguel walked to the bathroom and looked around in wonder at the total devastation that Gund's temper had brought. Stepping carefully over the shards of broken china that a moment ago had been a toilet and sink, he reached down and turned off the water that supplied the toilet.

The fountain of water stopped immediately, but there was still an untold number of gallons on the floor and in the hallway that needed to be mopped up before it caused more damage to the house.

Leaving the bathroom, the young man went to the garage to retrieve a trash can, mop, and mop bucket so he could begin. A long night of cleaning up his employer's temper tantrum lay ahead for the young man from Colombia, but that did not concern him. What Miguel was worried about was reporting on this development as soon as possible. The normal day for him to report was Thursday, four days away, and that was too late. There was a special procedure for making a report outside of protocol, but it was only for emergencies, and it could blow his cover. Still, a bug was found and disabled. If reporting that wasn't worth the risk, he didn't know what was.

CHAPTER XXII

Rehearsal Dinner

Thursday afternoon, Holmes was sitting in the offices of the firm, unable to still his mind. It had been three days without a single download from the device in Texas. The last thing transmitted came in late on Monday, and it sounded like something had bumped the microphone in the office. After that, nothing. Not even background noise that one might hear in the normal course of a functioning house.

Whether he wanted to or not, his mind ran through possible scenarios concerning the silent device, assigning each one a number indicating its probability. When he was finished, the numbers were not a comfort. In the best-case scenario, the device had simply run out of power and could no longer function. The number representing the probability of this was low; there should be another two weeks' worth of power in the device. In the worst case, that bump was someone removing the microphone from where Watson had planted it; the number, which indicated that probability was distressingly high.

The front door opened, admitting Watson to the office. Holmes didn't turn to see that it was his partner, having heard his distinctive

footfalls on the stairs outside. "You would chastise me for having my back to the door," Watson noted.

"I knew it was you as soon as you began climbing the stairs."

"Perhaps it was someone who just sounded like me?" Watson asked.

"I would know the difference," Holmes replied, sounding confident.

"How do you know I wouldn't know the difference?" Watson challenged.

"Because," Holmes began. "You are human, and I am not."

Knowing that there was no use in pursuing the topic, Watson changed subjects and asked, "Heard anything?"

"No. Nothing. The device is still silent," Holmes reported. "However, someone has been poking around, asking questions about us."

Watson nodded. He had helped Holmes set up certain triggers on the public face of the firm when it first opened. If people were looking at Holmes & Watson, Consulting Detectives, they would leave a digital footprint that could be traced back to the source. "Interesting," Watson replied. "Still could be a coincidence."

"You know my thoughts on coincidence. I'm afraid we can no longer deny that the device has been found and silenced."

Watson once again nodded his head, a grave expression on his face. "We need to keep Cass and Izzy in the loop," in a tone that indicated that this wasn't open for debate.

"Agreed. Pull them aside tonight and let her and Isabella know," Holmes instructed. "I will update Anne Gaumont."

"Should we be worried about the wedding?"

"I don't think so. It would be folly to attack us there, with all the other people around, including Isabella's two friends from the FBI. That would bring the world down on someone," Holmes meowed and then looked up at Watson for reassurance. "The Circle is murderous but not suicidal. They'll attempt to kill us after the wedding."

"You know, I can never tell when you're joking, Holmes," Watson replied.

"Neither can I," the orange tabby admitted.

Because the wedding and reception were to be held at the Cider Haus, the wedding rehearsal had to be held there as well. The tables, which were not needed until the reception had been moved off to the side, were moved, and the chairs were staged for the guests. As soon as the wedding was complete, the staff would move the tables back for the dinner. Holmes, Watson, and Cassidy's brother, Christopher, were sitting in the first row of chairs, trying to stay out of the way until they were told where they needed to stand.

Nobody was paying the Cider Haus events coordinator the least bit of attention as she rushed around at a frantic pace, looking at papers on her clipboard. She was trying to usher people into their correct places while checking them off her list as they arrived. To that end, she had three pencils to choose from; one pencil was stuck in her hair bun, one pencil was held in place by her left ear, and the last pencil was sideways in her mouth, like a horse's bit. Still, when Anne Gaumont arrived, the coordinator began using her free hand to search her pockets for something to check off the name. With a look of sympathy, Anne held up her hand to pause the woman's frantic search, reached over, and took the pencil out of the coordinator's mouth. "Here you go," Anne said with a smile, handing back her own pencil, complete with teeth marks.

Both Izzy and Cass were being pulled in opposite directions by their respective families to meet people as they arrived. The bedlam was very funny to Watson and Christopher, both of whom were making bets on whether the rehearsal would ever start. "So, how is veterinary school?" Watson asked Chris. This was the first time he had been able to speak with Cassidy's younger brother in quite a while. The tall, blond, skinny teenager with acne he remembered had become a tall, blond, muscular man with blue eyes and the looks of a movie star.

"The vet program is incredible. But I think it's more complicated than becoming a human doctor. Our patients can't tell you where it hurts or what is wrong. We also need to understand the basics of multiple species. Human doctors only have to worry about humans. Unless you're like Grandma Gaumont, my sister, or you, a cat meowing sounds just like a cat meowing." Chris said, giving Watson an even stare.

"I don't know what you mean," Watson replied uncomfortably, looking at Holmes, who gave the perfect cat approximation of shrugging his shoulders.

"Tyler. I've been around my Grandmother and my sister for my whole life, and I've seen them talk to cats like we're talking now. And, I've seen you talk to Holmes here like a person. Somehow, you three understand what cats are saying."

The panicked look on Watson's face made Chris laugh. "Don't worry, Tyler. I haven't told anyone. I don't feel like being sent to a psychiatric hospital for an evaluation." But when he looked at Holmes, sitting on the chair next to them, he did say, "Just promise me that one day I can open up that head of yours and see what is going on in there." That caused Holmes to smile and actually do the cat equivalent of a laugh.

"Your sister and grandmother have the gifts. I had to learn through repetition and being told I was stupid," Watson admitted, giving the orange tabby a little shove.

"And because of my expert teaching skills, you are a fairly competent assistant to my investigations," Holmes meowed, requiring Watson to translate what was said to Christopher.

Christopher's laughing was cut short when the wedding coordinator walked up and said, "Okay, Christopher and Tyler, come here. You stand here," she instructed Watson. "By Isabella's side. And Christopher will stand over there by Cassidy's side."

"What about Holmes?" Watson asked as he took his spot.

"Who?" the coordinator asked, looking down at her clipboard, which was twice the age of anyone there.

"Him," Watson replied, pointing at the orange cat sitting calmly on a chair.

"The cat?" the coordinator asked. "What about it?"

"That's Holmes. He's part of the wedding," Cassidy replied from one side of the wicker and flower altar.

"Are you joking? A cat won't follow instructions. It will ruin the wedding chasing after him," the coordinator said, looking panicky and wishing she had followed her mother's advice and become a librarian.

"No, he won't," Cassidy replied. "Holmes, you come over here and stand here," Cassidy indicated, a spot between both brides.

The coordinator watched, astonished, as the orange tabby stood up and casually walked over to the spot Cassidy had indicated and sat down. Looking at the coordinator, Holmes gave the woman a smug look before turning back to stare up at Izzy and Cass. Speechless, the coordinator put her pencil back in her mouth and bit down.

Cassidy's parents decided to have the rehearsal dinner at their home in Torrington rather than an impersonal restaurant. To that end, the caterer had done a marvelous job recreating a small, southern Italian café in the Macgregors' backyard. Round tables with chairs had been set up across the backyard of the big white house; each was adorned with a white tablecloth and lit candles or lanterns. Café lights were strung from tree to tree, lending the backyard a festive, bistro-like ambiance, while Italian café music played softly in the background. The effect was perfect. If you closed your eyes, you could think you were in a small town in Italy.

The menu also reflected the Italian theme, featuring appetizers such as fried calamari, arancini, and bruschetta. The main courses featured spaghetti prepared in the traditional southern Italian style, with anchovies and breadcrumbs. Broccoli rabe, pappardelle bolognese, and mussels sautéed with white wine and garlic. All in all, it was quite a spread.

By accident, someone had left the back door of the house open. So, now, three of the Macgregor's cats and the kitten, Lily, from Anne's home, were sitting on the back porch watching the festivities. Hamilton A. Cat, however, was at the buffet line, running back and forth, trying to make the caterers listen to his instructions. "No, no, no! You have to turn down the heat, or the broccoli rabe will overcook," Hamilton A. Cat meowed. Then, running to the other end of the buffet, he patted the arm of the man, adding ingredients to the spaghetti. "Stop," he meowed. "No more anchovy. The fish should accent the pasta, not overwhelm it." Then Hamilton ran to the food truck the caterers were using to cook many of the dishes and loudly meowed, "Don't fry any more calamari until the guests have eaten what we have. If you make too much, it will sit too long and become soggy." The caterers thought the round black cat was adorable and kept trying to offer him little snacks, thinking that was what he wanted.

The cook came to the door of the food truck and smiled at Hamilton. «Aquí tienes, gatito. Toma un trozo de calamari,» *(Here you go, little cat. Have a piece of Calamari),* the cook said and gave the black cat a calamari ring. Hamilton tasted the appetizer and meowed, "Excellent, but add a little more fresh lemon."

Like most food services, a large percentage of the catering staff were originally from Latin America. Holmes heard the exchange between the cook and Hamilton and noted the cook's accent, nodding as another piece of the puzzle fit into place.

Hamilton's three clowder mates and the kitten Lily from next door were watching their friend trying to be several places at once, with varying degrees of amusement, until finally, Holly Bear meowed, "Should we tell him that he can calm down. He looks like he's going to lose it."

"Are you kidding?" Belle meowed. "Hamilton is in heaven right now."

"I think I will go over and see if he needs me," Giblet purred.

"Yeah, right. You're going over to get a handout," Belle shrewdly guessed. "Come on, we'll all go," Belle purred at her clowder, rising to her paws, but before she could leave the porch, Holmes walked up and meowed, "I need a moment of your time, Protector."

"You guys go on," Belle meowed. "I'll catch up." Holly Bear and Lily went ahead to the buffet line while Belle stayed to hear what the detective had to say.

"I think I'll stick around too," Giblet meowed and sat next to Belle.

"What's wrong, Holmes?" Belle asked, in a tone that would have made Mittens proud. Holmes made note of the timbre of annoyance and worry in the Protector's voice and launched into a concise synopsis of the case and what the bug's going dead might mean.

When he finished, Belle glared at Holmes, but it was Giblet who spoke, "You really made a mess of things, haven't you?" he meowed angrily.

"This is the job and career that Cassidy has chosen. Your anger is misplaced. I am letting you know so the Protector can do her job," Holmes meowed back, defiant.

"You've delivered the warning, Holmes," Belle meowed, frowning. "We'll keep an eye on things around here, and won't keep you from solving **your** case."

Holmes knew he was being dismissed. No longer was this Protector a novice. She had matured into the role and was wearing the mantle of responsibility as well as any Protector in history. Mittens would be proud. Without another word, Holmes turned and left the porch. When the detective was out of earshot, Belle meowed, "I'm not patrolling tonight. I will stay with Cassidy and keep watch."

Giblet nodded, then added, "I'll stay with you both as well. But I feel powerless."

"Yes," was all the Protector could add.

After dinner, the guests enjoyed a variety of cannoli, tiramisu, and zeppole. Espresso, regular, and decaf options were also available. It was at this time that Watson was able to pull Cass and Izzy aside and tell them about the bug going silent in Texas. "So Holmes thinks, and I agree, the bug was probably found. That means the danger for all of us has just increased. Where are you two going to be tonight?"

"I'm going home with my parents," Isabella said. "They're driving me to the wedding tomorrow."

"Perfect," Watson said. "Your parents' house is the safest place around," he admitted, remembering the home from last year and the top-of-the-line security measures it had. "What about you, Cass?"

"I'm staying here with my parents and my brother," Cassidy replied. "And before you ask. Yes, I'm armed." Cassidy opened her dress jacket to reveal the Glock-19M that was Izzy's service weapon while in the FBI.

"Are you armed?" he asked Izzy.

Izzy opened her cross-body purse and showed Watson the Beretta she had carried undercover the previous year. "Should we be worried about the wedding tomorrow?" Izzy asked.

"No. Holmes said, and I agreed, there will be a lot of people around us, including your FBI friends. Only a madman would go after us there," Watson replied, but kept Holmes' admission that after the wedding, there was no telling what might happen, to himself. Cass and Izzy had enough to worry about.

Later, on the drive home, Watson asked his partner, "I saw you talking to Anne and that cat, Belle. What did they say when you told them about the bugging and your concern?"

"Anne and the Protector are both rightly upset with me," he meowed.

"They are just worried," Watson guessed.

"I know. But I wish I could make them see that we had no other choice if we were going to continue the investigation of Gund." The orange cat sat quietly for a while, then said, "I wish my brother were here."

"You mentioned that before," Watson noted. "Why?"

"Because, my dear chap. My brother has a first-class mind despite his laziness. He is an ideal cat to bounce ideas off, to find flaws." Holmes was silent for a while, then added, "We'll do our best and persevere."

It was two in the morning, and Cassidy had awakened once again. So far tonight, she hadn't managed more than about forty-five minutes of sleep at a time. A sleep researcher might call her restlessness Polyphasic Sleep and seek a physical reason for her disquiet. But Cassidy knew why she couldn't stay asleep tonight: wedding jitters. Despite her absolute love for Isabella, Cass found herself nervous about the ceremony today. Turning on her side, she looked up at her bedroom window and saw Belle silhouetted against a backdrop of stars. The Protector's perfect night vision saw that Cass was awake again, so she hopped down from the window to join her.

"There are no monsters under my bed. You don't have to stay here tonight," Cass told the Protector. "You should patrol."

"You are my mission tonight," Belle meowed with finality. Giblet and I aren't going anywhere." As if to punctuate that, they both heard Giblet let off a loud snore. "Although we may have to wake Giblet if anything happens."

"I guess Holmes told you about the case."

"Yes. And I wish you had chosen to be a librarian instead of an investigator," the Protector meowed.

"You and my mother, both," Cass admitted.

"Close your eyes," Belle meowed. "I've got you."

Cass did what she was told and shut her eyes. A moment later, she felt Belle lie against her and begin to purr. The gentle, rhythmic sound, coupled with the warmth of Belle pressing against her, soon had Cassidy asleep once again. Belle nodded but didn't close her eyes. She was on duty.

CHAPTER XXIII

Wedding Day

One of the first things Carlos DeLeón did when he moved to Connecticut to attend Yale all those years ago was to locate a Catholic church that still offered a traditional Latin Mass. In his village in Colombia, Carlos grew up listening to the Solemn Mass, with its liturgy of the catechumens and the Mass of the faithful, which featured the sacrament of communion. The ritual of the Latin Mass helped stave off homesickness and gave Carlos his first sense of community in the United States, so much so that he never left. His marriage to Abigail and Isabella's baptism, confirmation, and early schooling were each conducted at the same church that Carlos had found when he was a nineteen-year-old college freshman.

Religion played a big part in his life growing up. So ingrained were the teachings of the church in Carlos that he could not, in good conscience, follow his family into the cartel business. However, these days, Carlos, or Carl as he now liked to be called, had many more uncomfortable questions in his head concerning what it meant to be Catholic and what was truly right or wrong, especially when it came to his daughter's homosexuality. These were questions that the strict old priests of the Latin Mass could not provide comforting answers to when Carl asked. Their responses left him confused and upset, especially when one particular priest suggested that Isabella was engaging in evil, sinful acts, and her soul was in jeopardy.

Unlike his wife, Abigail, who accepted their daughter's homosexuality as soon as it was public, primarily due to the fact that she said she always knew, Carl was beset with worry. Was this truly the life Izzy wanted for herself? Determined to question their daughter, Carl waited until they were alone to ask if she had any doubts and assured her of his love no matter what her answer might be. In simpler language, Carl needed reassurance.

"Daddy, God made me who I am, and let me meet Cassidy and fall in love with her. How could that plan for me be wrong?" his daughter asked him with such sincerity that Carl felt his eyes welling up with tears. Immediately, he drew his only daughter into a fierce hug.

After the simple statement stuck with Carl and comforted him, every time worry bubbled up in his mind, Isabella's words enveloped him like a warm blanket. So, Carl DeLeón stopped going to the church he had known for thirty years, confident that God had a plan for his daughter and her new wife.

However, on the morning of his only child's wedding, Carlos DeLeón rose before anyone else in the house stirred, got dressed, and drove into New Haven to that church he had found on his first day in the United States. There, he would pray for God's plan for his daughter and her wife's safety and happiness.

The old church continued to adhere stubbornly to the old ways, with two Masses each day, one at 7:00 a.m. and one at 9:00 a.m. As usual, the early congregation was sparse and generally much older; the 9:00 a.m. Mass, or family Mass, was always better attended, especially on Sundays. When Carl arrived right before the service was to begin, there were nuns and older men and women already in the pews. All the women who weren't dressed in habits had their heads covered by mantillas or scarves, and most were praying the rosary. About forty-five minutes later, after the priest gave the Concluding Rites and final dismissal, Carl felt restored and content. His personal prayers to God, he was sure, were heard. Standing and stepping out of the pew, he faced the altar, knelt, and crossed himself. Turning to leave, Carl paid no attention to an old woman in the back of the church who had her head bowed and was still praying, which was just the way she wanted it.

The wedding was scheduled for 4:30 in the afternoon, followed immediately by the reception. Two hours before her wedding, Cassidy sat at her old desk in her bedroom as her mother finished her makeup and hair. Belle, Giblet, and Holly Bear were all sitting on Cassidy's old bed watching. Without sleep or food, the Protector had stayed on duty and hadn't let Cass out of her sight.

Cassidy's room largely remained the same as it had been while she grew up. There was an acid burn on her desk from some long-ago experiment, and there were still posters hanging on the walls. Not boy bands or popular entertainers, Cass's posters featured famous women scientists, including Marie Curie, Jane Goodall, and Barbara McClintock. The sole male scientist present was Albert Einstein, as depicted in the famous picture of him sticking out his tongue.

When the makeup was finished, Cassidy stood and turned to her mother and the cats. Shunning a dress, which wasn't really her style, Cass instead opted for a white single-breasted blazer with white pants and a vest. The vest was low-cut, with four pearl buttons, and was designed to be worn without a blouse underneath, giving the wearer a very sexy look. Cassidy stood in the center of the room and slowly turned for all to see. A chorus of meows and her mother joined together, saying how beautiful she was. Cassidy beamed and smiled at her mom and the cats. Then,

grabbing her clutch, she walked out of her old bedroom for the last time as a single woman.

Belle looked at Giblet, who was rubbing his paw against his face, and said, "You're crying," to the old tomcat.

"No, I'm not. I had dust in my eyes," He protested.

"Yes, you are, Giblet. You're crying," Holly Bear confirmed.

"Just don't tell Hamilton," Giblet meowed as he and the rest of the cats went to see their girl and the family off.

In New Haven, a similar scene was playing out. "Come on. Or we'll be late," Carl called up the stairs for the third time.

"We're coming. Keep your shirt on," Abigail replied.

"Here we are, Daddy," Isabella said, standing at the top of the stairs, wearing the dress Aimée had made for her wedding.

Carl stared, not fully prepared to see the beautiful, grown-up woman who was standing there. Isabella was wearing the white tea-length dress with a white lace mantilla that covered her head, the effect making her look angelic.

"You are so…so beautiful," her father finally said as he began to cry. "This is the dress Aimée made for you?"

"Yes. Do you like it?" Izzy asked as she came down the steps.

"Oh, yes. Your mother and I will tell her how much we love this dress," her father promised as he walked to the front door. "It makes you look all grown up."

"Aren't we taking the car? It's around back, in the garage," his wife, Abigail, asked.

"Are you kidding?" Carl said with a grin. "My little girl gets a limo for her wedding day." With a flourish, Carl opened the front door, and a long, black limousine was waiting for them in their circular driveway. A uniformed chauffeur was standing at attention, smiling at the bride and her mother.

Before they reached the car, the chauffeur tipped his hat and opened the back door of the limo. «Señora, Señorita,» he said, holding the door as they climbed into the car.

Something about the man's accent made Carl stop and look sharply at the driver. «¿Es usted colombiana?» *(Are you Colombian?)* he asked suspiciously.

The driver smiled and replied, «Sí, señor.» Then, switching to near-perfect English, he said, "But I've been living here for fifteen years. I became a citizen last year. I recognized your name as Colombian, so I thought I would use my mother tongue. I meant no disrespect."

Carl accepted the information, and his stern countenance softened a bit. "Oh, well. Congratulations on becoming a citizen," he managed to reply before joining his wife and daughter in the car.

"Thank you, sir," the driver replied with a smile. Once he was seated in the driver's seat, he asked, "Shall we go, sir?"

"Let's go," Carl said, and the black limousine pulled slowly away from the house.

The driver checked his passengers and started the engine. However, before he shifted the limousine into drive, he reached under his seat and checked. Yes. The Uzi 9mm was precisely where it was supposed to be. Satisfied, the car began rolling down the driveway towards the front gate.

Watson was finishing putting on his tuxedo while Holmes watched. Before he tried on the jacket, he put on his shoulder holster and then checked the cylinder of his 38 Special. Fully loaded, Watson holstered the weapon and then put on the jacket. When he went for his fitting, Watson had purposely asked the formal wear shop to find a tuxedo jacket that was large enough to conceal the gun. Looking at himself in the mirror, he smiled. "Not bad." Then, spinning and bringing up his hand to mimic holding a weapon, he said, "Bond. James Bond."

Holmes rolled his eyes and meowed, "Would you like me to tell you how much that series gets wrong about MI6?"

"And how would you know, oh furry one?" Watson asked, adjusting his bow tie.

"Because I worked with a MI6 Operative for several months in New York many years ago," Holmes replied matter-of-factly. "That whole Double-00 is a load of tosh." Holmes meowed.

"You know, you have a knack for sucking the joy out of almost any situation," Watson admitted.

"So, I've been told," the cat admitted, scratching at the black bow tie he was being forced to wear. "Shall we be off?"

Watson nodded and headed for the door, with Holmes following close behind.

Cars containing the guests began arriving in earnest at 4:00 p.m. The original Cider Haus barn had two levels; the lower level was approximately half the size of the main level and was where livestock was kept when the farm was in operation. The main level was used for apple storage and cider production. The new owners converted the lower area into several meeting rooms that could be used for almost any purpose. Today, two of those rooms were being used as bridal dressing rooms where Cass and Izzy could put on the finishing touches to their outfits and wait for the wedding to begin.

As soon as Aimée arrived, she found Izzy's mother running around and greeting guests as they arrived. Getting Abigail's attention, she asked, "Where's Isabella? I want to see if she needs anything for the dress."

Abigail DeLeón directed her to the rooms where the Brides were and then rushed off to greet another guest. Aimée watched Abigail scurry off and chuckled to herself. Having seen many weddings, both here and in France, she knew the MOTB, or Mother of the Bride, was an archetype that transcended borders.

Aimée went down the steps to the lower level and knocked on the door. "Come in," she heard a woman's voice call out. Entering, she found both Cassidy and Isabella in the same room, seated on a couch, talking. "I wanted to see if you need anything?" Then she added, "But I thought the brides weren't supposed to see each other until the ceremony."

"I think that is supposed to be the groom seeing the bride," Izzy remarked.

"And we're fresh out of grooms," Cassidy added with a laugh.

Aimée smiled at the joke and asked Isabella about her dress. "I think everything is perfect. I love the dress," Isabella said as she stood and twirled. "What do you think of Cassidy's suit? Isn't she beautiful?"

Smiling, Aimée asked Cassidy to stand as she walked around her, reached over to adjust the collar, and smoothed out the back of the jacket. "It is a pleasure to meet you, Cassidy. Isabella told me so much about you." Stepping back, Aimée gave a professional eye to the suit and said, "Your suit is perfect. Classic lines, elegant, and, on you, very sexy. You both are gorgeous brides."

Aimée began to head to the door, but Izzy and Cass asked her to stay. "You can tell Cassidy about some of the women you have designed for," Izzy suggested. Aimée understood. Both girls were nervous, and since they had no bridesmaids, they wanted someone with them. Taking a seat, she began telling them about some of the weddings she had designed dresses for. Both women listened, holding hands, as they waited for the ceremony to begin.

Outside the venue, Watson and Cassidy's brother, Christopher, was stationed at the french doors. Their job was to greet arriving guests and invite them to sit wherever they wanted; there wouldn't be a groom's or bride's side at this wedding. Still, like most weddings, instead of being seated right away, most of the guests were milling around, talking to people whom they recognized. Overall, it was quite an eclectic group of wedding guests gathering in an old apple orchard in the middle of Connecticut: some college professors, a couple of millionaires, and one Nobel Laureate. Added to that mix was Anne Gaumont, who arrived with the Macgregor family.

"Any trouble?" Anne asked Watson softly, for his ears only. The former homicide detective was still unsettled about the warning Holmes had given her the day before.

"No, none."

"Where's Holmes?"

"Checking the perimeter,"

"Keep your eyes open," Anne said before going in to find a seat.

Watson watched as a dark blue sedan was parked, and two people from Izzy's previous career got out and began a leisurely walk towards the barn. "Keeping out of trouble?" Mike Hann asked Watson, smiling.

"Always. You know me, I like the quiet life," Watson replied. "How's New York?"

"Overworked, understaffed, and underpaid," Ethan Kelly replied easily. Then, making the exaggerated gestures of sniffing the air, he asked, "What smells so good?"

"That's our dinner being prepared," Christopher answered. "We're using the same caterer that we used for the rehearsal dinner. It's Italian."

"We're looking forward to it," Kelly replied. Then added, "After the wedding, I want to talk to you about that topic from a few months ago."

"No problem," Watson answered. "We'll find each other."

The two FBI agents went inside, giving Christopher the opportunity to follow up on what he had heard. "Problem with the FBI?"

"No. It's a case from last year. They've been keeping us updated on it," Watson answered. While they were talking, Holmes came walking up and sat down. "Anything to worry about?" Watson asked.

"Everything is fine. I checked the perimeter and on the caterers," Holmes meowed. "Everything is just like we thought it would be." Watson got the message and nodded.

Christopher listened to the part of the conversation he could understand and shook his head in dismay. "Tyler, that is so weird that you and Holmes can understand each other."

"It also can be an epic pain in the ass," Watson admitted, turning to greet more guests.

CHAPTER XXIV

For Better or Worse...

At 4:30 on the mark, the wedding began. The Cider Haus had done a fantastic job decorating the interior of the old barn with flowers, bows, and ribbon. Instead of the altar being at the end of the old barn, a square raised platform had been constructed, allowing for the chairs to be placed around three sides of the altar, giving all those in attendance a spectacular view. In addition, the chairs had been positioned so that there were two aisles, each coming in at a forty-five-degree angle to the center platform, one for each bride to use. In a break with tradition, both brides would walk up the aisles simultaneously, each escorted by their father.

After everyone was seated, two members of the Cider Haus staff pulled white runners up each aisle and then sprinkled red rose petals along them. The effect made two marvelous bridal runways. Each chair along the aisles had magnolia and lilac affixed to the corner of the top rail. The scent of the lilac was intoxicating in the barn.

The Cider Haus staff constructed a wedding canopy on the raised platform. Four posts, covered in white fabric and flowers, held a delicate wood lattice over the altar. Around the altar, candles were placed.

The Fire Marshal wouldn't approve of lit candles for the ceremony due to the fire hazard; instead, Cassidy's brother found flameless LED votive candles that looked just like the real thing. The effect bathed the altar in warm, cozy light.

Pachelbel's Canon in D began in the background, and an older woman with short, salt-and-pepper hair began walking up one of the aisles. She wore a black doctoral gown with velvet trim and piping on each sleeve. Her name was Alexandria Hudson, and she was a professor from the Theology Department at the University. Cassidy had taken her class as an undergraduate and really liked her approach to religion. After Isabella had met her, the two women had asked Dr. Hudson to officiate at their wedding.

Next were Watson, with Holmes, walking by his side, and Christopher, each coming up a separate aisle and meeting at the Altar. Holmes was wearing the black bow tie Cassidy had picked out for him, and many of the guests were whispering about how well-trained the cat was. For his part, Holmes tried to ignore the comments his excellent hearing kept picking up and kept a dignified look on his face until he caught the look Anne Gaumont was giving him. It looked as though she was struggling not to laugh. This caused Holmes to shake his head and count the seconds until this ritual was over.

When Dr. Hudson nodded her head, the music changed to Air on the G String by J.S. Bach. All the guests rose to their feet as Cassidy and her father started up one aisle, and Isabella and her father started up the other aisle, timing their walk so they would both meet simultaneously at the center altar. The effect was stunning as both brides stepped up onto the altar and looked at each other, causing several in the audience to burst out in tears. Both fathers kissed their daughters on the cheek and withdrew, and Dr. Hudson told the guests that they could be seated.

"What is it to be married? To bind yourself to another person for life out of choice?" Dr. Hudson asked, beginning her homily. Holmes sat, and even though he hadn't intended to listen, Dr. Hudson's frank and, at times, funny sermon drew him in. She was good, the orange tabby cat had to admit.

Dr. Hudson looked at both brides and said, "Isabella and Cassidy, marriage is easy when times are good and things are working. When you're young and healthy, your careers are exciting, and it's just you two. Those are the times when it is effortless to remember your vows." Dr. Hudson paused for effect, then went on, "The challenge is to embrace your pledge to each other when things aren't going well. When one of you loses a job. When money is scarce. When the kids or one of you is fighting a serious illness. Those are the times when you have to dig deep and remember you two are in this together. And after getting to know both of you, I have no doubt you will."

"So, without further ado, Isabella DeLeón, will you take Cassidy Macgregor as your wife? To have and to hold, in sickness and in health…"

As soon as Dr. Hudson was finished, Isabella said in a soft but clear voice, "I do." Dr. Hudson turned and asked Cassidy the same question, to which she also replied confidently, "I do."

It was at that point that Watson handed a ring to Izzy, and Christopher handed a ring to his sister. It was also at that point that Holmes heard a very high-pitched frequency sound, well above the human audio range but not that of cats. The sound, sometimes referred to as coil whine, was indicative of an electronic timer being activated, and it originated from behind the black curtains behind the altar. Without hesitation, Holmes left the altar to investigate,

As Holmes went behind the curtain, he saw a man in a waiter's uniform going out the door at the back of the barn. The mystery man turned and saw the cat, then hustled out the door. There was no time to follow the man; he had to find out what he was doing behind the altar. Holmes followed the coil whine sound to a cardboard box, and using his paw, he pulled one of the flaps up…

Back at the ceremony, Dr. Hudson was just finishing up with a short poem. "Pastor, oh Pastor, you live in a delusion. All the people want to hear from you now is, "in conclusion. So, in conclusion, I am happy to be the first to present Mrs. Cassidy and Mrs. Isabella DeLeón Macgregor. Let's give a hand to the happy couple."

Everyone was standing and applauding when Holmes ran back around and meowed loudly, **"THERE'S A BOMB. WE HAVE TO GET EVERYONE OUT!"**

Watson and Cassidy both turned to Holmes, having heard him but not grasping what he said. The disbelieving look on their faces caused Holmes to scream at the top of his lungs, **"A BOMB. EVACUATE NOW!"**

In the first row with the parents, Anne Gaumont also heard the warning. Reaching into her bag, she withdrew the Chiefs Special she always carried and announced, "Everyone out! There's a bomb!".

Watson was the first to call out, **"We need to evacuate now. There's an emergency."** At that exact moment, the French Doors at the back of the barn burst open, and some of the catering staff ran in to get people moving. Two exceptionally large men dressed as waiters went straight to an old woman with a cane and virtually lifted her off the ground and hustled her out the doors to safety.

"What is it? What's going on?" Mike Hann asked with Ethan Kelly by his side.

"There's a bomb behind the altar on a countdown timer," Cassidy said, translating what Holmes was telling her. Both agents looked at the orange cat, skepticism on their faces, when Watson interrupted, "It's true. We need to evacuate."

Both agents nodded and moved to usher the crowd out of the venue. "Come on," Watson ordered, going to the parents and practically pushing them towards the doors. "Is there anyone behind the altar?"

"What? I don't know?" Christopher answered, thinking that Watson was talking to him, but it was Holmes who meowed, "Nobody. The person who I think set the bomb was going out the back door when I saw him."

The last of the guests were filing out through the French doors and making their way to safety, leaving Watson and Holmes as the last two in the barn. "When we get back to the office, I will describe the bomb, and you will write it down," the cat meowed, walking towards the doors. "We should be able to backtrack the parts and the explosive to find the culprit." Holmes looked up when he noticed that Watson wasn't following or responding.

Watson hadn't moved; he seemed to be staring back at the altar. When he turned and looked down at Holmes, he had a peculiar look on his face. The two partners locked eyes, and a hundred things were said between them in silence. Watson rushed up, reached down, and picked up the cat; immediately, Holmes knew what Watson intended to do. "STOP. NO WATSON. I DON'T..." The cat was meowing, twisting, and thrashing in his partner's hands when Watson kicked open the French door and, with all his might, flung Holmes as far as he could, away from the barn. Watson then closed the door and ran back towards the altar.

The adrenaline-fueled act of flinging the cat detective on a ballistic trajectory was quite spectacular. Holmes reached the vertex in a matter of seconds and then began the fall back toward the ground. When he hit, his momentum was such that he had to tuck and roll. Still, his head bounced off the brick pathway hard enough to cause temporary dizziness. Regaining his paws after what felt like hours, but was only about fifteen seconds, Holmes drunkenly began to move towards the barn, but he only made it a few feet when the bomb went off.

Holmes was blown back another twenty feet from the blast wave. The only thing that saved his life was that all the glass used to rebuild the barn into a meeting space was tempered safety glass. So, instead of lethal projectiles striking him, the window glass became small, rounded pebbles that, thankfully, mostly went over his head. But there still was a great deal of wood, plaster, and miscellaneous debris that struck the detective, giving him numerous superficial wounds and one particular nasty penetrating trauma to his rear thigh. When Holmes regained consciousness, he saw Christopher doing a quick triage on him to identify any immediate life-threatening injuries. He also saw Cassidy kneeling next to him, talking, but he couldn't hear anything. "I can't hear you," Holmes meowed calmly.

"He said he can't hear," Cassidy relayed to her brother, not caring that Christopher figured out how strange she was.

"Wood has pierced the biceps femoris," Christopher mumbled to himself, making sure to keep his hands away from the piece of wooden shrapnel protruding from Holmes' thigh. "I think the rest of the projectile wounds are shallow." Using his bloody hands to softly check for broken bones. "He could be hurt inside. Blunt force trauma from the explosion pressure wave. Bleeding from the nose and ears, likely concussed, and possible hearing damage. He needs an emergency vet right now." The last sentence came out, not as a suggestion, but as an order.

Cassidy nodded, then looked Holmes in the eye, knowing he could read lips. "Don't move. We will get you to a vet. Where is Watson?"

"Inside," Holmes finally meowed. Cassidy turned to look at the barn. The roof and walls had collapsed onto the structure, and the wreckage was fully engulfed in flames. The two-hundred-year-old timber was burning like matchwood. Cassidy immediately read Holmes and saw the mental images of Watson throwing Holmes to safety and going back inside.

"Oh, God, no," Cassidy said, too shocked to cry.

"Watson," Holmes called out, and then mercifully, he passed out.

CHAPTER XXV

Tipping Point

2021–GEORGETOWN, WASHINGTON, DC.: The Fixer was reading a report from one of his contacts concerning James Gund's newest *secret* business venture. The sad thing was that James Gund actually thought he was being clever, and The Fixer would not find out about this until he was ready to tell him. Pathetic. The Fixer knew because he didn't trust James Xavier Gund any further than he could throw him. So, he made it his business to constantly check on Gund and know whatever his patron might be planning.

When Kerwin Gund was in charge, he held little back from The Fixer. "What good are you to me if you don't know what the hell is going on?" the senior Gund used to say. Unfortunately, that sentiment wasn't passed down to the latest generation. James Gund continually sought to expand into various markets or opportunities, as he liked to call them, without confiding in The Fixer or seeking his guidance. Also, unlike the father, who had an unblemished record of success in the various ventures he undertook, James Gund kept failing…often quite spectacularly.

It would be The Fixer's problem to clean up. More family capital was wasted trying to fix and/or cover up the son's mess.

At fifty-eight years old, The Fixer was getting bone tired of James Gund and the Circle. Initially, there was genuine dedication and respect for Kerwin Gund and what they had accomplished. But since the son took over, he found his thoughts dwelling on the idea of leaving. Just packing up and disappearing to a secluded beach in Uruguay, where nobody knew him. Throughout his many decades of work for the Gunds, he had established more than one emergency exit, preplanned and ready to be used. All he had to do was initiate the plan. The only problem was that he probably wouldn't live long enough to enjoy that secluded beach. The Gunds would utilize their considerable resources, as well as those of the Circle, to locate The Fixer. Unlike the Mafia and their law of *ometră*, which was more a fanciful *opera seri*a than the actual truth, this was not the kind of job that one could walk away from. For The Fixer, the only viable retirement plan was death.

PRESENT DAY: James Xavier Gund was sitting at his desk, re-watching the news feed on his laptop, when The Fixer arrived for their meeting. The Fixer saw that his employer was probably now on his second tumbler of whiskey and seemed very pleased with himself.

"Good evening, Sir. I have the report on the pressure points for the remainder of the Circle." The Fixer set the manila file folder on his boss's desk and took a step back. "There is only one copy of this report, and all electronic files have been destroyed."

When Gund spoke, he did so without looking up from his computer: "You mean you wiped the files you used for the report?"

"No, Sir. I took the laptop I used and my notes to a shredding company, and I watched as the computer and notes were irrevocably destroyed. The paper file on your desk is the only copy of the report anywhere in the world."

"Except what's in your head," Gund replied with a snort. That chilling statement caused The Fixer to momentarily wonder about using one of his escape plans. Gund then softly chuckled and took a drink of bourbon. The Fixer wasn't sure what to expect from his employer tonight, but it certainly wasn't a soft chuckle. Gund looked up to see the confusion on The Fixer's face and said, "Come here and look at this." Gund hit play and spun the laptop around so it could be seen.

The news report was concerning a wedding in Connecticut that was blown up by a bomb. One person, Mr. Tyler Watson Baumann, a consulting detective with the Holmes & Watson Agency, was killed in the explosion. State Police and the FBI were conducting an investigation into the bombing, including looking into past cases Holmes & Watson had conducted.

The Fixer had actually heard about this in the news, but didn't pay attention to the names; now he wished he had. These were the same detectives that his boss had had contact with a couple of months ago, and they had even been in the house. The Fixer suddenly realized he needed to sit down and slowly sank into one of the chairs in front of the desk. "Did you do this, Sir?"

"Yes," Gund replied with smug satisfaction.

"Why? What changed?" The Fixer racked his brain about their last conversation concerning these detectives. Gund said he checked twice for a bug and found none. And there was the coincidence concerning an orange cat. "You realize that the FBI is going to come to your front door and ask a lot of questions."

Gund got a sour look on his face and barked, "I didn't like their attitude, and I don't like yours." Gund wasn't going to tell The Fixer about the bug that he found, especially after making such a point of saying he'd checked. The older Gund got, the less he could ever admit being wrong. The truth was for suckers and losers, and led to defeat. Gund was a winner. Furthermore, with his wealth and the layers of sycophants around him, Gund was protected from ever having to face the truth.

The Fixer watched the expressions on his boss's face and had a pretty good idea about what Gund was thinking. "Sir, what are you going to tell the FBI when they arrive?"

"I'm going to tell them the truth. They came and took a painting back to my cousin. High-priced delivery boys. And that they left here fine, and I haven't had contact with them since."

The Fixer took a deep breath and slowly let it out. Gund was unquestionably hiding something, and that was dangerous for a person who wasn't as smart as he thought he was. Furthermore, when Gund said he would tell the FBI the truth, The Fixer doubted that Gund even knew what the truth was anymore. "When the FBI calls for an appointment, make sure you have your attorney present."

"You mean, 'if' the FBI calls, don't you?"

"No, Sir. I mean, when the FBI calls. Have your attorney here." The Fixer knew the attorney who handled the delicate side of Gund's business. He was very competent and would provide The Fixer with a detailed report. There wasn't a chance in hell that The Fixer would be around if the FBI was going to show up.

"I'm going to leave, Sir. Please put that file somewhere safe." The Fixer saw Gund wave him away, so he went out the side door of his office and got into his car. While driving home, he racked his brain for the real reason Gund had ordered a hit on those detectives. Each time, it came back to something that had happened during their visit. Scenarios were considered and discarded. *What could they have done to make Gund mad enough to kill?*

The Fixer kept coming back to the same explanation: Holmes & Watson *had* managed to bug Gund's house, and they had heard something that would be very bad if it got out. Pride and humiliation made Gund lash out and kill the detective. For thirty-seven years, Joseph Goebel had dedicated his life to working for the Gunds. The first seventeen years were for Kerwin Gund, and the job was reasonably predictable. Kerwin was a more stable person, both temperamentally and in his reactions. For the last twenty years, he had worked for his son, who was more unstable and, therefore, more volatile. Indeed, the alcoholism wasn't helping. As The Fixer pulled into his driveway and waited for the garage door to open, he knew he was stuck.

The Fixer let himself into the house and entered his code into the burglar alarm. The beep from the control panel let him know the alarm was disabled, so he walked into the darkened family room and turned on the lights. Immediately, he saw a well-dressed man sitting in his favorite chair, fingers laced, staring at him.

«Buenas noches, Sr. Goebel. Por favor, tome asiento. Tenemos mucho que discutir» (*Good evening, Mr. Goebel. Please have a seat. We have much to discuss*).

The Fixer had no problems understanding the Spanish being spoken, and ever since Kerwin Gund hired the twenty-five-year-old Joseph Goebel, The Fixer always carried a small pocket pistol wherever he went. These days, it was a Beretta Tomcat 30X.32 ACP in the right pocket of his sports coat for close-quarters emergencies. Casually, Joseph let his hand dangle by his pocket, which caused the man sitting in his chair to actually smile and shake his head. «Por favor. Si te quisiéramos muerto, ya estarías muerto» (*Please. If we wanted you dead, you would already be dead*).

The Fixer considered that statement and slowly looked to his left, then to his right. Behind him, at four and eight o'clock positions, were men, both with suppressed Smith & Wesson M&P M2.0 9mm, pointed at him. Their placement was deliberate. If they had to fire, neither would be in the other's crossfire. That screamed professional. Slowly, Joseph Goebel held out his empty hands and sank into his chair to listen to what his uninvited guests had to say.

HEREFORD, ENGLAND: Captain Mary Augustine was sitting alone, sipping a cup of acceptably good coffee. Surprising, really, being that this place only seemed to know how to make tea. It was off hours for the Mess, and there were only a few tables occupied. The Captain had just returned from an overnight training sortie in the Beacons at 06:30 that morning. After checking in, taking three acetaminophen and a well-deserved nap, Mary needed the caffeine. After her second cup, the Captain was feeling almost back to normal. She was the lone officer accompanying the five senior enlisted soldiers on this training exchange between the 1st Special Forces Operational Detachment-Delta and Special Air Services, Hereford, England. A captain in an elite United States Army Unit, not bad for a formerly messed-up teenager.

Years ago, Mary had run away from home. Looking back, she realized she had dumped all her teenage anger and resentment on her mother, a woman who really didn't deserve it. Her mom was working two jobs to support her and her brother and didn't know how to deal with a sullen teenager, so the mom backed away, letting her daughter make her own decisions, which Mary took as rejection. After one particularly nasty fight with her mother, Mary saw the impact her presence was having on the family and brother, and what she didn't want to do, more than anything, was ruin his life. So, at sixteen, she left with her boyfriend for New York.

Two years of crashing with other runaways in abandoned buildings, working odd jobs, and panhandling kept Mary alive, but desperately unhappy. When her boyfriend, now a meth user, suggested she turn tricks to make some money for them, she knew she had to get away from him, so the next day, before anyone else in their runaway community was awake, Mary left. Finding her way to the U.S. Army Recruitment

Office in Harlem, Mary walked in, placed her driver's license on the Recruiter's desk, and stated that she wanted to join. The Sergeant First Class Dobbins looked at the girl in front of her and asked her to take a seat. For over an hour, she questioned the eighteen-year-old about her, her background, and why she wanted to join. Something about this dirty, skinny, young woman made Sergeant Dobbins remember her own background in Mississippi, and an old line about potential and second chances. So Dobbins decided to adopt this lost puppy and help her get into the Army.

When Sgt. Dobbins finally put Mary on the bus to Basic Training, the Recruiter told her to keep in touch. When Mary finished Basic Training, first in her class, her first call was to Sgt. Dobbins. After that, every milestone Mary achieved in the Army required a perfunctory call to Sgt. Dobbins. Other milestones, such as becoming a College graduate with a degree in languages, followed by graduation from OCS (again, first in her class), were followed by a call to the now-retired recruiting sergeant. Her final call to Sgt. Dobbins, now fighting cancer, came after her promotion to First Lieutenant and posting to 1st Special Forces Operational Detachment-Delta, the posting she had been working towards for five years, because Delta was the best.

When Patricia Dobbins hung up the phone and cracked a smile, a rarity lately, during these pain-filled days, her husband asked, "Who was that?"

"My old lost puppy. She's done really good," was her response. When Sgt. Dobbins passed away, Lieutenant Mary Augustine commanded the honor guard for the woman who became a second mother to her.

As ranking officer, Mary didn't have to go on the Fan Dance over the Pen y Fan mountain with her five soldiers. But she had a reputation to uphold in front of her SAS colleagues and her men. Captain, Mary Augustine (whose last name was the only thing that remained from a marriage that had lasted only ten months) had been in the Unit for ten years and in that time, had made quite a name for herself.

Fluent in Arabic and several African dialects, and as a black woman, she was able to travel unnoticed to many more places than her white teammates. Her Distinguished Service Cross and Silver Star were well-deserved for meritorious service; however, the actual details of the operations that justified those medals were a matter of national security. Therefore, the Army concealed the details to disguise the classified nature of the operation. Major Augustine could wear the medals on her uniform ribbon bar, but couldn't talk about them.

Mary knew she was nearing the end of her career as an active-duty operative for the Unit. What awaited her, if she stayed in, was a promotion to Major, a leadership role, and a desk job—*and a slow death from boredom*, she thought. Of course, the CIA would want to talk to someone of her skills, but the Army was her home; she wanted no other career. Taking another sip of coffee, she continued to scroll through headlines from the States on her laptop. She thought about going home, more than once to see her family, but was always restrained by the memory of her actions during that last fight with her mother, and the things she said. Earlier this year, Mary had read that her mom had passed away. Now, that reunion and plea for forgiveness would never happen. She continued to scroll through headlines when she saw a news report—**Bombing In Connecticut Leaves 1 Dead**. She clicked on it to see what it was all about. If it were terrorism, it might be something for her Unit. Quickly scanning the article, she came to an abrupt halt when the reporter identified the dead man as **Mr. Tyler Watson Baumann**. Mary froze. *No, it can't be,* she thought. Further down in the article, it was stated that the man was a private detective from Torrington, CT. Quickly, she accessed another news service and then even a local television station from the area; all the reports were the same: Mr. Tyler Watson Baumann, dead at 30 years old. Shock at reading the story soon turned to anger, and then, because of her thorough training, the anger was redirected into shaping a plan.

Captain Augustine had one more week in England before she could return to the United States and her Unit. Once there, she would request some of the leave she had accumulated. She planned on finding out how Tyler died, and who was responsible, and holding them to account.

Shock & Anger

It was 11:30 at night on their wedding day, but Mrs. Cassidy and Mrs. Isabella DeLeón Macgregor were not on their way to the Bahamas. Instead, they were sitting in the Macgregor family room with both their parents, Anne Gaumont, and Christopher. "What are you working on that caused this to happen?" Carl De Leòn asked again, worry and anger etched on his face.

"I really don't know," Cassidy replied, meeting her father-in-law's gaze. By mutual agreement, Izzy and Cassidy had decided during the drive over to Cass's parents' house not to inform anyone about the Gund case or the possibility that the bombing was related to it. "There's nothing they can do about it, and it would only make them upset," Isabella said, staring out the windshield of the car. Cassidy didn't respond, only nodded her head.

"You haven't been talking to your grandmother anymore, have you?" Carl asked his daughter. "Was this because of her?"

"No, Daddy. I haven't," Izzy replied, "You made it very clear last year about how dangerous her world was, and I haven't contacted Abuela at all."

Not slowing down, Carl went on, "Well, someone wanted this, and now your friend Tyler is dead."

At the mention of Tyler's death, Izzy began to cry again, prompting Cass, who was also tearing up, to reach down and grasp her hand. "I think you've made your point," Abigail said, frowning at her husband.

Belle and Giblet had been sitting on the kitchen table, listening to the humans talk. When Mr. De Leòn mentioned Tyler's death, Belle wanted to go over and slap him. It was Giblets' restraining paw that stopped her. "He almost lost his daughter today. He's scared, upset, and very worried," Giblet softly meowed.

"If he's disrespectful about Tyler or my family again, he is going to have a face full of Protector," Bell promised.

"Until we get the police report, we don't know who or why the bomb was placed." Anne Gaumont pointed out knowing how these investigations work. She spared a glance over at Izzy and Cassidy, seeing both nod. Anne had been briefed by Holmes about the danger during the Rehearsal Dinner. Now Watson was dead, and Holmes was in the Hospital. Anne had been a cop a long time and had learned to compartmentalize things that happened on the job. However, it was a lot harder to do this when the people who were hurt were, to all intents and purposes, your family.

Shirley Macgregor, who until this point had mostly stayed on the sidelines, spoke up, "Anne is right. Right now, we don't know what is going on. We're all upset, worried, and tired."

"How is their cat, Holmes?" Russell Macgregor asked his son.

"He was fine when I left. He was sedated and out of surgery to repair his leg. The Vet promised that they would call Cassidy with news if anything changed overnight."

"Thank you again for taking him," Cass told her brother once more.

"No problem. I like that cat," Christopher admitted.

Everyone was quiet for a time when Anne stood up and said, "I'm going home and going to bed. Please call me if you need anything or have news about Holmes."

"Do you want me to walk you home?" Christopher asked.

"No. It's just across the yard. Good night, everyone," she said on her way out the door.

"We should get going as well," Carl De Leòn said, also rising.

"You can't drive all the way back to New Haven tonight. Stay here. We have a great extra bedroom with its own bath that you can stay in," Russell Macgregor insisted. After the usual back-and-forth about not wanting to be an inconvenience, Carl and Abigail agreed to stay.

"I'll show you the room. And I think I have some PJs that will fit you just fine, Abigail," Shirley offered, heading up the stairs to the bedrooms.

Christopher also went to his bedroom, leaving Russell Macgregor alone with his daughter and daughter-in-law. "I know you haven't told us everything," Russell said, mainly directed at Cassidy, who had the good manners not to deny it, but to stare down at the floor. "But, I trust you. Please stay safe."

Rising to his feet, he said good night and went upstairs. As soon as he had left the room, Belle and Giblet came over. "We're going to patrol around the immediate neighborhood. You two should go to bed," the Protector instructed.

"I think you're right," Cass said to Belle as she stood and reached her hand down to her wife. Together, they also went upstairs.

"Let's go," Belle said to Giblet. The two cats went to the basement and out the one window that the Protector had been using for years to get outside. Once there, they began their patrol. The neighborhood was quiet, and with no moon tonight, the darkness seemed even more impenetrable. There was a house directly across the street from the Macgregors' white clapboard house, which was a rental property. Typically, visiting professors rented the home while they were in town for a semester of guest teaching. When Giblet and Belle walked past the house, there were no lights on, and all looked normal. However, if Belle and her companion had gone around the back and looked in the basement window, they would have been surprised by what they would have seen.

A man was sitting at a desk in front of four video monitors, each displaying a different real-time feed of the Macgregors' house. The man sipped his coffee and continued to watch. On the desk next to him was a suppressed Heckler & Koch MP5 machine gun, a round chambered, and the safety was on. His two companions were upstairs, both asleep, but equally well armed. They could react, if need be, on a moment's notice. So far, all the action had happened that afternoon at the wedding, which suited the man watching the monitors just fine. But if trouble came to the Macgregors' house tonight, he would be ready to handle it.

Floating. No pain or discomfort; in fact, no discernible features that could be used as a reference point. In fact, he had no sense of a body. "Pure thought. Existence without corporeal form. Is that even possible?" Holmes asked aloud. However, he wasn't sure if he was verbalizing or thinking the question. An ataraxia, the likes of which he had never experienced before, held him. No, that wasn't quite true. One of Holmes's very first memories, before his eyes were even open, was being groomed as a newborn by his mother. Her tongue massaged him while her body kept him warm, and her soft purrs rumbled all around. Such perfect contentment and serenity, the likes of which he never knew until now.

"I must be dead. It is the only possible explanation," Holmes meowed into the void.

"You're not dead, Holmes. At least not yet," a female voice replied to him.

Turning his head towards the familiar elocution, or at least thinking he was turning his head, he saw a Maine Coon scrutinizing him. It took Holmes a minute to realize he knew this cat. "Mittens," he meowed at her. "What are you doing here? Where am I?"

"I live here," the former Protector meowed matter-of-factly. "The question is, what are you doing here?"

The question took him aback. What was he doing here? The detective, who was never unprepared for repartee, was suddenly at a loss for words. "There was a bombing at Cassidy's wedding," Holmes replied tentatively, struggling to remember the details. "I think Watson ran back into the building, and I was thrown back by the explosion." A look of frustration on his face made Mittens laugh. "Why is it so hard to remember?" he wondered.

"Because, Holmes, those things happened in the mortal world. When a spirit transitions, all the worry and grief are left behind. This is a realm of peace. Here, only the strongest spirit can usually remember anything of their prior lives."

"You say I'm not dead, but here we are. You look decades younger than the last time I saw you," Holmes told the former Protector.

"So do you," Mittens replied. "In fact, you have two full ears," she informed him. Then she watched as Holmes reached up with a paw and felt his left ear. The end that had been clipped off was back. "As to why you're here, the reason is, as you say, elementary. You need something from me."

Holmes was quiet, thinking about what Mittens had said to him. A couple of times, he almost spoke, but then fell back into silent self-reflection. "Wake up, Holmes," a familiar voice sounded, breaking his concentration. Turning to Mittens, he asked, "Excuse me. What did you say?"

"I didn't say anything," the Protector replied. "But I have a feeling that your work isn't done in the mortal world," Mittens offered. "Until we meet again," she meowed before fading into the ether.

Once again, the familiar voice sounded all around him, "Please wake up…"

CHAPTER XXVII

Familia

It was the next morning, and both Izzy and Cass were waiting by the door when the veterinarian and his technician showed up to open the practice. The two women were led to the examination room, and once there, joined by Doctor Ewan Gallowglass, VDM. The technician brought the unconscious orange cat to the exam room, set him on the table, and departed. Holmes was lying in an open plastic bassinet, similar to what was used in hospitals for newborns. As soon as Cass and Izzy saw Holmes, head partially shaved, leg bandaged, and with an I.V. line running into him, Cass took in a sharp breath while Izzy's eyes began to tear up. They were at the best emergency veterinary hospital in Hartford, where Chris Macgregor had rushed the unconscious cat twenty-four hours before.

The doctor began checking Holmes's vitals by first examining the color of his gums; they were bright pink. Then, using his stethoscope, the doctor checked the heartbeat and respiration. Both were fine. Finally, the doctor checked to ensure that both pupils were reactive to the penlight; they were. "Aye, everything's awricht an looks stable," Dr. Gallowglass told the visibly upset women. "Ye cat nae any immediate danger." Cass and Izzy relaxed slightly after translating the Doctor's thick Scottish Brogue.

Yesterday, Cassidy and Isabell wanted to travel with Chris to the veterinary hospital after the explosion. They were in shock about Watson's death and felt that they needed to do something to make sure they wouldn't lose Holmes as well, but the authorities had other ideas. They made it abundantly clear that the women needed to stay at the scene to answer questions about what had happened.

"Go. Go, get Holmes to the hospital," Izzy said. "You can't wait for us," Cassidy added. So, after scooping up the unconscious cat and taking it to his car, Christopher drove like a madman, disregarding posted speed limits, to the best trauma vet hospital he knew, which happened to be in Hartford. Christopher had a profound sense of déjà vu in the situation because it was just last year that he and his family had hurried to Hartford, following behind the ambulance transporting Cassidy after she had been stabbed. "I hope this is not becoming routine," he said to himself.

After determining that Holmes was stable, Dr. Gallowglass continued his assessment of his patient. "His X-rays are fine. Naebody broken, and no skull fracture," he said. "The ultrasound confirmed nae internal bleeding or organ damage, and blood work looks braw. We've had him on intravenous fluids tae keep him hydrated, an as ye can see, we shaved pairt o his heid whaur he needed stitches." The doctor paused to see if Izzy or Cass had questions, then continued. "Dinna fash. Oweraw, he looks frail an like he's been through the wringer, but I've seen cats wha looked a lot waur, an they a' pulled through juist fine."

"Why hasn't he awakened?" Cassidy asked, always the scientist, looking for an explanation.

"It's the concussion," the vet replied. "It micht tak a couple o days tae regain consciousness. Blether tae him. Hearin yer voice micht help."

Cass looked to her wife to see if she wanted to ask anything, but Izzy shook her head. "Thank you, Doctor," Cassidy replied to the vet.

"Bide as lang as ye like," the doctor said as he left the room.

The two women were silent for a while when Izzy said, "You know if it wasn't for Holmes, we may never have met."

"You're right. Perhaps we should add match-maker to his list of skills," Cass agreed, summoning a small smile.

Izzy reached over and gently stroked Holmes, saying, "Wake up, Holmes," her face streaked with tears. Cassidy stood next to her wife, matching her despondent look. "Please, wake up."

As they watched, the detective's eyes suddenly popped open. At first, there was a look of total confusion as he tried to focus and understand where he was and if this was real. When he caught sight of Cass and Izzy staring at him, he raised a paw and drunkenly tried to reach for them. Izzy reached her hand down and took the paw. Physical contact seemed to calm the cat, and he tried to find his voice but only succeeded in coughing. "It's okay, Holmes. We're here," Cassidy said reassuringly.

Once more, the detective tried to speak, but without success. When he finally managed, it was in a raspy-sounding voice, "Cassidy, Isabella, you need to listen to me very carefully..." he began.

Only Watson remained unaccounted for since the bombing. All the rest, guests and staff, had been confirmed and questioned by police, then released. When the site was finally cool enough for forensics to enter the crime scene, they found that nothing remained of the old barn except the stone foundation and a few small pieces of twisted, blackened metal. Everything else had been reduced to ash by the incredible heat the fire generated. The Fire Marshal and the Chief of the Division of Criminal Justice for Connecticut, DCJ, were wearing their white protective suits and discussing the case. "Any development on the lead about the man dressed like a waiter?" the fire chief asked. During their interviews, several people mentioned seeing a man dressed like a waiter carrying a box into the church. When the investigators questioned the caterers, they said the person was not one of their employees.

"No," the chief of DCJ replied. "Of course, in the chaos of the bombing, any number of people could have simply walked away."

"Were there cameras? Is there any video?" the Fire Marshall asked.

"No. Why would you need them at a wedding/meeting venue?" The DCJ answered and was about to elaborate when a voice called from across the ruin, "Chief. I found something."

"Come on," the Chief said, and together they began picking their way across the debris. They found the tech taking pictures of the charred remains of a pistol. A yellow evidence marker and ruler were placed next to the pistol to provide scale. A few pieces of what might have been bone were also in the vicinity, but everything else was ash.

Squatting down but not touching the gun, the Fire Marshall said, "That was a 38 special. The victim carried that kind of pistol, didn't he?"

"Yes. We should be able to get a serial number off the barrel." The DCJ chief replied. Then, addressing the tech, he said, "When you're done with the pictures, get that bagged up and back to the lab. I want their report ASAP."

"Yes, sir," the tech answered before getting an evidence bag out of her kit.

Despite his determination to leave, Holmes was kept at the veterinary hospital for two days while they monitored him for complications from his concussion. The attack on Isabella's and Cassidy's wedding received national and international news coverage, none of which the women wanted. News organizations also reported that there was only one casualty from the bombing: Mr. Tyler Watson, of Torrington, Connecticut, a partner in the Holmes & Watson Consulting Detectives agency. DCJ investigators located Watson's remains at the epicenter of the blast. They theorized that he was attempting to disarm the bomb when it went off. Because of the heat of the conflagration, the body was all but incinerated. Therefore, identification was made by the serial number stamped on the barrel and frame of the recovered 38 Special. A quick check of state records showed the gun was registered to Tyler Watson.

The plan to conduct a DNA comparison between the few bone fragments recovered and the verified DNA from Mr. Watson was thwarted due to the high temperature of the fire. Fires over 550 degrees Fahrenheit usually destroy most of the DNA in tissue. The Fire Marshall estimated the fire at the Cider Haus barn was in excess of 1100°F, based on the state of the remains.

Over the next few days, Izzy and Cass were required to sit through multiple follow-up interviews conducted by various law enforcement agencies, including Isabella's former employer and the FBI. Mike Hann and Ethan Kelly were as gentle as possible when they asked the same basic questions everyone else did: Do they know who might have done this? Was somebody threatening the firm or Watson? Each time they were asked, they kept their answers within the bounds of what they had all agreed to with Holmes.

After the last interview with the FBI and before he left to return to New York, Ethan pulled Izzy aside and asked if she would talk to him alone for a minute. "Outside, in private," he suggested.

"Sure, Ethan. Let me tell Cass I will be right back."

Burlington, Connecticut, was a tiny, picturesque, and very rural town to such an extent that their five-person police department didn't have its own building and ended up sharing space in the town hall with other municipal departments. The various agencies that came to Burlington to investigate the Cider Haus fire had been given temporary space in the already overextended Burlington town hall to conduct their work and interviews. To ensure a private conversation, Izzy and Mike walked out of the town hall and proceeded across the lawn in front of the building.

It was a beautiful September afternoon, and the sun warmed Izzy's face. Walking next to her former boss, she wondered how anyone could have a problem on such a day. As soon as they were far enough away that they wouldn't be overheard, Ethan began, "Izzy, this wasn't a random act. Somebody was coming after you, Cassidy, and Watson. Based on what happened last year, I think we both have a good idea who that might be." Izzy didn't say anything to confirm his suspicions, but didn't deny anything either.

Nodding, Ethan continued, "We both know you wouldn't be in this situation if you hadn't been coerced into that ill-contrived undercover operation. Because of that, the FBI has an obligation to your safety."

Izzy had been in the FBI long enough to guess that wasn't true. "Is this official policy?"

Ethan smiled and nodded at her discernment. "You know that it isn't, but you are still one of my people." Reaching into his pocket, he handed her a card, "Here," he said. "My personal number is on this. If you need something, call me. Day or night. Don't call the FBI office. This is strictly off-book."

Izzy looked at the card and nodded. "Thank you, Ethan. I will keep this handy," she promised.

A good FBI agent, especially one who has more than twenty years on the job, knows when someone is holding back, and Izzy is definitely holding back, he thought. "What are you going to do now?" he asked.

"We're going to pick up our cat. The vet said he could come home." Izzy replied, then headed back to find Cassidy.

Before Izzy and Cass could leave with Holmes, the vet wanted to go over a list of instructions for the orange tabby cat. "Abune a' else, keep him calm, an dinna let him rin aboot or play ower hard," to which Holmes raised an eyebrow from inside the carrier. "He's still healin," the doctor reminded them. When they finally made it to their car, Holmes growled, "Macgregor, get me out of this infernal cage!"

When Cass opened the carrier door, Holmes stepped out and settled on the car seat. However, with his rear leg still in bandages, his hesitant movements were unlike his regular, graceful motions. "Are you dizzy?" Cassidy asked, her face filled with concern.

"I'm fine," Holmes answered unconvincingly. Irritation was clear in his voice. "Did you do what I told you to do?"

"Yes. We swept the office, Watson's home, and our home. We found bugs in Watson's home and the office. There are three different types, but our apartment, strangely, is clean. We didn't touch the bugs, per your instructions," Cassidy said.

"Three different types," Holmes mumbled to himself. "We have a bigger radio audience than Churchill had during the Blitz."

"Why leave them? What are we waiting for?" Izzy wanted to know.

"We leave the listening devices in place because we know about them, and our adversaries don't yet realize we know. That is a tactical advantage for us. Now, we need to bustle off to your apartment. The rest of the players for this drama are waiting to be identified."

"Why isn't our home bugged?" Izzy asked.

"The answer is elementary," the orange cat replied, but refused to elaborate.

CHAPTER XXVIII

The Players

Cassidy, Izzy, and Holmes sat in the newlyweds' apartment waiting for, as Holmes said, "Company." Izzy was sitting upright at the end of the couch, her hand within inches of her loaded Glock 19, sitting on the lamp table. Cassidy was reclining against her wife, but both women were keeping a wary eye on the front door. Only Holmes seemed at ease, lying across the coffee table in the center of the room. "You won't need the weapon," Holmes meowed for a second time while Cass translated.

"After everything that has happened, forgive me if I don't believe you," Izzy replied with an uncharacteristic snap, glaring at the cat.

The group fell back into an uneasy silence. Though they were expecting it, when there was a knock at the door, both women jumped. "I'll get the door," Cass said, starting to get up.

"We'll get it together," Izzy said, following her wife to the door, her pistol in her hand but pointed at the floor. When Cassy put one hand on the deadbolt and the other on the doorknob, she looked at Izzy, who gave a small smile and nodded. Slowly, Izzy changed her grip on the Glock to the Weaver Stance but still kept the gun pointing at the floor. Slowly,

Cass turned the deadbolt and opened the door…And found herself staring into the upper chest of a man who was at least a foot taller and a hundred-and-fifty pounds heavier than she was. He was wearing a white shirt and black pants. No weapon was visible, but Cass was absolutely sure the man could produce one at a moment's notice.

«Buenas noches, señorita. ¿Está presente el Sr. Holmes?» the man said in a deep, rumbling voice, emanating from somewhere in his broad chest. When he saw Izzy holding the Glock, he smiled and said, «No hay necesidad de eso, Sra. DeLeón. ¿Podemos entrar?»

"Uh, what?" Cassidy replied, not fluent in the language.

"He said, Macgregor, that he is looking for me, and can he come in?" Holmes meowed from behind her. "Oh, and he also said that Izzy does not need her gun."

Still confused, Cass looked at her wife, and Izzy nodded, lowering the gun, but not putting it away. "Let them in, I guess," she said and went back to the main room with Cass following.

The big man at the door nodded and came into the apartment. Cass watched, wondering if he would have to duck under the door jamb, but there turned out to be plenty of room. Instead of walking in, the man stopped about six feet from the door and removed a black bag from his pocket. Looking at Isabella, then to Cassidy, he said, «Sus teléfonos, por favor».

"Why do you want my phone? What's with that bag?" Isabella asked.

"That is a Faraday bag," Holmes informed them from his place on the coffee table. "It prevents a cell phone from clandestinely recording and then downloading a conversation. Our guest wants this meeting to be private."

"No," was Cassidy's simple answer, looking at her wife for confirmation. Izzy nodded in agreement and shifted the Glock in her hand to emphasize her reply.

Instead of arguing, the big man turned back to the open door and made the 'all clear' signal. Soon, an old woman appeared in the doorway.

She looked to be about seventy-five and was dressed in what might be called business casual. The woman's hair was gray and styled in a blunt bob. She looked very fit for her age despite appearing to need a mahogany cane to help her walk.

However, it was the eyes of the old woman that drew the observer in. Not cruel eyes, persê, but very determined. Holmes rose to a sitting position and quietly observed this woman. In turn, the woman stopped and stared at the orange cat. After a minute, she asked, «Sr. Holmes, ¿qué ves cuando me miras?» *(Mr. Holmes, what do you see when you look at me?)*

Immediately, Holmes utilized his unparalleled observational skills and began cataloging what her appearance revealed to him. "Your shoes were chosen for practicality, not fashion. The sole on the right shoe was worn at an angle because your right foot rolls out when you walk," he meowed. "Undoubtedly, because you have had damage to your right knee in the past, which is also the reason for the cane. Your wedding ring is on your right hand, indicating your spouse has passed away."

"Surrounding the diamond are two black onyx jewels and one blue sapphire jewel. The two black onyx gems are for your two dead sons, although they were not added at the same time because they were killed separately, and a couple of years apart. This is evident because the gold tines holding the gems are each slightly different in shade and configuration, obviously not from the same casting. The Blue Sapphire stone is for your last remaining son, Carlos, and is his birth month, which is September."

Holmes's meows were being translated into Spanish for the woman as soon as they were spoken. However, Cassidy wasn't the one translating. Instead, a young girl, between the ages of five and seven, who had joined them in the apartment, was translating from Cat language to Colombian Spanish, with all the inflection and cadence of Holmes's usual tone. Whereas Cassidy sometimes had to wait until Holmes was finished and then summarize what was said, this little girl was doing an instantaneous translation as soon as each meow was uttered. A singularly impressive display and mastery of Cat language.

"There are creases on your clothes and a faint musty odor, indicating a long period of storage between uses. I deduce that these clothes are not your usual attire, but they spend most of the time in a closet. Your uncomfortable demeanor tells me that you would usually be found wearing practical clothing, a blouse, blue jeans, and alpargatas, perhaps." As Holmes continued his impressive display of observation, the old woman nodded and began smiling.

"Finally, the scar on your neck, fully healed but not erased by plastic surgery or hidden in some other way, indicates that you were held at knife-point at some point in the past. Your determination not to cover the scar or have it removed serves as a visual reminder, ensuring you never forget the confrontation. But it is your eyes, while I'm talking about the scare, that tell me that the man who did this is no longer living and that his death came at your hands." Holmes finished, then sat and watched the woman for a reaction. Throughout Holmes's recitation, Cassidy leaned over and whispered to her wife what was being said.

Satisfied, the old woman said, «Tienes razón. Es tan brillante como me prometiste,» *(You are right. He is as brilliant as you promised)*. The old woman spoke, but it wasn't obvious to whom she was addressing until the white cat gracefully jumped on the couch, having entered the apartment silently and unseen. "I told you. He's perfect," the white cat meowed, a wicked smile on her face.

"Irene Adler!" Cassidy exclaimed, surprised at seeing the white cat from Philadelphia here in their apartment. Cass turned and whispered something to her wife, and Izzy nodded in response. Only Holmes showed no shock at the arrival of *That Female*.

A second bodyguard, equally large and formidable-looking, came in and stationed himself by the door, making sure nobody else could enter. It was then that the old woman turned her attention from Holmes to

Isabella. She walked over and stood before Izzy, looking at her with such intensity as if trying to commit every part of her face to memory.

"Can I help you?" Izzy asked. She wasn't upset by the old woman's scrutiny, but she didn't understand it either, especially the look she was giving her. There was love behind that hard stare that confused Izzy. Why was the old woman so interested in her? And why was there something in her voice that sounded so familiar?

The old woman continued smiling and said, «Mi corazón. Qué alegría verte en persona. Permíteme decirte que estabas preciosa de novia. Por favor, dame un abrazo» *(My Heart. It is so good to see you in person. May I say, you were a lovely bride. Please, give me a hug).*

«¿Abuela?» *(Grandmother?)* Izzy said, not really believing what she heard. «¿Qué haces aquí?» *(What are you doing here?).*

The Spanish was being spoken much too fast for Cassidy to follow, but she recognized the word "grandmother" that her wife used and instantly knew who this must be. Standing in her apartment was the woman who ran the De Leòn Cartel and employed Diego, the man who almost killed her.

When her grandmother held out her arms to her granddaughter, Izzy backed up a step, not wanting to hug this woman. Unrebuffed, the woman turned to Cassidy and said, «Tú debes de ser Cassidy. Yo soy Antonella De Lêon. Es un placer conocerte» *(You must be Cassidy. I'm Antonella De Lêon. It is a pleasure to meet you),* and she held out her hand. Seeing that Izzy was in shock, Holmes quickly provided a translation for Cassidy's benefit.

Cassidy heard the translation and saw the woman's outstretched hand, but there wasn't a chance in hell that she was going to take it. "Your man, Diego, almost killed me," Cassidy snapped at the old woman, her voice rising and her hands balling into fists. Then she turned to Holmes as realization dawned upon her. "You knew she was coming here today. You knew she was involved. What else have you been keeping from Izzy and me?" The anger she had felt a moment ago toward Antonella

DeLeón was now directed at the orange tabby cat sitting on her coffee table. Izzy reached over and put a soft hand on Cass's shoulder, but Cassidy shook it loose. She wasn't having any of that. She was angry at what happened at their wedding, about what happened to Watson, about being stabbed a year before, about all of it. "It's okay, my girl," Izzy said softly as Cassidy broke down in tears and Izzy held her. Izzy rocked back and forth, cuddling Cassidy and stroking her hair. When it sounded like the tears were spent, Isabella lessened her embrace but didn't let go. Finally, the two of them sat down on the edge of the couch and glared at the orange tomcat.

Holmes knew how furious they were with him and that they demanded answers. He let the anger wash over him. It was better that they get this out of their system now, considering the work coming up that needed to be done. "I understand your anger," he meowed, looking from Cass to Izzy. "But it wasn't until your wedding that my speculation turned into fact. The only human I shared this with was Watson, and he agreed with me. I was going to tell you after the ceremony, but the bombing that Gund orchestrated threw a wrench into the works and significantly altered our timetable. If everyone will please take a seat, I will explain. We have a mutual enemy and a lot of work to do."

The Fixer woke up with a dry mouth and a pounding headache. He was lying on a metal-framed bed in an otherwise empty room. He knew it was daytime because a single window in the room was letting in filtered light. There were two wooden doors on the opposite walls, both of which were closed. He tried to sit up but immediately abandoned the effort when his headache intensified. Instead, The Fixer closed his eyes and tried to think. He had left his meeting with Gund and returned home to find three men waiting for him. Two held him at gunpoint while the third questioned him about his work for Gund and the Circle. After about ten minutes, The Fixer felt a pin-prick on his neck, and then he woke up here, wherever "here" was.

Listening, The Fixer didn't hear any noise from outside the room, like one would expect from an urban environment. As soon as his head stopped pounding, he opened his eyes again. The room appeared to be of older construction, with a hardwood floor, wood baseboards, and the aforementioned wooden door; however, this time, he noted that the doorknob was tarnished brass. Also, there was a certain unevenness in the walls, the same kind of look The Fixer remembered from his grandmother's house when he was little. "Plaster walls!" he croaked, the dryness of his mouth making his words sound hoarse. That meant the room was built before or during the 1950s.

Apparently, his speaking drew the attention of someone outside the room. The door opened, and one of the men from last night came in with a paper cup of water and two white pills. The Fixer sat up and swung his legs over the edge of the bed; that was when he noticed his right foot was chained to the metal frame. «Toma. Bebe esto y coge estas» *(Here. Drink this and take these)*, the man said.

The Fixer looked at the pills suspiciously, so the man added, «No te preocupes. Son aspirin.» *(Don't worry. It's aspirin)*.

The Fixer nodded and did as he was told. The guard took the paper cup and withdrew. After a few minutes of sitting on the edge of the bed, looking at his manacled foot, he saw that the edges of the cuff were padded around his ankle so it wouldn't cause abrasions. "Very considerate," The Fixer mumbled. Standing, shuffled over to the window and parted the drapes. There were trees in the immediate vicinity, and in the distance, he could see blue water. He stared at it for a moment when the door opened, and an unfamiliar man came in.

"If you want some fresh air, the window's unlocked, Mr. Goebel," he said by way of a greeting in accented English. The man appeared to be about forty, well-dressed, fit, and of Latin American descent.

"Aren't you worried about me wandering away, especially if I get out of this cuff?"

"Not particularly. We are on a private island off the coast of Connecticut," He replied. "We don't have a boat stationed here; it has to come out to us from the mainland. You look relatively healthy, but a fourteen-mile swim against an ocean current would keep you from making it to shore. Besides, you're not stupid. You're a survivor, and you're wondering what this is all about."

"So, what is this all about?" The Fixer asked. "And, what is your name?"

"You can call me Matías. Someone will be along to ask you some questions. You will answer them truthfully. If you lie, you will wish you hadn't."

"And then you will kill me," The Fixer added, matter-of-factly.

"Not necessarily. I imagine it will depend on how useful you are." Matías took out his phone, punched in his code, and handed it to Goebel. The Fixer looked at the screen and saw a live image of a man sitting in a chair, bound and gagged. "Do you know him?" he was asked.

The Fixer stared at the screen and recognized a person he had seen around Gund's ranch from time to time. "He works for Gund," The Fixer replied honestly. "I don't know his name."

"He's been following you for the last couple of weeks. In fact, he was outside your home when we collected you last night." Matías waited a couple of beats, then asked, "Did you know your employer was having you watched?"

Goebel was quiet for a time as the realization sank in that two different groups had been following him for at least the last couple of weeks and that he hadn't picked up on it. *Maybe I should have sold tickets,* he thought bitterly to himself. Sloppiness like that usually is a death sentence. Matías watched The Fixer's face as the realization sank in.

"No. I didn't realize I was being watched. But I'm not surprised," Goebel finally said, deciding that being honest about this subject would not cost him.

Matías nodded, then said, "The toilet is through that other door. Food will be brought to you in about an hour. Good afternoon, Mr. Goebel." He turned and left.

Joseph Goebel sat on the edge of the bed and wondered what he should do when a single pistol shot from somewhere close by broke his train of thought. He guessed that the man on the phone, his shadow, had just kicked the oxygen habit. That realization created a new set of problems to consider.

CHAPTER XXIX

Gund & Diego

TWO YEARS BEFORE: Diego paced around the Music Stand gazebo in Tower Grove Park, waiting impatiently for the other man to arrive for the meeting. After the last body of one of his men, or rather 67% of the body, was dumped on Diego's doorstep, a temporary truce was ordered so that an encuentro could be arranged. So far, this turf war had cost Diego three low-level but good men and had put their St. Louis distribution operation into disarray. «¿Qué hora es?» (What time is it?), he barked at his lieutenant.

«Son las tres menos diez, jefe,» *(It's ten to three, Boss)*, his man Luis replied.

So far, Diego had kept the DeLeón family back in Colombia from knowing about the problems in St. Louis. The three men who were killed were local recruits, not Colombian men. The last thing he wanted was for the DeLeón family to think he couldn't do his job. To that end, the remaining men in the St. Louis operation were sworn to secrecy about what was happening. Anyone foolish enough to go behind Diego's back to report knew what would happen because of Diego's well-founded reputation as a maniac.

Six months prior, the St. Louis operation began hearing whispers and noticing strangers in the neighborhoods they controlled, offering competitive products and undercutting their prices. These streets were controlled by the DeLeón Cartel, and competition was not tolerated. When these interlopers were followed back to their sede principal, an old gas station in south St. Louis, Diego made his usual prosaic decision to use violence to send them a warning. After Pepe finished airing out their rival's headquarters with his AK-47, he was heading back to report when his car was stopped, and witnesses said he was dragged from his vehicle.

That was the last confirmed sighting Diego had of his man until Pepe's remains turned up in Pontiac Square Park in Soulard. Typically, a single body being found does not get the police all that excited. However, it was the condition of Pepe that got the Major Case Squad, along with all the St. Louis news organizations, up in arms. Pepe was found staged, leaning against a tree, with his own head in his hands. In addition, there was evidence that he had been tortured before being beheaded, probably with a machete, according to the St. Louis Medical Examiner.

Diego already knew his man was dead before the body was found, because he had received a text from Pepe's phone. «Admiro tu valentía, pero no tu sabiduría» *(I admire your courage, but not your wisdom)*, Diego mumbled to himself concerning what they did to Pepe. Clearly, this new faction wasn't going to be intimidated easily. Still, whoever they were, they hadn't gone up against the DeLeóns before. It was then that Diego offered a reward for anyone who could deliver the body of the leader of this new gang to him: two thousand dollars dead or three thousand alive, so he could have some fun. However, try as they might, finding the person pulling the strings remained elusive.

Instead, there was a string of tit-for-tat murders on both sides that hurt business and woke up a few more cops. It was during this time that Diego discovered the leader's name behind this new group: a gringo from Texas named Gund. Apparently, he was a prominent figure, looking to expand into new markets. When it looked like this war would continue unabated, Gund suggested a ceasefire so that they could meet and perhaps make some kind of accommodation.

By arrangement, only the Jefe and one trusted lieutenant would be present for the meeting, and nobody was to be armed. The encuentro was to be held in Tower Grove Park, a Victorian-style walking park in south St. Louis, Missouri. For the safety of both parties, the meeting was scheduled for three p.m. on Saturday, when the Park would have plenty of witnesses. Naturally, Diego had no intention of obeying the meeting's stipulations. On the best of days, Diego was belligerent and quick to temper, and there was no way he was going to meet up with this gringo without a gun. So, he and Luis were both armed, and for good measure, he put two of his men in the food truck parked on Magnolia Street with a long gun. All Diego had to do was remove his hat, and his men would open fire.

At three p.m., a middle-aged man wearing jeans, a white shirt, cowboy boots, and a Stetson hat walked up to the Pavilion. He was accompanied by a bodyguard dressed all in black. The bodyguard wasn't your average muscle; Diego guessed correctly that this man had the air of professional training about him. The man in the Stetson stopped six feet away and said, «Soy James Xavier Gund, y tú eres Diego Jiménez, del Cartel DeLeón» (*"I'm James Xavier Gund, and you are Diego Jiménez, of the DeLeón Cartel."*), in passable but highly accented Spanish.

Not to be shown up, Diego replied in English, "Yes, I am. And you're James Gund from Texas." Then Diego went straight to business. "The St. Louis region is DeLeón territory. You don't want to be in a war with the DeLeón Cartel."

Gund smiled. The fact that Diego didn't mention the Circle or Gund's association with that organization proved that he wasn't informing his superiors in Colombia about the trouble he was having. Had he done so, they would have told Diego they had done business with Gund in the past.

Long before there was a DeLeón Cartel, there was the DeLeón family, who were honest but poor sugar cane farmers in a small village in Colombia. When Prohibition took hold in the United States, organized crime needed sugar to make molasses for their bootleg rum, a very popular drink in the southern United States and California. Overnight, all across South America, farmers were being paid very well for their sugar, and for the first time in their lives, the DeLeón family was making a substantial amount of money. Besides growing the cane, the DeLeón family generated additional income by providing drivers to bring the cane across the border and into Texas, where Gund and the Circle provided protection from the authorities.

When Prohibition was repealed, the business arrangement between the DeLeóns and the Gunds faded into history; both families went their separate ways until James Gund once again attempted to branch out into a new business that he could run and call his own, outside of the Circle. That the distribution of Chinese narcotics, produced by Tong gangs in Southeast Asia, was by far one of the most dangerous businesses to try to break into didn't worry James Gund. In fact, the danger made the whole operation exciting for the Texan.

Standing across from Diego, Gund saw a kindred spirit in the young Latino; arrogant, dangerous, and eager to be his own boss. After reaching an agreement that divided up the St. Louis region between them, James asked, "Where do you see yourself in five years, Diego? Still working for the DeLeóns?" Gund saw that the unexpected question caught the young man off guard, and his face revealed his apprehension. "Afraid to talk in front of your man here?" Gund asked, gesturing to Luis.

Luis looked surprised to suddenly be included in the talks, but it was Diego who answered. "No. I confiad Luis," he said. Then, he added, "I trust him, or he'd be dead."

"Do you want to be your own boss someday?" Gund asked, already knowing the answer.

"Why do you want to know, Señor Gund?"

"Because I am a businessman, and I've made a fortune out of seeing and exploiting opportunities," Gund said with a straight face. The fact that James had inherited almost all of his money and had yet to start a successful business on his own was left off. "I see you as a tremendous untapped opportunity." The flattery worked as Gund had hoped, as Diego's body language changed in proportion to the compliments.

To his credit, Diego counted to ten in his head before he replied and worked at keeping his voice casual, "What are you offering, Señor Gund?"

"The DeLeóns have you running a small midwestern city. How would you like to run half the country?" Gund let that sink in, then sweetened the pot. "With the opportunity to run it all after I retire?"

"Why would you do this? What's in it for you?" Diego asked.

"I am already rich and couldn't spend what I've got if I tried. When you reach a certain point, you look for new ways to bring the excitement back to the game." Gund watched as Diego thought about it. "I don't need an answer now. But let's keep this conversation to ourselves and stay in touch," he suggested and held out his hand.

Diego took Gund's hand and felt the firm grip. Then, feeling the need to exert a little of his own bravado, he said, "I was ready if this had been a trap."

"You mean the two men you had stationed in the food truck?" Gund asked. "Take a look."

Diego turned to look at the food truck sniper nest he'd set up, but the large concession window wasn't open anymore, and there was no sign of the men. "They're alive. Although you will have to untie them after we leave," Gund informed him. After a pause, he added, "Look down at your chest." Diego did so and saw the small red dot of a laser sight, unwavering, over his heart. "You have good ideas, Diego. But you don't have the means to take them to the next step. If you work with me, that won't be a problem."

CHAPTER XXX

Truths & Half-Truths

Everyone was quiet as Antonella DeLeón finished her long story about Diego, his betrayal of the DeLeón family, and the beginning of his association with James Gund. While it would probably never be a convivial atmosphere among those present, at least there appeared to be an uneasy détente setting in.

"When did Diego tell you this?" Cassidy asked Antonella.

"When he was brought back to Colombia, we talked."

«¿Dónde está ahora?» *(Where is he now?)* Isabella asked, to which Antonella simply raised one eyebrow at her granddaughter and gave her a *"are you serious?"* look.

«Está bien. Pregunta tonta,» *(Okay. Dumb question),* Izzy replied, sitting back into the cushion of the couch and folding her arms over her chest.

"Use English, My Heart, so your wife can understand you," Izzy's grandmother said, admonishing her. Antonella DeLeón was sitting in the armchair, facing Izzy, Cass, and Holmes, while the young girl she had brought was on one end of the couch closest to her with the white cat, Irene Adler, in her lap. Irene seemed to be enjoying being petted and purred, but otherwise remained quiet. The only time the little girl spoke was if Holmes or Irene Adler meowed something, and then she would immediately translate it for Antonella in perfect Spanish or English.

"Did you know all of this when you sent me to St. Louis to 'clean house' as you put it?" Izzy asked her grandmother.

"I had suspicions, nothing more. Diego, despite his other faults, managed to keep the situation in St. Louis quiet. However, when you contacted me, I saw an opportunity to use you to uncover the truth in St. Louis." Antonella replied, not the least bit contrite.

Isabella was angry and hurt that her grandmother would put her into that situation, and her face displayed her emotions. "Remember, My Heart. You came to me," Antonella reminded her. "Besides, Guillermo was there to keep you from getting hurt. That is, until you tied him up and left him during your escape."

"What did you find out about the connection between Diego and Gund?" Cassidy asked. "How deep were those two in business together?"

"It appears that Diego was being groomed to run a narcotics business for Gund, as well as human trafficking. With Diego gone, it has delayed Mr. Gund's next step," Antonella observed. However, he isn't giving up on his plan."

"What is his plan?" Cassidy asked.

"The more I dug into Mr. Gund, the more interesting it became. The organization he is part of has tendrils that reach into virtually every industry in the United States and many layers of government as well. I believe he intends to take over that organization, eliminate anyone standing in his way, and make himself into the Napoleon of business and crime in the United States."

"The Circle," Holmes meowed, and simultaneously the little girl translated it. "He wants to run the Circle."

"Circle?" Antonella questioned.

"The Circle is a confederation of four families from the United States Gilded Age. They are fabulously wealthy and powerful, and between them, they run most of the US. Gund wants to take over the Circle as well." When Holmes finished and the little girl translated, Antonella nodded.

"Who is this child?" Izzy asked, changing the subject. "And what is she doing with you?"

"Beatriz is from our village. Her mother is dead, but she was found to have a unique ability to understand cats." Antonella answered. "I found the need for her talents when my original translator was killed."

"Who was your original translator?" Cassidy asked, already suspecting the answer. "And, how was she killed?"

"Her mother was my first translator. It seems that the talent is sometimes handed down, mother to daughter, but interestingly, never to sons. She was killed by an unknown assailant in Philadelphia while she was supporting Ms. Adler in her undercover work. I've kept her daughter by my side ever since and set up a courier chain to bring the intel to her, so as not to put her in danger," then, Antonella added, as an afterthought, "Your Mr. Watson was unique in his ability to learn how to understand cats. I have never found anyone else who could do that."

Antonella's mention of Watson's name and the fact that he wasn't there was like a gut punch for Cassidy, no matter the circumstance. Seeing her reaction, the matriarch of the DeLeón cartel quickly added, "You all have been under my protection for the last year, as I moved my people into position."

"What do you mean?" Cassidy asked.

"She means," Holmes began, "that it was your Grandmother who planted Irene Adler at Cynthia Delacourt's home. The suggestion that Cynthia Delacourt hire us to find the painting also originated with your Grandmother." Holmes looked straight at Antonella and meowed, "You also have an asset in Gund's home. Is your agent still viable?"

Betrix did her uncanny job of translating Holmes without appearing to think about it, while Antonella replied, "Unfortunately, not. When Gund found your listening device, Miguel blew his cover, getting word back to me."

"The servant at the luncheon. The young Latino man." Cassidy stated, recalling the flash of memory she had seen from him at the Gund's lunch, and the image of an older woman sitting behind a desk, quickly piecing together the truth.

"You did that with very few clues. Well done, young lady," Antonella remarked.

"What do you mean that we've been under your protection?" Cassidy asked, seeking clarification.

"I've had my people around you since the attempt on your life last year. But when Gund found the bug, I knew he would react. So I increased your protection."

"The chauffeur, the caterers," Izzy said, remembering things she heard and saw.

"Quite right, My Heart."

"So why are you here now?" Cassidy wanted to know.

Antonella replied, "Because we've reached an inflection point. We are now engaged in open warfare with Señor Gund. His utter disregard for collateral damage when he bombed your wedding has forced us to update our timetable." She looked at Holmes and said, "We have taken his Arreglador, so he knows he's under attack."

Holmes translated the word in his head and meowed, "I want to be there when you question the Fixer."

"That has always been my intention." Antonella agreed.

"So what is the plan? You can't just keep people around us forever," Izzy questioned.

Antonella was quiet for a minute and then said in a chilling voice, "The DeLeón family is going to destroy Gund and the Circle. You and your Mr. Holmes here are going to help."

Everyone was quiet in the room until Holmes meowed, "The enemy of my enemy is my ally."

Epilogue

It had been a successful summer for tours at Magnus House in County Durham. From June through September, eager tourists, many of them exploring Britain's lesser-known regions, would end up staying in the small market town of Darlington. Once there, these travelers would be informed about the Magnus Estate and have the opportunity to sightsee a real 17th-century manor house; all it would cost is £20.00.

Given a brochure at the front desk of their lodgings in Darlington, these people would make the twenty-minute car ride to Magnus House and wait for the next tour to start. Today was the last day the house would be open this season. At four p.m., the house and grounds would be closed down, and only the old caretaker would remain to keep an eye on things through the winter, until next June, and Lord Magnus could make money off his estate once again. As the last tour gathered at the front door, the cheerful young woman began her well-rehearsed speech about the Magnus family and how the Crown granted these lands to Percival Magnus for his gallantry in battle in the American War of Independence. At this point, the young guide with strawberry-blond hair would smile and wink at any Americans in the group and ask jokingly for their forgiveness.

The tour would begin in the two-story entry hall, where suits of armor and medieval weapons adorned the walls. What was never mentioned was that the armor and weapons were inexpensive reproductions from China, purchased by Lord Magnus, to enhance the appearance of his property. From there, they would turn left and enter the Library, with its floor-to-ceiling book stacks. The path through the Library was contained by two red velvet ropes that kept people from wandering afield. Next, a right turn into the Drawing Room, with its massive fireplace, couches, and chairs. Curled up on one of the upholstered chairs was a male tabby cat, apparently totally indifferent to the tour moving past him. The cat had been born on the estate and usually accompanied Lord Magnus to his London address at the end of the season.

A couple of the guests pointed at the cat, and one even tried making a meowing sound at the sleeping cat (which really didn't sound like a meow to a cat). However, the tabby cat continued to sleep, utterly oblivious to the humans. As the tour continued into the chapel, one guest remained casually behind, watching the sleeping animal.

As soon as the man was alone in the Drawing Room, he cleared his throat and called out, "Mycroft?"

The tabby cat's ear twitched at his proper name being used. The cat's eyes slowly opened, and casually raised his head to silently examine the human calling to him. He seemed completely unimpressed that a stranger knew his name, as if it were a frequent occurrence.

"I have a message for you," the man said and waited for a response. But the tabby only continued to scrutinize him. The human felt as if he was under a microscope; the cat's piercing stare sought to memorize every detail about him.

After a respectful period, the man ducked under the red velvet rope and approached the cat. Reaching into his pocket, he removed a small piece of paper, unfolded it, and laid it before the tabby. There were no readily identifiable words on the paper, just dots, dashes, and a variety of unknown characters, some of which would only mean something to him or his brother. The tabby cat recognized the code immediately as one that he and his brother had made up during their kittenhood. It was one of the brothers' easier codes; still, it would take a cryptographer months, even with a supercomputer, to crack. Furthermore, some of the characters would only be meaningful to a cat. After digesting the message, Mycroft nodded at the note, and the man retrieved it, putting it back in his pocket.

Mycroft got to his paws and stretched in a very familiar way; first with his front legs reaching out and his paws opening up to reveal very sharp claws. Then, taking a step, he stretched out his back legs. His ritual complete, he hopped down to the floor and walked to the man. "Very well. Shall we be off?" he meowed, knowing the man could understand him.

The man nodded and turned to go back to the front door, with Mycroft walking next to him. As they reached the car park, Mycroft asked, "And what shall we call you, Yank?"

"You can call me Watson," the man replied.

The End.

Hamilton A. Cat Presents

Recipes from Our New Book

Hello, mystery readers. Hamilton A. Cat here to present the new recipes for our book, *The Bridge Too Far*. Having heard back from many of you, I am told that this is one of your favorite parts of our books. We are delighted that you enjoy these recipes as much as we enjoy sharing them with you.

Today, we have three new recipes that appeared in *The Bridge Too Far* story, which are very tasty and deceptively easy to make. So put on your aprons and join me in the kitchen.

Sincerely, Hamilton A. Cat.

SWEET POTATO PUREE

This is so easy to make that your diners will think you spent a lot more time on it than it actually took. But when presented alongside your protein and vegetables on the plate, the taste, color, and beautiful consistency will be a winner.

Ingredients:
3 pounds whole sweet potatoes
salt and ground black pepper to taste
½ cup sour cream*
½ cup whole milk–warmed*
3 tablespoons Irish butter, softened
*Note–Buttermilk can be substituted for the sour cream, and
    2% can be substituted for the whole milk; it just won't be
    quite as rich.*

Move your oven rack to the center position and preheat the oven to 425º F. Take a metal baking sheet and line it with aluminum foil. Wash and poke the sweet potatoes with a fork and spread them out on the sheet. Bake for 45–60 minutes until tender. You can check this with a toothpick and the thickest part of the potato. You should be able to insert the toothpick and withdraw it without difficulty.

Remove the potatoes and let them cool. When they are comfortable to handle, peel and cut them into 1" cubes and place in the food processor with the butter and sour cream. Begin pureeing the potatoes, adding the milk slowly through the processor's feed tube. Whip the potatoes until they are smooth and velvety. Salt & pepper to taste.

PORK TENDERLOIN
WITH MAPLE GARLIC GLAZE

This is another deceptively easy dish that your family and guests will love, and leftovers make incredible sandwiches.

Ingredients:

4 tablespoons Dijon mustard

2 teaspoon sesame oil*

4 cloves garlic, minced*

fresh ground black pepper to taste

2 cup real maple syrup

1½ pounds pork tenderloin

Note—Peanut oil or extra light olive oil can be substituted. Avoid using extra-virgin olive oil, as its flavor can be overpowering for this dish. Also, try to use fresh garlic and mince it yourself. Fresh always beats processed garlic or powder.

For the marinade, combine 1 teaspoon of oil, 2 minced cloves of garlic, 2 tablespoons of Dijon mustard, and 1 cup of maple syrup in a bowl. Whisk and set aside.

Rinse and pat the pork tenderloin dry. If you buy two tenderloins, simply double the marinade ingredients. Place the tenderloin in a shallow baking dish and brush half the marinade over the meat. Flip and brush the remainder over the other side. For the best results, marinade the pork the day before, then refrigerate it to allow the flavors to meld. When you wake up, flip the tenderloin in the marinade. Remove the meat from the refrigerator 1 hour before grilling so that it reaches room temperature. Mix the second batch of marinade to brush on the tenderloin while cooking and to drizzle across the carved tenderloin.

I grill the pork tenderloin outside, over a charcoal grill. However, it can be done on the stovetop in a saucepan over medium heat. Avoid using high heat, as it can burn the marinade. Regardless of the method, cook the pork until the internal temperature reaches 145°F on an instant-read thermometer, which takes about 18–24 minutes. Note that charcoal is harder to regulate heat, so the tenderloin may cook faster.

Carve the tenderloin across the grain into about ¼ to ⅜" thick, round medallions, drizzle a little marinade across the meat, and serve.

SICILIAN PAST CA' MUDDICA ATTURRATA
(Spaghetti with toasted bread crumbs and anchovies)

Believe it or not, this recipe actually came from my fellow human cook, Robert. He learned it while at University, and was friends with another student whose family served it at their Italian restaurant. This is the pasta envisioned at Izzy and Cass's Rehearsal Dinner in the book.

Ingredients:

1 pound spaghetti
6 tablespoons extra virgin olive oil
2 oz. Ortiz imported anchovy fillets in oil, chopped*
3 cloves garlic, crushed with the side of a knife
2 shallots, minced
⅔ cup toasted bread crumbs, or to taste
1 cup chopped fresh parsley
Kosher salt
Fresh, cracked ground black pepper to taste
Freshly grated Parmesan cheese

Note that I found Ortiz anchovies at the St. Louis Italian market on the Hill. Ortiz anchovies are pricey—especially now—but you also get enough anchovies in a resealable glass jar that you will have extra. They can be stored in the refrigerator for up to six months. If the Ortiz is too expensive, a 2-oz tin of King Oscar anchovies will work fine.

For the breadcrumbs, you will need 2 tablespoons of extra-virgin olive oil and ½ teaspoon of salt. You will need enough stale French or sourdough bread, broken into pieces, to fill 3 cups. Please try to avoid processed white bread found in supermarket bread aisles.

Lay parchment paper on a cookie sheet and preheat the oven to 350°F. Place the three cups of bread in the food processor and pulse a couple of times until you have bread crumbs that are ¼" to ⅛" in size. You don't want smaller breadcrumbs, like the ones that come from the market, because they will absorb more of the liquid, drying out the pasta you serve.

Before emptying the food processor bowl, drizzle the contents with olive oil, making sure to cover as much area as possible, and sprinkle with a pinch of kosher salt. Toss a couple of times, and then spread out on the parchment paper. Bake for 10–15 minutes, or until golden brown.

In a large pot, pour in a gallon of water and add one tablespoon of kosher salt. Bring to a boil and slowly add your pasta, making sure that the pot does not boil over. Cook about 9 to 10 minutes, until the pasta is al dente. Remove the pasta from the water and set aside. Reserve the pasta water for later.

In a medium saucepan, add 4 tablespoons of olive oil, the anchovies, smashed garlic, and shallots. Over medium heat, stirring constantly, cook the anchovies until they sizzle and the garlic is delightfully fragrant–about 2–3 minutes. Do not overcook the anchovies, or they will disappear in the oil.

Stir in the hot pasta into the anchovy sauce, adding some reserved pasta water until the spaghetti is creamy and coated. Then add the breadcrumbs and toss a couple of times until all the pasta is evenly coated.

With a set of kitchen tongs, pick up a portion of spaghetti and begin lowering it into the middle of your bowl or plate. As you slowly lower the pasta, gently spin the bowl so that the pasta forms a ball in the middle. Use the tongs to pick up and move any errant spaghetti back onto the ball. The ball of pasta should be about 2½" in diameter. Sprinkle with freshly grated Parmesan cheese, parsley, and cracked pepper.

Present the perfect plated Sicilian Pasta Ca' Muddica Atturrata to your family or guests.

Buon appetito, Hamilton A. Cat

Author's Note

Thank you for purchasing and reading *Holmes & Watson, The Case of the One Bridge Too Far,* the second book in the *Holmes & Watson Circle* series. I hope you are enjoying Holmes' exploits as much as I am writing them. This is the place where I usually thank the people who've helped me put this book together: the Wonderful People list. You all know who you are, and I hope that, through my words and deeds, you have come to understand your importance to me.

However, I would like to address a different topic in this author's note. This book was dedicated to *Acceptance,* and the Epigraph is a quote from Emerson about trusting yourself that there is a place for you in this world. I believe that.

Black, brown, or white. Gay, Straight, or Transgender, the world is big enough for all of us, and there is a place for you. Please don't think the vitriol spouted by some politicians and churchmen for their own gain is indicative of the majority. I believe that a majority of people are kind and accepting. But their recognition and tolerance are drowned out by the din of hurtful rhetoric spouted by the minority.

Most of us will never know the individual pain caused by the hurtful words directed at these marginalized groups. We can't be there during your darkest time to say it will be alright, that it will get better. I sincerely hope there is a support system you can turn to for help.

Perhaps, one component of that support system could be a cat from a shelter. When you find the right cat, you will know it. A cat may take a little while to get to know you, but when they do, their love is unreserved. Speaking from personal experience, a cat will greet you when you come in the door and settle on you in the evening, content with the physical contact. They will listen to your day without interruption and will purr to show they care. Cats are not apathetic; on the contrary, they are small, furry antidepressants in a turbulent and indifferent world.

I hope these words, though inadequate, help.

Sincerely,

Lily and the Great Vampire Hunt

"Slowly, methodically, the vampire cat searched the bedroom, the scent of fresh kitten blood driving its hunger." Giblet paused and looked at his audience. Lily was leaning forward, her tail vibrating with fear and excitement, while her two friends, Squeak and Casper, sat on either side of her for comfort and protection, but also captivated by the story. They were all on the back porch of the Macgregors' big white house, listening to the latest spooky story from Giblet during the Halloween season.

The Macgregors already had five cats when Belle brought home a newborn orphaned kitten and named her Lily. Belle became the de facto mother to the kitten, even producing milk to feed her. When Lily was old enough, it was decided that she would move to their next-door neighbor's house, where the Macgregors' grandmother, Anne Gaumont, could take care of her.

Continuing the story, Giblet meowed, "Hiding under the bed, Darla the kitten had a glimpse of the vampire cat's paws, still covered with dirt from digging itself out of the grave. Those paws circled the room, getting closer and closer. Finally, the vampire cat stopped right in front of where Darla was hiding. Daring not even to breathe, the kitten decided there was only one way she was going to survive this." Giblet once again knew just where to stop for the best effect. All the cats agreed, Giblet was the preeminent storyteller in the neighborhood. The old tomcat knew how to hold an audience.

"Then what happened, Uncle Giblet?" Lily asked in her high, kitten voice, unable to sit still.

"Yeah. Then what happened, Uncle Giblet?" asked an older, and a lot more annoyed voice from behind him.

Turning his head, he saw Belle staring at him, her head cocked to the side, a look of reproach plain to see on her face. "Ah, err," Giblet mumbled, seeming to have lost his place in his story.

"What have I told you about your spooky stories. Lily will have nightmares," Belle scolded.

"Oh, Ma'ma. I'm not afraid," Lily protested. "Let Uncle Giblet finish." Squeak, the orange kitten, and Casper, the black & white kitten, also added a chorus of mews, letting Ma'ma Belle know they also wanted to hear the rest of the story.

"Okay. What happens next, Giblet?" Belle asked, raising an eyebrow.

Every cat stared at Giblet, waiting for him to finish. Finally, Giblet cleared his throat and said, "Then the vampire cat left, and Darla lived happily ever after. The end."

"That's not the way it ends. Oh, Mama, you ruined it. Why'd you make Uncle Giblet stop?" Lily bemoaned.

"Because, little one, it's time you go back to Grandma Gaumont's house for dinner, and Squeak and Casper need to go home as well."

It was Monday, October 27th, and Halloween was just a few days away, and Lily was all worked up. At six months old, this was going to be her first fun people holiday; the Fourth of July had been too loud for her, so she hid under the bed. However, Halloween would be different; she was very excited about the chance to see real ghosts-cats, ghouls, and especially vampire-cats.

For the entire month of October, Lily had pestered Giblet every time she saw him to tell her more about vampire cats. What started out as harmless storytelling had turned into a real problem for Lily. Grandma Gaumont informed Belle that Lily was having bad dreams because of Giblet's inventive storytelling. "She's too young for these stories," Anne told Belle, who then confronted Giblet. "Don't you have something a little less frightening?" she asked the old tomcat.

"Oh, it's okay. All kittens like spooky stories," Giblet meowed, dismissing Belle's concern with a wave of his paw. "When you arrived, you liked stories about Protectors, and things that go bump in the night, as I remember."

"This is different," Belle insisted.

"No, this is the same. You are different." Giblet waited a moment, then added, "Because you're a mom and want to protect Lily. However, for you, I will tailor the stories to suit your daughter's kitten age.

Lily sat and listened to the two best friends argue, but her mind was elsewhere. She was determined to see these vampire cats herself, and what better time than on Halloween? Lily made plans with Squeak & Casper to sneak out after everyone had gone to sleep. She would show Mama that she was no scaredy-cat. This was going to be so much fun!

Halloween arrived on Friday, and Mother Nature seemed to want to join in the festivities. A cold wind blew in from the north, dropping the temperature and causing the leaves on the ground to swirl around the trick-or-treaters as they made their rounds. The leaden sky with low clouds contributed to the gloomy feel. "Perfect weather to see vampire-cats," Lily meowed to her two friends.

"Where are we meeting?" Squeak meowed.

"We all meet at the entrance to the cemetery," Lily reminded them.

"Are you sure we won't be in trouble?" Casper asked, always the cautious one when it came to Lily's schemes.

"It will be fine," Lily assured her. "We'll leave after everyone is asleep and be back before they wake up."

The back door opened, and Anne Gaumont called, "Lily. Come on in, it's supper time. Tell your friends you'll see them tomorrow.

"Okay," Lily loudly meowed to Anne. Then, in a sotto voce, she said, "See you tonight," as all three kittens reached out their right paw, one on top of the other; their secret paw shake. Then the three friends each headed to their homes.

Lily helped Anne hand out candy to all the little trick-or-treaters that came to the house, and even meowed her approval to several of the costumes. But by eight-thirty, it was over, and Anne blew out the candle in her jack-o-lantern and turned off the porch light. "Let's go to bed, Lily," Anne said and climbed the stairs to her bedroom. After reading for an hour, Anne turned the nightstand lamp off, and it was quiet in the house.

At a quarter to midnight, Lily quietly jumped off the bed and made her way to the pet door so she could meet up with her friends. Having never been out this late at night, Lily was nervous and jumped at every sound as she made her way to the old Torrington cemetery. A pair of wrought-iron gates built into impressive stone walls marked the entrance to the two-hundred-year-old graveyard; it was there that she found Casper and Squeak, both as nervous as she was.

"I don't think this is a good idea, Lily," Casper meowed. "We're going to get into trouble."

"We're here now, we need to see if we can see a vampire cat," Lily insisted. "Right, Squeak?" she asked, but didn't hear an answer. Turning her head, she saw her friend. Squeak was shaking like a leaf, and her eyes were huge. "We'll be okay, Squeak," Lily began, but it was too late.

"Nope, nope nope," Squeak began meowing, as she backed away, turned tail, and ran as fast as her little legs could carry her, for home.

"Well, I'm going in," Lily announced confidently and walked through the gates and into the cemetery.

Casper looked up the street, but Squeak was no longer in sight. Not wanting to be by herself, she reluctantly followed Lily under the gates. Once inside, the little bit of light available from the street was gone, making it a lugubrious experience to identify the surroundings. Gradually, the kittens were able to see the old tombstones, some of which were so weathered that the etching on their faces was barely visible. The cold wind whipped through the graveyard, causing the bare branches of the trees to sway. Casper thought they looked like skeletal hands trying to reach down and scoop them up. She was sure that nightmarish creatures were moving all around them, just out of sight.

"Where do you think the vampires are?" Casper whispered.

"We probably have to go further in to find them."

About a hundred feet down the path, the kittens came to a grave where the dirt was disturbed. "Something was digging here," Lily observed.

"You mean something dug itself out?" Casper asked, her voice pitching up, as she meowed. "What...what is it?"

"I don't...," Lily began, but was overidden by a cold, gravely voice that said, "Blood!"

Lily turned to look at Casper, thinking it was she who spoke, but Casper shook her head, indicating that it wasn't her, as she began to tremble.

"BLOOD!" the voice repeated, more insistent. Looking around, Lily and Casper suddenly saw a large, jet-black cat, its fur in shambles and covered in dirt, the same dirt that came from the grave, but that wasn't the most unnerving sight. What was terrifying was this cat's canine teeth, which were each twice as long as any normal cat's. "I SMELL KITTEN BLOOD!" the vampire cat called once again, advancing on the two kittens in jerky movements, as if it were trying to remember how to walk again after being dead.

Lily turned to Casper to say something, but her friend was no longer there. Casper was already halfway down the path towards the cemetery gates, running as fast as his paws would carry her. "Wait for me," Lily shrieked, as she took to her paws to follow her friend out of the cemetery.

"How does Frank do that with his teeth?" Giblet asked from his perch on the graveyard stone wall.

Sitting next to him, Belle responded, "He has a way of curling up his lips so his front teeth appear longer. But if you asked those two," Belle said, indicating the two kittens running up the street towards home. "They would tell you those fangs were at least an inch long each."

"How did you know she was going to sneak out?"

"Are you kidding me? Have you met my daughter?" Belle asked with a grin. "I'm going to help Frank clean himself off and thank him," Belle said as she jumped easily to the ground. "You follow those 'brave' vampire hunters and make sure they get home." Gilblet nodded and meowed, "Okay. See you at home."

November 1st was still as grey and cold as Halloween when Giblet saw Lily sitting with Casper and Squeak, on Anne's back porch, apparently having a serious conversation. Walking up, he meowed, "Lily. Now that

Halloween is over, I don't think your mom would mind me telling you more vampire stories, if you want."

Lily's pink nose suddenly turned very white, and she stammered, "No, that's okay, Uncle Giblet. I think I have to go inside, see you later, bye," she meowed in a rush and turned tail and headed through the pet door.

"How about you two? Want to hear about the time I came paw to paw with a real vampire cat?" Giblet asked Lily's friends. However, both Squeak and Casper said they had to go, and beat a hasty exit, heading for their homes.

Giblet watched as all the kittens left and smiled, then went back home for his nap.